SYDNEY HARBOUR HOSPITAL: AVA'S RE-AWAKENING

BY
CAROL MARINELLI

HOW TO MEND A BROKEN HEART

BY
AMY ANDREWS

MILLS & BOON

Carol Marinelli recently filled in a form where she was asked for her job title and was thrilled, after all these years, to be able to put down her answer as 'writer'. Then it asked what Carol did for relaxation. After chewing her pen for a moment Carol put down the truth—'writing'. The third question asked—'What are your hobbies?' Well, not wanting to look obsessed or, worse still, boring, she crossed the fingers on her free hand and answered 'swimming and tennis'. But, given that the chlorine in the pool does terrible things to her highlights, and the closest she's got to a tennis racket in the last couple of years is watching the Australian Open, I'm sure you can guess the real answer!

Amy Andrews has always loved writing, and still can't quite believe that she gets to do it for a living. Creating wonderful heroines and gorgeous heroes and telling their stories is an amazing way to pass the day. Sometimes they don't always act as she'd like them to—but then neither do her kids, so she's kind of used to it. Amy lives in the very beautiful Samford Valley, with her husband and aforementioned children, along with six brown chooks and two black dogs. She loves to hear from her readers. Drop her a line at: www.amyandrews.com.au

SYDNEY HARBOUR HOSPITAL: AVA'S RE-AWAKENING

BY
CAROL MARINELLI

MILLS & BOON

For Anne Gracie. Thank you for your friendship and support.
It means a lot. Carol x

First published in Great Britain 2012
by Mills & Boon, an imprint of Harlequin (UK) Limited.
Harlequin (UK) Limited, Eton House, 18-24 Paradise Road,
Richmond, Surrey TW9 1SR

© Harlequin Books S.A. 2012

Special thanks and acknowledgment are given to Carol Marinelli for her contribution to the *Sydney Harbour Hospital* series.

ISBN: 978 0 263 89188 1

Harlequin (UK) policy is to use papers that are natural, renewable and recyclable products and made from wood grown in sustainable forests. The logging and manufacturing process conform to the legal environmental regulations of the country of origin.

Printed and bound in Spain
by Blackprint CPI, Barcelona

**Welcome to the world
of Sydney Harbour Hospital
(or *SHH*… for short—
because secrets never stay hidden for long!)**

Looking out over cosmopolitan Sydney Harbour, Australia's premier teaching hospital is a hive of round-the-clock activity—with a *very* active hospital grapevine.

With the most renowned (and gorgeous!) doctors in Sydney working side by side, professional and sensual tensions run sky-high—there's *always* plenty of romantic rumours to gossip about…

Who's been kissing who in the on-call room? What's going on between legendary heart surgeon Finn Kennedy and tough-talking A&E doctor Evie Lockheart? And what's wrong with Finn?

Find out in this enthralling new eight-book continuity from Mills & Boon® Medical Romance™—indulge yourself with eight helpings of romance, emotion and gripping medical drama!

Sydney Harbour Hospital
From saving lives to sizzling seduction, these doctors are the very best!

PROLOGUE

SHE would call him.

Ava Carmichael sat in her office at Sydney Harbour Hospital and stared at her phone, willing herself to pick it up and call her husband. She had just spent the best part of the last hour counselling a couple—telling them to talk, to open up to each other, that if they just forged ahead with communication then things would begin to improve.

As a sexual dysfunction specialist—or sex therapist, as everyone called her—Ava got to say those lines an awful lot.

Well, it was time for the doctor to take her own medicine, Ava decided, reaching out and picking up the phone and dialling in his mobile number. At the last moment she changed her mind, and hung up. She went back to twisting her long dark hair around her fingers—just unsure what it was she should say to him.

That she missed him?

That she was sorry?

Ava didn't know where to start.

Her husband, James, had been away for three months

in Brisbane. He had taken a temporary teaching place-
ment at a school of medicine there, which was ridiculous. James was an oncologist and completely hands-on
in his work. He loved being with his patients more than
anything. Had it been three months of research, it might
have made some sense—Sydney Harbour Hospital was
cutting-edge and James kept himself right up to date,
but James liked reading about findings rather than dis-
covering them. He liked being with his patients and
James, her James, wasn't a teacher.

She smiled at the very thought.

The medical students got on his nerves.

He hated explaining his decisions.

He was a man's man, a gorgeous man, her big honest bear of a man who would come home and flake on
the sofa sometimes and moan because he wanted it to
only be him in the room with his patient, especially
when giving bad news.

'It's a teaching hospital,' Ava would point out, lying
on the floor, doing her Pilates. 'They have to learn.'

'Yeah, well, how would you like to have a couple of
students sitting there watching when you're trying to
talk to someone about their bits not working?' There
was rather more to her work than that but he'd made a
very good point, and he had made her smile too, especially when he checked his own bits were there for a
moment, indignant at the very thought.

Well, there *had* been conversations like that one,
lovely evenings that had been shared, talking easily

about their day, their thoughts, *them*, but those evenings seemed like an awfully long time ago.

Yes, he loved his patients and they loved him back, and the real reason he had taken the position, they both knew, even if they hadn't voiced it, had been because they'd needed space from each other—they'd needed those three months to hopefully sort out their heads.

James and Ava had been married for seven years, but had been together for ever. They had met at university and, quite simply, at the age of eighteen the awkward and rather shy Ava Marwood had discovered love. James had been twenty-one, good-looking, funny and the first person in her life, it seemed, who actually wanted to spend time with her. Like James, she was an only child, but unlike James, who had grown up with parents who adored him, Ava's parents had made no secret she'd been an accident, an inconvenience really. It had been a parade of young nannies who had raised Ava—her parents had been far too busy with their lives, their careers, their endless extra-marital trysts, which, they'd both agreed, kept their relationship alive.

It had been a confusing, lonely childhood and then she had met James and her world had changed. Ava had found a whole new definition for love. It had been completely unexpected, thoroughly reciprocated and though they had their own friends and lives, there was no doubt they had met their match. Everyone thought them the golden couple and it had been golden for a very long while. A thirty-six-year-old James still made her toes curl just looking at him, and he had always made her laugh. And even if he wasn't particularly romantic, it was a love that went so deep Ava had considered it invincible. But over the last two years their marriage had slowly unravelled. With each miscarriage Ava had suffered, they had grown further and further apart and now they were barely talking. In fact, if it weren't for email they would hardly be corresponding at all.

Still fiddling with her hair, she looked at her computer and then went and reread the last email he had sent her.

It was just his flight details really, and all so impersonal it might just as well have come from Admin.

And then, loathing herself, she did it again—checked their bank account with suspicious eyes.

She saw the boutiques he had visited and couldn't quite envision it—James, of all people, in male boutiques!

James, who got a wardrobe update each Christmas and birthday when she went and did it for him, had taken himself off to several trendy shops these past few weeks and from the amount spent he had been having quite a good time of it.

And what was it with all the cash withdrawals?

James never used cash or rarely, but now it was a couple of hundred dollars here, another couple of hundred there, and what was this weekly transfer? A few minutes' research later she found out.

Her husband, who liked nothing better than to lie on the sofa and laugh at her doing her exercises, had, a couple of months ago, gone and joined a gym.

She didn't know if she was being practical or being a fool to believe that James wouldn't cheat. And things must be bad because she was even thinking of turning to her mother for advice!

Call him, Ava counselled herself. *Call him now from your office.* Because each night at home she went to call but couldn't, and each night was spent in tears. Perhaps she could be more upbeat, logical and truthful if she sat at her desk.

More direct.

'Hi.' She kept her voice bright when he answered the phone.

'Ava?' He sounded surprised, well, he would be, she told herself, it was six-twenty in the evening and so rarely did she ring. 'Is everything okay?'

'Of course it is. Does there have to be a problem to ring for a chat?'

'Er…no.'

She could feel his wariness, but she forged on. 'Look, James, I know things haven't been—'

'Ava, can I call you back?' He sounded awkward and James was never awkward. She'd timed the call carefully, knew that he wouldn't be teaching now.

'Is someone there?' she asked, and there was a long silence.

'I'll call you back in ten.'

She sat trying to ignore the unsettled feeling in her stomach that was permanently there these days—he might have a colleague with him, she told herself, but that had never stopped him talking before. They were a very open couple, or had been; he wouldn't give a damn if someone was around—and he wasn't seeing patients so it couldn't be that.

'Sorry about that.' He had called her back five minutes later.

'Why couldn't you talk?'

'Just…' She could almost see his wide shoulders shrugging the way they did when he closed off. 'What did you ring for?'

'Just…' She shrugged her shoulders too.

'Ava.' She could hear his irritation. 'I'm sorry I couldn't talk before, but I can now—you just called at a bad time.'

'Well, when's a good time?' she snapped. 'I called you the other morning and you couldn't talk then either…' He had hardly been able to breathe. More to the point, he'd hardly been able to breathe! She'd rung him at seven and he hadn't answered and she'd called him straight back, and he'd picked up then, trying to pretend he'd been asleep, but he'd been breathless. She knew he was having an affair, except she didn't want to know it. Ava had always thought that their marriage ending was just about them—a private affair, not a real one.

She wasn't stupid. They hadn't slept together since God knows when, more than a year at the very least. As if James wasn't having the time of his life in Brisbane. She was mad to think otherwise.

'Do you want me to order a cake for your mum's birthday?' she asked instead.

'Please.'

'What about a present?'

'I don't know…just think of something.' And that annoyed her too. Veronica Carmichael was a difficult woman; she and Ava had never really got on. A widow, James was her only child, and she was never going to like the woman who, in her eyes, had taken him away and, worse, a woman who couldn't give her grandchildren. Ava had organised a small family gathering for Veronica's sixtieth, which was next weekend, and would on Saturday go out and buy her something lovely for her birthday, something really beautiful. And she'd wrap it too, and then Veronica would unwrap it and thank James, and would go on and on about what a thoughtful son she had when, had it been left to him, there would have been a card bought on the way to her house and no party.

So she and James chatted for another thirty seconds about his flight home on Monday and then she hung up and stared at the view she loved. SHH looked out over Sydney Harbour and the sexual dysfunction centre was on one of the higher floors—the floor was shared with Psychology and Family Counselling. Nobody would ever get out of the lift otherwise, James sometimes joked when he came up to visit her some lunchtimes, though again, that hadn't happened in a while. Still, every morning that she came into work Ava pinched herself at the view from her window, and she gazed out at it now, to the opera house and the Harbour Bridge, the blue of the ocean and the white sails that dotted it, and she waited for the view to soothe her.

Unfailingly it worked.

It really was a wonderful perk of her job.

It was the same view she looked at the next morning after another tear-filled night when Ginny, her receptionist, came in carrying a huge bunch of flowers from James.

'Ahh…' Ginny beamed and handed her the bouquet. 'He's so romantic.'

Ava *knew* at that point that he was having an affair. Knew that she wasn't simply being paranoid.

Not once in the seven years they had been married and not even when dating had James sent flowers, not one single time. It just wasn't him. *What do I need to send flowers for?* He'd shrug. *I've done nothing wrong.*

She read the card.

Miss you.

See you on Monday

James x

And she remembered a time, took it out from the back of her memory and polished it till she could clearly see.

It had been two, maybe three years ago.

Yes, three years ago and it had been their wedding anniversary and they'd both decided they were ready to try for a baby. Ava's career had been in a really good place and she'd felt confident she could juggle work and motherhood far better than her mother had. James had bought her a ring, the large amber ring that she was wearing now, because, he'd said, it matched her eyes.

And he'd taken her out for dinner, the perfect night, and they'd had the same old good-natured joke as they'd got back to the apartment and she'd moaned about the lack of flowers.

It hurt to remember and she tried not to, but the memory was out there, all polished and gleaming and allowing for total recall.

Tumbling in bed together, making love as they once had.

His big body over hers, his chin all stubbly, those gorgeous green eyes looking down, and she saw in that image what she hadn't seen in a very long time. James was smiling. 'Men only send flowers when they've something to feel guilty about.'

'In your own words, James,' Ava said, and looked at the flowers and wanted to bin them. If her window had opened she would have tossed them out there and then, except her window was sealed closed, and then in came Ginny with a huge vase.

'Put them out in the waiting room,' Ava suggested. 'Let the patients enjoy them.'

'Don't be daft,' Ginny said, and plonked them right there on her desk. 'He sent them for you.'

And there they sat, for appearances sake, their sweet, sickly fragrance filling her nostrils, the violent colours perpetually in her line of vision. She wished they'd just wilt and fade.

Like her marriage.

CHAPTER ONE

'THEY'VE cancelled the surgery.' Ava said nothing for a moment, just stood quietly as her colleague Evie Lockheart leant against the corridor wall, her eyes closed as she struggled to keep in the tears, utterly defeated by what had happened. Ava had seen her walking dazed along the hospital corridor. Even if she didn't know Evie particularly well, she liked her—they had shared the odd conversation and everyone in the hospital knew that Finn Kennedy was having his surgery today.

Complicated surgery that was extremely risky. Ava already knew his operation had been called off—news spread fast around SHH and she couldn't even hazard how Finn must be feeling to have been told an hour before such major surgery that it wasn't going to go ahead.

'It hasn't been cancelled,' Ava said, her voice practical. 'It's been postponed.'

'Well, it might just as well have been cancelled,' Evie said. 'He just told them not to bother booking it again, then he told me to get the hell out.' Evie shook her head. 'I shouldn't be troubling you with this.' She was clearly in distress and not used to sharing her private life, and Ava was more than used to situations like that.

'Come back to my office,' Ava suggested. She could see a couple of nurses turning their heads as they walked past—Evie and Finn were hot topics indeed. Finn was the chief of surgery and a formidable man at best, well known for his filthy attitude and ability to upset the staff, but no one could question his brilliance. His voice could be as cutting as the scalpel he so skilfully wielded, except lately he hadn't been operating and it had done nothing to improve his mood, and today poor Evie was wearing it. 'We can get a coffee there. I'm sure you might like a bit of privacy now.' She walked Evie back along the corridor and to the left and then up in the lifts they went without a word. She walked along the corridor, nodded good morning to Donald, one of the therapists, and then through to her own centre and shook her head when Ginny told her she had a message from the spinal unit.

'I'll call back later,' Ava said. 'I'm not to be disturbed.'

She and Evie entered her office—well, it was more a room. Yes, she had a desk, though it was terribly messy, but the room had a couple of couches and a coffee table, and a small kitchenette where Ava would make her clients a drink, or herself one, if they needed a moment to pause, and she gave Evie that moment now as she went over to make them a drink.

'Finn would never forgive me, you know...' Evie gave a pale smile as she sat down on one of the comfortable couches 'If he knew I was stepping into a sex therapist's office to talk about him.'

'I'd be patronising you if I laughed.' Ava turned around and smiled. 'I hear the same thing I don't know how many times a day. She put on a gruff male voice. "'Well, I never thought I'd find myself here. I really don't need to be here..."' Ava rolled her eyes and poured coffee, taking a little longer than perhaps she needed to, to give Evie a chance to collect herself.

'Well.' Evie gave a wry laugh. 'At least we know that's one type of therapy that Finn doesn't need.'

Ava chose not to correct her—Finn had been using women as sticky plasters for a very long while, there was certainly something going on in that brilliant head of his. Still, that wasn't what Evie needed to hear today. Finn's and her on-again, off-again relationship was clearly taking its toll on her.

'What a view...' Evie noticed her surroundings for the first time. 'Maybe I could ask them to consider moving Emergency up here.'

'The paramedics would never forgive you,' Ava said. 'Do you want me to leave you?' she offered, handing Evie a steaming mug of coffee—Ava wasn't a nosy person at all and she certainly never gossiped. It was why, perhaps, she often found herself in situations such as this one. 'The cleaners have already been in.' She glanced at the desk, wished those blasted flowers were gone, but apart from a couple of wilting roses that the cleaner had removed, they were still there and still taunting her. 'I haven't got any patients for another hour, so you won't be disturbed.'

'No.' Evie shook her head. 'You don't have to go. It's actually nice to talk, just to be up here and away from the prying eyes.'

'It must be an extra pressure on Finn,' Ava mused. 'Having to have his operation where he's the chief of surgery. Still, there's no better place.' SHH was the best hospital for this sort of procedure, there was no question that it might be done elsewhere. It was experimental and even with the best surgery, the best equipment, there were no guarantees that Finn's ability to operate again could be saved. Indeed, there was a good chance that he would be left a quadriplegic.

Ava knew that, not because of the gossip that was flying around the hospital but because, unbeknown to Evie, Finn had actually been in for mandatory counselling prior to surgery. The team had discussed who should see him and Ava had immediately declined. She didn't know Finn particularly well, but they lived in the same apartment block, Kirribilli Views—his penthouse apartment was directly above hers—and though they barely greeted each other if they met on the stairs or in the lift, still, it could surely only make things more awkward for Finn.

He'd seen Donald instead.

And even though Donald was terribly experienced— he did both family counselling and sexual dysfunction and his patients adored him—Ava wondered if his brusque approach would mesh with Finn in such a delicate matter.

Ava dealt with spinal patients a lot. Her work gave her much pleasure, seeing relationships saved, helping people to learn that there could be life, a satisfying sex life even, after such catastrophic events. Her work was, in fact, moving more towards trauma and post-traumatic stress disorder patients, it was how she and Evie had first started talking. Evie worked in Accident and Emergency and had dropped by for a chat about a 'patient'. Ava was sure, quite sure, that the person they had been discussing was Finn. Finn's brother had been a soldier like Finn. His brother had died in Finn's arms and shrapnel from the bomb that had killed his brother was still lodged in Finn's neck, and it was that that was causing his health issues.

Sometimes Ava wondered if Finn had ever heard the rows between her and James, not that there had been many, really, before he'd gone away to Brisbane. They had been so deep into injury time by then that she and James hadn't talked much at all, but Finn had never intruded, there had been no chatting on the stairs or anything, just a very occasional 'Good morning'. And not once had Finn questioned her about her red, swollen eyes, neither had he done the neighbourly thing and popped around to see if she was okay when she'd lost the last baby. Ava cringed at the memory—Finn had been in the lift that day—the cramping had started on her way home and she had just wanted to get into her apartment, to call her doctor, to lie down, but there had been this awful sudden gush and then a crippling, bend-over pain and, terribly practical, Finn had helped her to her door, had taken her inside and had then called James. They'd never discussed it further—instead it had been a brief nod in passing and Ava had been grateful for that. Grateful now that Finn never stopped to ask when James was returning, or how she was getting on.

No, they just shared the same brief nod and greeting.

Grief recognising grief perhaps.

Respecting it.

Avoiding it.

'I can't believe we're going to have to go through all this again.' Evie broke into her thoughts. 'I really don't think he'll consent to surgery a second time.'

'Why did they cancel the operation?' Ava asked. 'I thought they had everyone on board, it's been planned for weeks.'

'This piece of equipment they need,' Evie explained, 'they're having trouble calibrating it. There's a technician coming over from America so it looks like it will be another week before the surgery can go ahead. They just can't risk even a single mistake.'

'What did he say when they told him?'

'Not much—a few choice words and then he took out his drip, put on his suit, told me where to go, and not very nicely either, and now he's back at work—he's doing a ward round as we speak, no doubt chewing out everybody in his path. Ava…' Evie's eyes were anguished '…the thing is, with Finn and I, I know it's very on-and-off, I know how appalling he can be, but

in the last few days we've been close. Last night we…'
She let out a startled half-laugh. 'I can't believe I'm
discussing this.'

'You won't make me blush,' Ava said.

'We had a really nice night.' Evie was awkward. 'I
mean, it was really intimate, amazing. It wasn't just
sex, it was so tender, we were so close.' Ava said nothing, reminded herself she was thinking as a friend, not
a therapist, and she let Evie continue. 'And now, just
like that, he's told me to get out, that he doesn't want
me around.'

'Give him some time,' Ava said. 'He would have
been building himself up for this surgery, and to have
it cancelled at the last minute—'

'But cancellations happen all the time and you don't
see couples breaking up over it,' Evie interrupted. 'He
said that now he knows a bit how the patients feel when
we cancel them at the last minute.'

'Ooh, are we going to get a new, compassionate
Finn?' Ava was pleased to see Evie smile. A cheerful
person, Ava found that a little dose of humour helped
in most situations.

Most, not all.

'Finn compassionate?' Evie rolled her eyes, and then
sat quietly as she finished her drink. Ava sat in silence
too, a comfortable silence that was perhaps needed by
Evie before she headed back out there, but after a moment or two in their own worlds it was time to resume
appearances, to play their parts. Evie drained her drink
and stood. 'Thanks so much, Ava.'

'Any time,' Ava said.

'Oh.' Evie suddenly remembered. 'That gorgeous husband of yours comes back today, doesn't he?'

'This morning.' Ava nodded. 'He's heading straight in to work. That's James.'

'Well, you can see him tonight,' Evie said. 'He's the luckiest guy in the world, isn't he? Married to a sex therapist...'

Ava grinned. 'Again, I'd be patronising you if I laughed, if you had any idea of the amount of times I hear that each day...'

She was *sick* of hearing it.

So too must James be.

The assumption that they must have most amazing sex life and wonderful relationship was a pressure in itself. As if people thought her job followed her home, as if the smiling, cheerful, practical Ava, who was open to discuss everything, who managed to deal with the most sensitive subjects with barely a blink, translated to the Ava at home.

Finn would never say such a thing, Ava thought as she saw Evie out.

Or maybe he would, she mused—nervous, embarrassed, new to a wheelchair, maybe Finn would crack the same old jokes if she offered her help.

She stood alone in her office and looked out the window at the glittering view and wondered if she could stand to leave it, not so much the view but her work here. She didn't want to start over at another hospital or open a private practice. Because SHH was so cutting-edge she got the patients in her office that she was most inter-ested in helping. It was no doubt the same reason James would remain here, but how hard would it be to work in the same hospital, to see your ex-husband most days?

Ex-husband.

There, she'd said it and she didn't like how it sounded. More than that, she didn't want to be James's ex-wife.

CHAPTER TWO

'Lovely flowers.' Elise was a bit flustered but George was friendlier this time. 'From your husband?'

'They are.' Ava smiled. 'Come in, take a seat.'

She had been seeing them for a few months now. For George and Elise it was a complicated process and not as simple as writing a prescription. George had been in an accident at work last year, an appalling accident where he'd seen a colleague die. It wasn't just George's physical injuries that had caused him pain. Over and over he had relived the moment of the accident and the depression and anxiety had been all-engulfing. He'd seen his GP but the medication for the depression had affected his libido, which had increased his anxiety, and by the time they had arrived at Ava's, the pair had all but given up, not just on their sex life but on themselves.

She was seeing them monthly as a couple and George was also having one-on-one counselling with Ava, but more about the accident and the flashbacks he was getting and his appalling guilt that the colleague who had died had been so much younger than him.

'How have you two been?' Ava asked.

'We're doing fine,' George said, handing over a folder. 'I've done my homework.'

Ava grinned and checked off their sheets. Her methods were a bit flaky at times, and with some couples she made things a bit more fun. With George and Elise she had them playing Scrabble, taking walks, doing little quizzes to find out more about each other, just little things, and she looked through the sheets.

'Elise?' She saw the woman's worried expression as she handed over a folder. She looked as if she was about to start to cry. 'Elise, the homework's for fun…'

'It's not that.' She was really flustered, Ava realised. 'You know you said we weren't to…' She could hardly say it.

'I suggested that you didn't try to have sex.'

To take the pressure off George Ava had suggested a sex ban, kissing and holding hands only—which apparently they hadn't done for decades.

'Oh, we haven't,' Elise assured her.

'Okay.'

'We did get a bit carried away, though,' George admitted.

Quite a bit carried away, it turned out! By the time their hour was up, they were all smiling. 'I'll see you again next month and, George, you in two weeks,' she said to the couple. 'And follow the rules this time.'

She grinned at her own success. Okay, they had a long way to go, but they were both determined to get there, and with a couple as lovely as them, they would, Ava was quite sure.

'Ava?' She heard a knock at the same time she heard her name, Elise and George had left the door open. She felt her stomach tighten at the sound of her husband's voice, and she turned round.

'James.' There he stood, tall, strong, gorgeous and *different*. His light brown hair, which usually fell rumpled and messy, now had a modern cut, and usually his chin was crying out for a razor, but he was clean-shaven today. Generally James wore jeans and a T-shirt or jumper, depending on the season. His patients, he'd explain, had more on their minds than whether or not the doctor was wearing a suit—but now and then he donned one and when he did, he quite simply took her breath away.

He wasn't wearing a suit today but, dressed in grey linen trousers and a black fitted shirt, he was a mixture between the two versions of James she adored and it almost killed her to see it. James never bought himself new clothes; they simply didn't interest him. Her heart stopped in her chest for a moment, seeing him in new attire, wondering who had bought them for him, or who James had bought them to impress. She had a horrible glimpse into her future if they both worked at SHH, watching the man she loved and knew so well change before her eyes.

'You've lost weight,' she said, because he had. He was a big man, and had never been *that* overweight, but he'd lost a lot and now stood broad, lean and toned.

'A bit.' He shrugged.

'How was your flight?' How stilted and formal she

sounded when really she wanted to run to him, to rest her head on his chest, to welcome him home, to say how much she had missed him, except she greeted him like a colleague and clearly it was noticed, because he didn't even answer the question, just shot her a slightly incredulous look that that was all she had to say after his three months away.

'I'll see you tonight,' James said instead, and then as he turned to go, he stopped. 'Ava, we need to talk.'

He'd been saying that for months—no, years—as more and more she'd shut him out, only this time it was a different conversation to be had. 'I know we do.'

'I'll speak to you tonight.' He didn't come over and kiss her, he just turned and walked away and headed out to work, to involve himself in his patients. Only it wasn't his familiar scent that lingered. Instead she smelt cologne. Ava wished she had patients scheduled this morning, that she could think about someone else's problems instead of her own.

Instead, she was giving a lecture.

She had her little case packed, filled with aids that would make the student nurses laugh at first, but she would push through it, hoping to get her message across, hoping that one day in the future her words would be recalled and a sensitive, informed word might be had by one of them to a patient, that there was help available.

Except she felt a fraud as she stood there, this cheerful, laughing, sexual dysfunction specialist married to the gorgeous James.

She couldn't remember the last time that they had

slept together and wasn't stupid enough to think in the three months he'd been away, in the years they'd been away from each other physically, that James wouldn't have seen someone else.

Someone he liked enough to lose weight for, to tone up for, to buy new clothes for and splash on cologne for—it wasn't the James she knew. She knew that she'd lost him long ago.

Lost them.

CHAPTER THREE

'Look at you!'

The reception that greeted him as he walked onto the unit for the first time in three months was far more friendly and receptive than Ava's had been.

'Where did you disappear to?' Carla, the unit manager on the day ward, asked.

'Brisbane,' James said.

'She meant this.' Harriet gave a friendly sort of pat to his stomach as she walked past and, yes, he'd forgotten that Harriet had been getting a bit too friendly before he'd gone away.

'Ava's got herself a whole new man,' Carla said, and winked at him, and he grinned back, because Carla would soon have a word if needed. 'Bet she's delighted to have you back.'

'She is,' James said, and as Harriet pulled on her gloves he watched her cheeks flood with colour as he made things clear. 'And I'm really glad to be back— I've just been up to see her.'

He'd read through files and results and it really was good to be back—at least on the unit. He tried not to think about Ava's lukewarm—or, rather, stone-cold—reception. A long breath came out of his nose as he tried not to think about it but, hell, he'd thought she might be at the airport, he'd even emailed his flight times as a prompt, and then when she hadn't been he had stopped by the flat, just in case she'd taken the morning off, but of course she was at work.

'We've a new patient this morning.' Carla handed him a file. 'Richard Edwards. He was supposed to be in on Friday for his first round of chemotherapy but he cancelled. I wondered if you could have a word with him as he's ever so anxious. Wouldn't be surprised if he refuses again.'

'Sure.' James read through the file and his colleague Blake's meticulous notes. Richard was nineteen and had been recently diagnosed with testicular cancer. He was stage one and all his markers were good, but after discussion with Blake he had decided to go ahead with chemotherapy, though he was clearly wavering on that decision now.

'Where is he?'

'He's in the coffee room. Do you want me to bring him through to your office?'

'I'll find him.'

James headed down to the patients' and relatives' coffee room and met with the young man and his worried parents. 'I'll have a chat with Richard…'

'We'll come,' his anxious parents said, but James shook his head.

'I'll speak with you all shortly, but first I'd like to speak with Richard himself.'

'He gets overwhelmed—'

'I'm sure he does,' James said. 'That's why I'll go through everything again afterwards.'

'Thanks for that,' Richard said as they took a seat in James's office. 'They've been great and everything, but...' He struggled to finish his sentence and James tried for him.

'They're not the ones going through it?'

Richard nodded. 'They don't understand why I wouldn't want the chemotherapy if it gives you more chance that it won't come back. Blake seemed to think it was the better option, but he did speak about waiting and watching,' Richard said. 'I've just started a new job, I've got a new girlfriend and she's been great and everything, but I just can't imagine...' He closed his eyes for a moment and James didn't interrupt. 'I always look after myself. I'm a vegetarian. I just think I might be able to take care of this myself. I've been looking into things...'

'It's called watchful waiting,' James said. 'There's no evidence your cancer has spread so if you adopt that approach then you'll come back regularly for tests— and if it does come back the treatment is still there for you. Some people prefer that, whereas others find it far more stressful and just want the treatment straight away.' He spent time with Richard, going through everything, giving him pointers to do his own research, and it was good to be back at work with real patients.

He liked informing his patients, liked them informed, and Richard was. He didn't, at this stage, want to go ahead with the treatment, but as they wound up the discussion, along came the question, the one he was asked so many times. 'What would you do if it was you?' There were variations to the question, of course—if it was your wife, your mother, your daughter, your son. So often James was asked what he would do in their place, and normally he answered it easily, but maybe he was out of practice, because he hesitated a moment before answering.

'What you're doing,' James said. 'I'd weigh up my options. Do you want to make another appointment so we can talk again in a couple of weeks?

'That would be great,' Richard said. 'Will you speak with my parents?'

'Sure.'

It didn't go down very well, but James took his time with them too, assuring them that it was a valid option, that Richard wasn't closing any doors—and sometimes, James thought as he headed back to the treatment area, it was the relatives who had the hardest time dealing with things.

'No go?' Carla asked.

'Not at this stage,' James said. 'I've given him some decent sites to look at and some reading material.'

As he wrote in Richard's notes James could fully understand Richard's decision. He was fortunate that he did have options, and chemotherapy wasn't a decision to be made lightly, or pressured into. He looked through the glass screen at the patients in for treatment this morning and recognised a couple of them.

There was Georgia, back to do battle again, her headphones on. She gave him a smile as she caught him looking over and James returned it, and then he let her be because she closed her eyes and went back to the affirmations she played through the headphones each time her treatment was delivered. Then he looked over at Heath, who didn't look over or up. He was still too busy controlling the world from his laptop, still insisting the world wouldn't survive without him for a couple of days…

It just might have to, though.

James must have dropped his suitcase off on his way to the hospital because when Ava walked into the apartment, laden with bags, there it was in the lounge.

She could smell that blasted cologne in the air, just a trace that lingered, and she opened a window to let in some fresh air. They had a two-bedroom apartment at Kirribilli Views. It was the perfect place for a young professional couple and several other medical staff from the hospital lived there. One of the bedrooms was used as James's study. Many times while he had been away Ava had found herself in there and she found herself in there now. It was always messy. James had forbidden her from tidying it, insisting he knew where everything was. There was their wedding photo on the desk and Ava couldn't help but think how young and happy they looked. She wandered into their bedroom—well, for the last year or so it had been her bedroom. She kept her home far neater than she kept her office, though it was hard to keep anything tidy with James around, even though they had Gladys, the cleaner, coming once a week. Really, for the last three months Gladys must've thought herself on holiday—well, she'd get a shock when she came in this week now that James was back.

She wandered into their en suite. Gladys would have a fit when she saw it, because for the last three months it had been spotless. Ava routinely wiped down the shower after use and folded towels and put them back. James left his clothes where they dropped and his towels too. Funny, that even though he slept on the sofa, he always used the en suite. There was a small bathroom in the hallway, a guest bathroom, and James probably didn't want to be a guest in his own home.

God, she was nervous, and she jumped when her phone bleeped a text from James telling her he'd be home about seven.

Well, he wasn't exactly racing home his first night back.

So she put the shopping away and marinated some chicken and tried to tell herself it was ridiculous to feel so nervous. It was just James coming home.

'Sorry about that.' She jumped as she heard James's key in the door. 'I dropped into Mum's.' He was balancing containers of food from Veronica, who seemed to think he needed rations to fortify him. He gave her a kiss but he was still holding the containers, so it was rather hit-and-miss.

'No problem.' Ava was used to him being late, so she didn't put the vegetable steamer on till she heard him come through the door. 'Dinner won't be long.' It felt strange to be cooking for two again. The last three months she'd been eating mainly frozen meals, healthy ones, though, and with extra steamed vegetables, and she'd taken up exercising again and lost a little bit of weight too. Still, cooking for two really meant cooking for two in this house. James liked jacket potatoes and butter with *everything* and he hated steamed vegetables, which were what Ava liked. She'd started eating really healthily when she'd lost the first baby, and she couldn't quite let go of it, but she *was* trying to get her old self back.

'Do you want veggies?' she asked as she served up, and he gave her the oddest look. 'I mean, you've lost weight, I thought maybe you're on a diet.'

'I joined a gym.' James shrugged. 'I can eat what I want now,' he said. 'It's great.'

No, she wanted to correct him, because it wasn't just about that, but she didn't want to start the night with nagging. She'd already pursed her lips when he'd come home with cartons of chicken and stir-fried rice from his mum's.

'You look like you've lost weight too.' James followed her into the living area and they sat down at the table for the first time in a very long time. She felt more awkward than one of her patients on their first visit. 'I've been riding,' Ava said, 'and swimming.'

'That's good,' James said. 'That's good, Ava.'

It was good, except she felt as if she was giving up on her dream… She'd given up so many things trying to hold on to their baby. Their first pregnancy the doctor had said that of course she could ride, given that she regularly did, and she was incredibly fit after all. So she'd carried on riding and swimming each morning and they had made love lots, as they always had.

The second pregnancy, she'd given up riding, figuring that it seemed stupid to risk a fall.

The third pregnancy, she had felt as if she were on a tightrope and had given up swimming, and by the fourth she had given up James.

And when she'd lost that one, Ava simply knew she couldn't go through it again. It had been a relief to go on the Pill, to decide that children weren't going to happen for them, to get on with their lives.

Except they hadn't.

She sliced her grilled chicken, tried not to think about it. She didn't want to think about babies. It was hard not to, though. She never had any problems getting pregnant. It was staying pregnant that had proved impossible. Six weeks, nine weeks, seven weeks and then ten weeks once…

She remembered Finn dragging her to the door.

Remembered his voice as he'd called her husband, but by then it had already been too late.

'So what did you get up to in Brisbane?'

'Not much. The teaching was pretty full on.'

'You seemed pretty busy.'

He stood to get another bottle of water.

'Might treat myself to sparkling,' James said, and she knew it was a dig, because after three months apart they should be popping corks.

'Can you check I turned the oven off?' She watched his shoulders stiffen, knew it drove him crazy when once it had made him laugh, but she was forever checking things like that.

'Well?'

'It's off,' he said, cracking open the sparkling water, filling his glass and then raising it. 'Cheers!'

She was quite sure he hadn't checked but didn't say so, very determined not to start a row.

Or face *that* conversation.

'I got you Mum's present for her birthday.' God, but it was awkward. They hadn't seen each other for three months so they should be at it over the table right now, completely unable to keep their hands off each other. Instead, there had been no contact and, worse, the conversation was strained. They simply had nothing to say to each other—it was worse than a first date.

'How's your work?' James asked.

'Busy.'

'I heard about Finn's operation being cancelled.'

'Postponed.'

'Ava.' He'd finished his chicken and she had barely started hers. 'While I've been away, I've been—'

'I had a chat with Evie…' They didn't speak at the

same time. James started and she interrupted and then stopped. 'Sorry.' She knew she had to face it. 'You were saying?'

'It can wait,' James said, because he didn't want to face it either. 'How was Evie?'

They watched a movie, or tried to, but it was a crime one and she hated those, so midway through Ava gave up and went on her computer, writing up patient notes, fixing other people's lives instead of her own.

'I'm going to bed.' She didn't bend her head to kiss him and James hardly looked up, neither quite brave enough to have *that* talk.

He sat in the semi-darkness, teeth gritted, and tried to concentrate on the film, because if he didn't he might just march into that bedroom and say something he'd regret.

Some welcome home.

He was a night person, and once Ava had been. She'd been a morning person too—up at the crack of dawn and swimming on weekdays, riding at weekends, and he was glad she was doing that again. It was the early nights he couldn't stand and she was going to bed even earlier. Now it was lights down at ten, like some school trip.

James hauled himself from the sofa and wandered into his study, saw the wedding photo on the desk and he barely recognised them so he closed the door, went back into the living room, opened up his case then headed to the cupboard and took out a blanket and pillow and tossed them down.

God, but he hated that sofa.

There was a small bathroom in the hall and he was quite sure she'd prefer that he use it, but he refused to, so he took out his toiletry bag from the case and walked into the bedroom where she lay pretending to be asleep as he went into the en suite.

James took off the shirt and discarded the linen pants on the floor, then he rinsed off the cologne and looked at her make-up bag, saw the little packet of pills that was supposed to have been the solution. He thought about having a shower, but decided that it could wait till morning. There was a show he liked starting soon, so he put a towel around his hips and walked past her bed on the way to the sofa. They'd talk tomorrow, he decided, or maybe they should wait till after his mum's birthday. He was starving. One piece of grilled chicken and a baby potato with a tiny knob of low-fat sour cream—there hadn't been butter in the apartment for years, another thing that was banned. Maybe he should ring for a pizza; that would really get under her skin...

And then he stopped.

He just stopped.

Because he could do this no longer, because it had come to *this*. He was sick of the sofa and sick of not wanting to come home—and, as hard as it was, he had to say it—he was an oncologist after all, should be able to stand by a bed and deliver a grim diagnosis.

'Ava.' He stood by the bed. 'I need to talk to you.'

Her eyes were still closed but he carried on. 'These last months while I've been away in Brisbane, I've been doing a lot of thinking.'

'James.' She turned on her side. 'It's late, can we talk tomorrow? At the weekend maybe?' She didn't want to hear it.

'No,' James said. 'We're going to talk now. You know how we agreed about no children, that we weren't going to have babies…'

She didn't want this conversation, just didn't want to have it, but James pressed on regardless. 'When you went on the Pill, I thought it was supposed to take the pressure off, supposed to be a relief, but if anything it's made things worse.' She could feel him standing over her, could feel tears building behind her eyes, and then as he carried on, she grew angry. 'I mean, even if we only had sex because you wanted to get pregnant, at least we did it…'

'Oh, poor James.' She opened her eyes now—angry eyes that met his. Three months apart and a whole lot of thinking and that was all he could come up with, that they weren't doing *it* any more. 'So you're not getting enough!'

'I know I'm not good at this.' James hissed his frustration. 'I know that I say the wrong thing, but will you just hear me out? Every day you tell your patients to talk things through,' James said. 'Every night you come home and refuse to.'

'What do you want to talk about, James? That we're not doing *it*? Well, sorry…' And she stopped. She just didn't have the energy to argue any more, couldn't drag up any more excuses, and she sat up in the bed and looked at the face she had always loved, and he was looking at her as if he didn't even know who she was.

'We're finished, aren't we?' James said it for them and it made her want to retch, but instead she just sat there as he answered the question for them. 'I mean, how much more finished can you be if after being away for three months I'm automatically heading for the sofa?'

'Some sex therapist!' She made the stupid joke for him, the one he must hear every day, when no doubt people nudged him and said how lucky he was. If only they knew. She wanted to reach out to him but she didn't know how. She'd tried so many times to have the conversations that ran in her head with him, to mourn the loss of their babies together. She had tried to tell him how she was feeling, that it wasn't just the baby she grieved for but the chance to be a mother, to fix what had been broken with her own mum. She really had tried. At first she'd cried on him. James all big and strong, telling her things would be fine, that there would be other babies, except that wasn't what she had wanted him to say.

Neither had it helped when he'd told her that they'd try again soon because she hadn't wanted him to say that either.

He was an oncologist, for God's sake; he should know how to handle grief!

She could remember how excited he had been the

first time she had been pregnant. He'd told her how much he wanted children, how much he was looking forward to being a dad. He'd shared his dreams with her and she felt like she'd ended them.

'What happens now?' She looked over at him.

'I don't know,' James admitted. 'I guess we both get a lawyer.'

'We don't need lawyers.'

'That's what everyone says, isn't it?' James said. 'Let's just get a lawyer and get it done.'

He headed out to the sofa and she called him back. 'It's your mum's birthday next weekend—should we do it after that?'

He gave a short nod. 'I'll go to a hotel tomorrow. I'll tell her after, well, not straight after...'

'Okay.' She couldn't stand it—she couldn't stand to look at what she was losing so she moved to turn out the bedside light. 'Night, then.'

That incensed him. He strode over, his face suddenly livid, and as she plunged them into darkness he turned the light back on and stood over her. 'You can't even squeeze out a tear, can you?' James accused.

'Don't say that.' Because if she started crying she thought she might never stop.

'You're just glad it's done, aren't you?' James said. 'Well, you know what? So am I. It's been hell...'

'It wasn't all bad.'

'No, Ava, it wasn't all bad,' James said, his voice rising, 'but it wasn't all good either, so don't try and sugarcoat the situation. This last year has been hell and I just want done with it.' She winced at his anger, at the hurt that was there, and then he stopped shouting. 'Sorry.' he ran a hand through his hair. 'I'm sorry, okay? I don't want to fight.' He sat down on the bed and took her hand. 'We'll do this civilly. I don't want any more rows, we'll finish things nicely… You're right, it wasn't all bad.' And he looked at her. 'There was an awful lot of good.'

'I don't want to fight,' she begged, because she hated fights, she hated rows, they made her feel ill, and James knew that.

'We won't,' he promised. 'We'll just…' He gave a shrug. She could see all his muscles, he'd really toned up, he looked amazing, he felt amazing on her skin as his hand met her arm. 'We'll remember the good times,' James said. 'We don't want to end up like Donna and Neil.'

And they both shared a pale laugh, because they'd had Donna and Neil over many times, at first together and then, when their marriage had broken up, separately, where they'd sat bitching and moaning about their exes—and James and Ava had shared many cross-eyed looks in the kitchen as they'd topped up drinks or put out dips…

'"He makes out he's so easygoing…"' She put on Donna's voice.

'"Don't know what she spends it on."' He put on Neil's.

'"He was crap in bed…"' She was still Donna.

'Well, you won't be saying that,' James said, but in his own voice now.

'No,' she admitted. 'Though you might.'

'No,' James said, and he smiled. ''Cos when we were good…' She knew what was happening as he leant over, she knew what she was doing as she put her hand to the chest that was so very close, and she didn't push him away this time, but felt his skin beneath her fingers, and her fingers lingered as she returned his kiss. She knew it wasn't a last-ditch effort to save a relationship, it was a kiss goodbye, and sex because you never would again.

She thought about it quite logically as for the first time in a year their mouths met properly, so logically for a moment that she knew it had been the same for Finn and Evie, the wonderful night Evie had recalled had been goodbye sex from Finn—while he still could.

Goodbye sex where you tried to imprint every detail as you kissed the other goodbye.

And logic went then.

His mouth was the same as the one she'd first kissed at uni, and his chin was a little stubbly now, not smooth as it had been this morning. God, but she'd loved his mouth. His shoulders were broader too, she thought as her fingers traced them, and she loved the solidness of him, loved the new toned James beneath her hands, and she pulled him further into her. And even if they hadn't been together in a very long time, still their bodies knew and recognised each other, still they matched the other's wants, a delicious familiarity, and she didn't care if he'd been with another, because she'd got to love him first.

She'd started wearing pyjamas in their year apart, big, baggy things that were buttoned to the neck, and James very slowly took them off. He looked at her body, which was way too slender now, but he had loved it for more than its shape and he kissed her ever harder.

Even if he'd lost weight he was still big, big and strong. He pressed her into the pillow and pulled the sheet down as he kissed her deeper till his towel was long gone and he was over her and here she could cry, his mouth on her salty cheeks as he slipped inside and moved inside where only he had ever been. She remembered the first time as their bodies meshed for the last time. She remembered so many times. Their first kiss on the beach, the night in his room when they had first made love, a carousel of images that flashed through her mind, and they flashed through his too—the first time, how many hours, days, weeks it had taken her to unbend, to give in to him, and the bliss he had felt when she had. He told her with words and with moans how good it felt to be there. They had always been noisy, James the most, just a delicious, uninhibited lover, and she'd miss their sounds, miss the one she was making now as her body throbbed its admission as to how much she had missed him. He moaned as he came—a deep, loud moan with her name on the end of it—and she'd miss that too, and then they lay there, conjoined, neither speaking for a while, till he rolled off and lay looking up at the ceiling, waiting for the carousel to slow down.

'Well,' Ava said finally, 'that was very civil.'

'Yeah, I can be sometimes.'

She curled up into a ball and faced away from him, wondered if he would head to the couch now, but he pulled her over to him, tucked her right into him and shielded her through their last night.

She woke to the dark, as she often did, and wriggled from his arms and lay on her back, trying to sort out problems in her head—sometimes she laughed out loud as she sorted them, but she wasn't laughing this morning; instead, she lay there fearing the dawn.

He hated the clock. He hit the snooze button, then thought better of it, leant over and turned it off. He climbed out of bed and headed to the shower. His toiletry bag from his time away was still unpacked and he went to get the razor, but couldn't be bothered. He'd only have to pack it again, so he went into the shower instead.

Maybe they could make it. Maybe after last night now they could somehow talk. He was supposed to be packing a bag and leaving for a hotel, except for the first time in more than a year there was a glimmer of hope. Yes, he knew last night hadn't been about rekindling them but somehow it felt as if they had. He thought of her body and how it had responded to him as he washed himself, thought of her warm and half-asleep in the bed just a few steps away from him, wondered about going back to her, just sliding in beside her still wet from the shower. He was hardening just thinking of her. Maybe, James thought, they should just talk; maybe they should just get angry and have a row. He knew how much she hated them, but maybe they should just shout it out, or maybe he should go in and just… He decided otherwise. It wouldn't be particularly sensitive to go in there and try to save his marriage with a throbbing hard-on, so instead of shower gel he picked up her conditioner and lathered himself with the scent of her, because that was what he often did, then bit down on his lip so as not to call out to her—when a couple of years ago he would have.

'Hey, sex therapist,' he'd used to call out from the shower, 'I've got a bit of a problem here…'

He leant his head on his arm against the shower wall as he recalled it, how she'd slipped into to the shower to 'take a closer look'. He remembered the time, before babies and miscarriages and depression and hell, his hand moving faster and the carousel was back and spinning faster now. He backed against the wall, using both hands now, remembering her hands cupping… And then he stopped.

Everything just stopped for a moment.

Even the water seemed to, because it all just seemed to go still and silent till his senses returned again and he could hear the cascade of the water, and could feel the lump in his hand. He tried to detach, to examine it clinically, and he almost managed to—could feel the lump that was certainly suspicious, except now there was no clinical detachment, he could feel sweat running down his head too, running down his back, and it wasn't the water…it was the cold sweat of fear.

'James?' He heard her voice and looked up. He heard

the concern in her voice too, and Ava was far too open-minded to care what he got up to in the shower, and in that moment she knew.

CHAPTER FOUR

'I DON'T need to leave a specimen,' James said. 'I'm not exactly in the mood.'

'Well, you'd better get yourself in the mood,' Donald said brusquely. 'Of course you will still have one testicle, but if you need chemotherapy...'

'We both decided ages ago that we're not having children.'

'James.' Donald was always blunt. He had a completely different approach from Ava. She sat there beside James for the counselling session that the surgical oncologist had insisted on, and she didn't like being on the other end of it. Ava wanted to get the hell out. 'Your marriage is over.' He looked over at Ava, who sat with her face rigid. 'You've pretty much said that you're just together for appearances' sake.'

'We didn't say that,' Ava snapped. In fact, it had been James who had said it almost the moment they'd sat down, had told Donald straight that their marriage was finished, had said up front that he didn't even know why Ava was in there with him.

'You wouldn't be here if I didn't have cancer,' James said. 'I'd be in a lawyer's office now and so would you.'

'Well, in here you can forget appearances' sake. You wanted to put off this operation so you didn't ruin your mother's birthday—for God's sake, man!'

It was Thursday. James had already had a battery of tests and there were more still to come. Blake was the oncologist that James had chosen for his treatment, thought it would be the surgical oncologist doing the operation tomorrow. He would have his testicle out, and a nice prosthetic one put in. There was one on Donald's desk now, like a strange worry ball, and she was sorely tempted to squeeze it now, though she had handed it straight to James like a hot coal when Donald had first passed it, like some bizarre game of pass the parcel. James had given it a very cursory squeeze and put it back on the desk and they both sat trying to ignore that little saline-filled ball. Ava stared out the window instead, at a view that had once soothed, as Donald spoke on.

'It's often a very treatable cancer. You may well recover from this—have the two of you thought about that? Have you, James?' Donald asked. 'Have you even let yourself consider a wonderful future, one in which you're well—where you meet someone else and fall in love and you both want to have children?'

Ava felt as if she was choking. She had this sudden vision of James running around the garden in the house they'd intended to buy when they had children.

They'd wanted a weatherboard and hopefully one with a massive garden.

'Three bedrooms,' she'd said as they'd looked through the real-estate pages.

'No, four.' He'd kissed her, patting her belly because they'd wanted loads of kids. They'd put the flat at Kirribilli on the market when she'd first got pregnant and had then wandered around homes trying to choose the one that would suit their family. She could see it in her mind's eye now, a gorgeous old weatherboard and loads of white iceberg roses and wisteria too—could see James running around the garden, clearly at one with his saline ball, children hanging off him as she trudged past on her way back from the shops, with her frozen healthy meals for one and a tin of cat food.

She hated it that he took the specimen jar.

They walked down the long corridor, James with the jar and pathology slip, and he was shown to a room. She didn't kiss his rigid, tense face, neither did she offer him a *hand*. Instead, she just stood there.

'I'll be in in the morning to see you.'

'There's no need to come in,' James said. 'It's a very simple procedure...'

'Your mum will be there,' Ava said. 'It will look strange if I'm not.' She wanted to be there, she wanted him home with her tonight, not checked into the hospital because he was first on the list and he wanted the bliss of a sleeping pill.

'James, please,' Ava said, 'please, can we talk?'

'Talk?' He gave an incredulous laugh, 'That's the

one thing we don't do, remember? Or rather one of the many things we don't do.'

And he walked into the room with the specimen jar that would soon hold his future and it terrified her that he might have one. Of course she wanted a future for James but she wanted it to be with her. Ava wanted to walk into the room and be with him now, wanted to make this hell somehow easier for him, but instead she had to head for home.

Her head was pounding, it really was.

Every root in her scalp throbbed a pulse. They'd been together so long every step was a memory.

It was here she'd started to lose the last pregnancy. That first low cramp that she'd tried to ignore and pretend hadn't happened and then a block later she'd got the next.

The sun was hot and her blouse clung to her and home just seemed too far, and she didn't want to retrace her footsteps so she walked into Pete's instead, but it was a place she and James had often gone together, and it had been ages since Ava had been there. She sat at a table and ordered a glass of sparkling water and rummaged in her bag for some headache pills, but of course she had none.

'Ava!' She heard her name called but she ignored it, and there must have been something on her face that told people to stay away, because no one came over. Pete's was filled with hospital personnel. It was a place where many met. She couldn't face going up to the bar and seeing anyone so she sat alone at her table and looked out of the window, watching all the people walking past, just getting on with their day as if it was just another day, except her marriage was ending and James had cancer and she wanted to be with her husband so badly that even the phone ringing felt like an invasion.

She answered her phone. 'He's fine, Veronica. He said he doesn't want visitors tonight.' She did her best to answer her mother-in-law's endless questions, but Veronica wasn't just a nosy old boot, she was a perceptive one too.

'It's because he's a doctor,' Ava said, when Veronica pointed out that these days people went in in the morning and James had told her it was a day-case procedure and nothing to worry about. 'They're just doing him a favour so he can get a bit more sleep. He'll have a sleeping tablet and be knocked out. It's better than him being at home, stressing.'

Except James didn't stress.

It was one of the things she had so loved about him. Arrogant, some said; male chauvinist, a few others, but he wasn't—he was just this big bull of a male and she loved him for it. This man who didn't sweat the small stuff, who didn't care about clothes and flowers, and it wasn't that he expected her to do the washing-up: he'd happily leave it undone.

'Can I get you anything else?' She blinked as she saw the waiter taking away her empty glass. She couldn't remember even drinking the sparkling water.

'A glass of wine,' Ava replied, and then she had to go through whether she wanted red or white. She stabbed her finger at a random one on the menu. She didn't care what she had, she simply couldn't face going back to the flat, to lie in bed without him.

But they had been sleeping apart for months, Ava reminded herself as the waiter came back. She sipped on her drink.

'Ava!' It was Mia and Luca walking into the bar, friends they had often shared a drink and a meal with, but they were so in love, so together, it made Ava want to weep.

'We heard about James.' And they were a nice couple, just up front, and she should be grateful that they faced it, that they didn't pretend that they didn't know. Except she was starting to cry—she was sitting in the middle of Pete's and starting to cry.

'Ava,' Mia put her arm on her shoulder but she pushed it off and stood.

'Leave me, please…' She didn't even pay for her wine, just stood up and walked out. She saw Mia's eyes close in regret for her handling of things, except they hadn't been insensitive, they were doing what everyone said you should: facing it, bringing it out in the open, talking about it.

She never wanted to hear those words again.

She walked home, thinking of the babies James would have with another. She had so often blended their features—amber-eyed babies with light brown hair, or green-eyed babies with their hair dark—but now she had to take herself out of the picture.

Her blouse was sticking to her again, and as she

stepped into the air-conditioned lobby at Kirribilli she shivered as she waited for the lift. Tears were really starting to come and she didn't know how to stop them. She pressed the lift button again, relieved when the doors opened. As she stood inside, pressing the button for her floor, someone raced to catch it, and she was quietly relieved that it was only Finn.

And because it was Finn, of course he ignored her.

He was having surgery first thing tomorrow too, but unlike James he was spending his last night at home.

Ava glanced at the bottle he must have gone out to purchase, figured a sleeping pill would be the safer option, but it was none of her business.

Neither nodded.

Neither bothered pretending it was a good evening.

They just both wished the lift would start moving. She was holding on to her tears for dear life, but they kept slipping out and her breath was coming out in little shudders and she just wished the lift would move.

'Looks like we're walking.' Finn broke the tense silence after several of Ava's frantic attempts at pushing buttons.

'Looks like it,' Ava said through gritted teeth.

She pushed open the stairwell door, and didn't hold it open, which was maybe a bit mean with his crippled arm, but she was past caring and started climbing. She could hear Finn behind her, determined to keep up with her, probably to prove he wasn't in pain.

She wanted to start running.

She just wanted to be in her flat so the tears could

fall more readily, but even if she wanted to run her legs seemed to be turning to lead. She gripped the hand rail, moved one foot in front of the other, could hear Finn catching up, and she couldn't move a step further. She was doubled up in pain, not bleeding this time as Finn came up behind her. The pain wasn't physical, but it paralysed her just the same.

'Leave me,' she sobbed as he walked past her and she sat on the stairs, grateful that if someone had to see her like this it was Finn, because he was perhaps the only man who would walk straight past, because no doubt he just wanted to get up to his flat too. It was a relief to hear his footsteps pass, to just sit with her face buried in her hands and to weep, to give in to the tears and just let them fall. Later she would try to summon the energy to move.

She didn't hear him come back down, as she was crying too hard to notice his about-turn. She just sort of felt him on the stairs beside her, but she was too far gone to stop.

She hadn't cried like this in years.

Oh, there had been nightly tears for a long time now, but she hadn't actually broken down, not since she'd had the second miscarriage.

She hadn't sobbed so hard she thought she might vomit, that she might never again be able to breathe, in ages, but she did it now, sat on the stairs with Finn beside her and shuddered her pain out, and it seemed to echo through the stairwell. Surely people would come soon and tell her to shut the hell up, but she was shutting up anyway. Somehow the sobs were slowing down.

'Do you want some?' She glanced over as he opened the bottle.

'I really wish you'd just kept walking.'

'Believe me, I tried.' He handed her the bottle and she took a sip. She hadn't had whisky in years, hadn't had a glass of wine in years either. She had just kept on giving up everything she liked in the hope of keeping a baby inside her, and never going back to them again—just giving up all the things that made her her. And she didn't like who she was any more.

She didn't like the nitpicking, low-carb, healthy version of herself.

And she cried some more, but not so violently now. Finn just sat there and let her, and she took another swig of his drink.

'I don't want to talk,' Ava said.

'Good,' Finn answered. 'Because neither do I.'

They sat, him in silence, Ava still catching her breath as the tears started to slow, her body shuddering with little hiccoughs as it slowly calmed. Then she remembered it was his drink and Ava handed the bottle back to him. 'Should you be…?' And then she stopped herself because it wasn't her business and he too wanted silence and she was surprisingly grateful that he was there, but he declined when she offered him his drink.

'I think you need it more than me.'

She didn't. She took the lid and put it back on. They sat a while longer, her tears slowing down, the hiccoughs silencing, and it had actually been better here than alone. Finally, she could think about moving those last steps to her door as she sat there, still catching her breath from her crying marathon.

'I think the chivalrous thing to do would be to put my arm around you,' said Finn, 'except I can hardly feel it.'

She turned and gave him a very watery smile and after a moment's pause he returned it.

She'd never really looked at him, never really understood what Evie saw in him. James was macho, but Finn could be a bastard at times, yet he'd always been quietly nice to her and he was being quietly nice to her now.

And Finn looked at Ava. He'd never really been able to work her out. He liked James a lot, he was a bloke's bloke, and they'd shared more than a few nights at Pete's. But Ava—she was a funny little thing. At times he'd heard their rows, but she was always so prim and guarded when they met in the corridor. Even when she'd had the miscarriage, she'd hardly said a word, just 'Call James,' but surely she wasn't so prim and guarded? He knew what she did for a job. 'Lucky guy,' he'd ribbed James at times when they'd shared a drink at Pete's. 'Married to a sex therapist.'

Except he knew now how stupid those words had been. He'd had to see that Donald a couple of weeks ago, a requirement for the surgery he was having, and hadn't liked one bit the details that Donald had gone into. He had firmly decided he wouldn't be seeing him again.

His smile turned wry as both sat on the steps, staring at the other, and it was Finn who broke the strange silence. 'You know, we could really mess things up here,' Finn said, removing his gaze from her and looking at their surroundings. 'We could have drunken sex on the stairwell...'

And she actually found herself laughing.

'Except I'd hate myself even more in the morning,' Finn said.

'Hate yourself?' Ava frowned.

'Guilt.'

'I didn't know you possessed such a thing.'

'Neither did I. But it'd be there tomorrow—you know, when Evie tries to come and see me to wish me well for the operation.'

She doubted a man like Finn had ever felt guilty before, had ever felt so loyal to a woman before, and he looked at her for a very long moment and she looked back at him. And then he spoke. 'And I'd hazard a guess that the only person you want to have sex with is your husband...'

It was true, so very true.

He stood up; he'd done enough sentiment for one night.

'Here.' She handed him the bottle, but he shook his head.

'Better not. Better still that the lift isn't working and I'll have to climb up these stairs again if I change my mind.'

He headed back up towards his penthouse suite as she sat on the step. 'Hey, Ava?'

'The answer is no.' She turned and smiled as

she hauled herself up to go home, except his face was serious.

'If I end up in a chair...if I...' He closed his eyes. 'I don't want Evie and I coming in to see you for help, don't want to be sitting in your office being told... I don't want to do that to her.'

Ava went over to him. 'Let her in, Finn.'

She saw the conflict knit his face closed, knew then how badly he wanted Evie there and understood too why he was pushing her away.

'And I'd help you,' she said, and wondered how she would deal with such a complicated, private man, because there was something about Finn, something about his brilliance that was intimidating. But she knew that if it came to it, and if he let her, she would help him.

'I don't want all that for her.' He shook his head. 'I saw that Donald...'

'You'd see me,' she said firmly. 'And *I* would help you, I would help both of you,' Ava promised as he shook his head to decline. Sometimes a bit of humour *was* needed. 'On the condition that you promise not to make one of those awful jokes.'

'What one's that?' Finn asked.

'Well, I never thought I'd end up in here.' She put on a macho male voice.

'You'll need the biggest one!' Finn gruffed back.

'They all say that.' Ava laughed.

'I *would* help you,' Ava said, joking over now, and her voice was kind as she did what she never thought she would to this dark, moody man—gave him a cuddle. And he put his good arm around her and they stood and held each other for a moment.

'We'll go back to ignoring each other tomorrow,' Ava assured him.

'I'm back to ignoring you now,' Finn said, but as he let her go, as he turned to go, he paused. 'Ring him,' Finn said, because he knew how cold and lonely James must be feeling tonight.

'Ring her,' Ava said, except she knew Finn wasn't going to take her advice. Was she going to take his?

Ava had a shower and washed her hair. It would be dry and frizzy tomorrow because there was never any conditioner in this place. She pulled on her robe and went through to the lounge and looked out of the window to the hospital where tonight James lay. She scanned the windows and tried to work out which was his room, wondered if he was looking out now towards their home.

She should be with him, Ava realised.

They should be in bed right now, making love—because she loved him and she had to tell him, and it was pure need that drove her impulse to pick up the phone.

'James.'

'Ava.' he sounded in no mood to talk. 'They've just given me a sleeping tablet.'

'I love you.'

'Look.' He was very practical, had anticipated that she must be feeling as guilty as hell by the timing of everything. 'We'll talk about this another time. We're over, Ava. You don't have to—'

'I want you here.'

James frowned as he heard her carefully formed words. 'Have you been drinking?'

'Yes.'

'How much?'

She looked at the bottle. 'Not much, but I haven't had anything for ages.' And then she remembered. 'Oh, and I had some wine too...'

'You lush!' She could picture his smile.

'God, James, I wanted to come to that room and help you...'

'You really have been drinking!' He grinned, remembered the times in their marriage when they would share a bottle of wine, and she carried on talking, told him she loved him, and even if they weren't going to make it, it was nice to hear it tonight, to talk to her, to hear her voice.

She wandered as she spoke, walked into the bedroom and then to the en suite, where there were towels all over the floor, and about four razors because there was no way a nurse was shaving him.

'Are you bald?'

She should have shaved him and she said what she was thinking.

'I should have shaved you.'

'Ava.'

'No, I should have...' And she told him how she would have.

'Hell, Ava.' His hand was under the sheets. 'I'm

going to have to press the bell and get them to bring in another specimen jar soon.'

They were both laughing.

'My wife the sex therapist.'

CHAPTER FIVE

'WE NEED you over on the trolley.'

Ava stood outside with Veronica as James was transferred to the trolley that would take him to Theatre. The warmth from last night had gone and she wasn't so shallow as to try and rekindle it. This morning wasn't about them, it was about James. He had been gruff and impatient when Lily the nurse had come in to take his obs and was equally gruff with his responses as she checked off the theatre list. Not that she seemed to mind. Lily was a friend of theirs—or rather Lily's husband Luke was a friend of James's and she and Lily always said they must catch up—they'd been to Luke and Lily's wedding. It just made it all the more awkward, though, but apparently not for Lily—she smiled over to where Veronica and Ava stood and Ava tried not to look at Lily's pregnancy bump. 'Just one of you can come down to Theatre with him.'

'I'll be fine,' James said.

'Don't be ridiculous,' Ava said, and Veronica said she might go for a wander, but, as she walked alongside him, she wondered if James actually wanted her there, if she was just making this harder than it had to be. James stared up at the ceiling as she walked alongside the trolley to Theatre and his responses were just as curt as the theatre nurse now checked off the list.

'Two crowns,' he said for perhaps the tenth time since last night. 'Front two,' he said again. And Ava could not help but remember the rugby accident when he'd been at uni where he had lost his two front teeth and broken his nose. A few days later his father, Edward, had died, and he'd had temporary crowns for the funeral…

There was so much of their history in each box the nurse ticked.

'No,' he snapped when she asked if he had any allergies, though he was, in fact, allergic to Play-Doh. Veronica had told her that he'd had came home from school when he was five, all covered in welts—not that the nurses needed to know that. Maybe it was good that she'd come up with him after all—she could just imagine Veronica chiming in, which wouldn't have been the best with James in this mood!

Still, all too soon he was all checked off to their satisfaction and was ready to be wheeled through, and it was time to say goodbye.

'Say goodbye, have a kiss,' the cheerful theatre nurse said. 'He'll be out soon. The operation usually takes about an hour, sometimes a bit more, but we'll page when he's in Recovery and about to head back to the ward.'

Ava leant over him and stared into those green eyes.

'Good luck.' How paltry those words sounded. She

went to kiss him but he turned his face so all she got was the edge of his mouth and his cheek and then he closed his eyes and said nothing, and she wanted five minutes away from everyone, just five minutes of his time, but since he'd found that awful lump they'd had none.

That dreadful morning was burned into her brain.

'James?' She could hear her question that morning, knew in an instant what he'd found.

She'd sort of dragged him to the bed, all sensible and reassuring, with her heart hammering in her chest. She'd felt for the lump and, yes, there was one, and she'd been all practical and agreed that, yes, he should get it seen to, except James had snapped into action by then—had been off the bed and ringing a colleague, and from that moment on it had been round after round of tests and scans.

And because it was James it had all been rushed through. They didn't do biopsies for testicular cancer—instead, it was ultrasounds and blood tests and CTs and counselling. And then he'd had to go round and tell his mother and then his mother had told the rest of his family and of course there had been uncles and cousins and just too many people coming over at night.

And when they went, so too did James's smile.

He was back on the sofa—his choice now, and using her own excuses against her.

'I'm tired, Ava.' That was one of them. 'I need space.' The other.

So she stood for a moment, watching him being wheeled away behind the black plastic doors, and as she turned around to go she saw Evie standing next to Finn. She was trying to talk to Finn, but his face was as closed as James's, staring over her shoulder, and then Finn's eyes met Ava's for a very brief moment and maybe last night had affected them both because she watched as he did turn to Evie.

As he let her kiss him.

'I'll always be there for you, Finn.'

And she wanted to step in.

Wanted to tell Evie just to kiss him.

Wanted to somehow explain that her saying she would always be there for him was what terrified Finn most.

But as she looked at the black plastic doors, she wanted to run to her husband, wanted to say the same words to him.

Except he'd assume he was being given the sympathy vote.

Even though Ava's heart and mind were consumed with James, she couldn't help but feel for Evie as Finn was wheeled off. She felt for Finn too and, based on their conversation last night, the best she could do for Finn was to go over as Evie stopped trying to be strong. She felt the other woman almost implode beneath her fingers as she put her hand on her shoulder.

'Come on,' Ava said. 'We'll go to my office.'

Evie held it together till they were there but once away from the sympathetic stares and curious eyes, she broke down. 'I'm sorry,' she sobbed. 'It's your *hus-*

band that's having surgery and I'm not being much help at all.'

'It's fine,' Ava said, because she'd had her tears yesterday and could at times be terribly, terribly practical, and also because she did not want to think of the paltry last words she and James had exchanged, did not want to spend the next couple of hours going over what was happening in Theatre, because she could not stand to think of him being operated on now. As complicated as Evie and Finn's relationship was, right now their problems were easier for Ava to deal with than her own. 'This is the easy bit for James. It's going to be hell waiting for the results and then finding out what's going to happen in the way of treatment, but today's really quite straightforward. Finn's surgery is far more serious.'

'Still...' Evie attempted.

'Hey, I spend the next couple of hours in here, or back on the ward with Veronica.' She rolled her eyes. 'My mother-in-law.'

'Don't you get on?' Evie was dabbing her eyes now. For all her tears she was much calmer today than Ava had been last night. Evie was a tough thing really, Ava thought. Though she'd probably had to be, given the family she'd come from.

'Not really,' Ava admitted. 'I don't think I've fulfilled the role of James's wife very well in her eyes. By now I should be a stay-at-home mum and have given her at least two little Carmichaels.'

'Don't you want children?'

And Ava had her lists of answers for that one, as if

printed out in her mind so she could reel off the one that suited best. *Not for ages* or *Maybe someday* or *Not you too!* Or, said with a wry laugh to her more feminist friends, *I'd have expected better from you.* But today she didn't have the list handy. Today she was aching inside, today she was touched too, that from the innocence of Evie's question she knew Finn really had never told anyone about that time. And maybe it was time to be honest.

'We'd have loved to have had children,' Ava said. 'It just didn't work out that way.'

'Ava!'

'Evie, please.' Ava put her hand up. 'Can we talk about you and Finn, because I can't break down today, I truly can't— I don't want to go in to see James all upset. I'm sure he's worried enough as it is without me breaking down on him.' Oh, God, how easily she could—she could kick the wall in this very minute because yet again another block had been put in their path to parenthood.

'What did Finn say when you said goodbye?' Ava asked instead as she filled a glass of water from the sink and drained it and then managed to turn around and play calm.

'He said, "Bye, princess."' Evie gave a very watery smile. 'He calls me that, sometimes nastily...' Ava could imagine. Evie's father had donated so much to the hospital and everyone had once assumed that Evie had had some sort of free pass in the hospital so it was a bit of a nickname around the place and she could well imagine Finn using that barb.

'But he didn't say it nastily today. I know Finn can be a complete bastard...'

And had Ava not sat on the stairs and spoken with him last night, she might have inwardly agreed, except... 'There's a lot more to Finn than that,' Ava said. 'And this operation is just huge. I can't imagine what he's going through.'

'We're not going to know the outcome for ages,' Evie said. 'He's asked me not to visit. How am I supposed to stay away?'

'I don't know,' Ava said. 'Maybe...' Despite her best efforts she couldn't stop thinking about James, couldn't stop comparing the two men, which was ridiculous as they were completely different. 'Maybe just give him space,' she advised, but her heart wasn't in it because she could not stand that now for James and herself—and maybe sometimes it was better to admit the truth.

'I don't know, Evie. I don't know what to suggest. I think you just have to get through this bit for now.'

It was terribly hard to take her own advice, though.

'How much longer?' Veronica was pacing when Ava came down.

'It shouldn't be much longer now,' Ava said.

'And then the real wait begins.' Which it did, because they'd have to wait to find out for sure what they were dealing with.

'I know it's hard.'

'No, Ava, you don't,' Veronica said. 'He's my son.'

Ava tried not to take it personally but, hell, it felt personal and terribly so, as if unless she was a mother she didn't really know love, and of course Veronica hadn't meant that, but it stung, that was all.

'He's all I've got,' Veronica said, and it took all Ava's might to bite her tongue, to not point out that at least she'd had a child. There was a froth of anger inside her, like the type that washed up on the beach after a filthy storm, and Ava hated what the last days had done, not just to James but also to her.

'I'm just going up to Theatre to get him.' Lily popped her head around the door. 'I shouldn't be long.'

She wasn't. About ten minutes later Ava and Veronica stood outside in the hall again as James was transferred back to his bed, and then they waited outside while Lily did his obs and made him comfortable. Finally they were allowed in.

'Hey.' She bent her head and he was too groggy to turn his face away this time. She could smell the fumes of the anesthetic and she was so pleased to see him back. 'How do you feel?'

'Tired,' James said, and promptly went back to sleep.

And Veronica had been right, because now the real wait started, and time seemed to be moving terribly slowly. When his next set of obs were done half an hour later, Veronica gave in to a headache and said that she would go but would be popping over to the apartment that evening. 'Do you need me to bring anything?'

'We're fine,' Ava said. 'I'll text you when we get home.'

And there were more obs and he woke up and was sick once, and he got annoyed with her and told her to go. Then he woke up again and was more like James.

'You might as well go.' James said it a lot more nicely this time. 'I'll be a few hours yet.'

'I'm not going anywhere,' Ava said. 'Well, I might go and get a drink and I'll text people, let them know you're okay.'

'Get some lunch,' James suggested.

She did, except she didn't have it in the canteen. Instead, Ava bought a salad sandwich and a bottle of water and sat outside in the sun. It was nice to be out-side, Ava realised. She didn't do this nearly enough. Most of her lunches she took in her office.

She looked out at the water. They hadn't been on the water in ages. They used to get the ferry, just hop off wherever and get breakfast when James had a weekend off. She would love to do it this weekend, but of course he wouldn't be able to, but maybe next, Ava decided, or maybe the weekend before he went back to work.

If they weren't over by then.

She felt like a fighter pilot, scrambling for a plan when already it was too late, but she sat in the sun, making lists in her mind of all the things they would do. They'd play Scrabble, and talk, or she'd just lie on the bed beside him and read. And, please, God, that the results weren't too bad, because there were so many things James had to do and so many things she wanted to do with him, and it was simply too hard to think like that today, so she stood and binned her half-eaten sandwich and then headed back to the ward.

When she returned the door was closed and as Ava walked in, Lily called from behind a drawn curtain and asked Ava to wait outside as she was just checking James's wound. That just seemed stupid to Ava—she'd seen it all before!—but she turned around obediently and went out to the corridor.

'Won't be long.' Lily popped out but closed the door behind her, and as she headed off to the supplies trolley she gave Ava a smile. Perhaps a bit rudely Ava didn't return it. Instead, she stood bristling in the corridor as Lily returned, holding a couple of medical packs.

She was being petty, Ava knew that. She and Lily shared a mutual love of horses and at Christmas dos and the like they sort of gravitated towards each other. Today she had been nothing but nice but Ava could not return her smile.

'Blake's going to come down and see him,' Lily said.

'Why?' Ava snapped, because Blake was an oncologist like James and this operation was being dealt with by the surgical team.

'He just wants to check in on him,' Lily explained.

'And then we can go home?' Ava checked, because she wanted so badly to be home with him, alone with him. Maybe when they got there she could ring Veronica and say that James was asleep and not to worry about coming over. But instead of answering her question, Lily gave that noncommittal smile that nurses did so

well and disappeared back into the room, leaving Ava
still standing in the corridor, tears stinging in her eyes.

She couldn't help it. She was jealous of Lily—her
pregnancy, her happy marriage and healthy husband.
She'd dealt with not being able to have a baby of her
own, but today everything felt so raw that she was even
jealous that it was Lily in with her husband now. So
jealous of Lily, who would no doubt trot and canter her
way through a textbook pregnancy.

Oh, God, what was wrong with her? Why was she
thinking such horrible things?

Ava didn't know how she felt.

She hardly managed a smile when Blake appeared.

'I'm just going to take a look at him, Ava.' And after
a few moments she was called into the room and she
still didn't know how she felt as she stood there.

'The surgeons say that everything went really well
today,' Blake said. 'However, he's still got some con-
siderable pain and is nauseous, so we're going to keep
him in overnight.' Blake confirmed what she'd guessed
was happening—knew the little powwow he and Lily
had had behind that closed door. 'He should be fine to
go home tomorrow morning.'

'Thanks, Blake.' James shook his hand from his bed
and then Blake left the room.

'I'll come back with your injection shortly,' Lily said,
and left them alone.

'You didn't say you were in a lot of pain.'

'I didn't want to moan,' James replied. 'You might
as well go home.'

'I can stay.'

'There's no point,' James said. 'I'll just be sleeping once I get the needle. When you get home can you ring Mum and tell her that they're keeping me in?'

'You know she'll just want to visit,' Ava said.

'Of course she will,' James said. 'I'm her son.'

'Here's your injection, James.' Lily came back in carrying a little kidney dish and she was going to swoosh that curtain any second, Ava knew it, and ask her to step outside, but it was James who spoke next.

'I'll see you, then, Ava.' And she knew that she was being dismissed. Ava didn't bother with the kiss goodbye for appearances' sake. Sure, he probably was in pain, but at the bottom of her heart Ava knew, and she knew that Lily knew, that James had told her and Blake that he'd prefer hospital to home.

She rang Veronica and told her of the development and, of course, Veronica informed her that she was heading back soon. 'I might take him in some dinner.'

Ava didn't bother with dinner—she was, in fact, exhausted.

She had a shower and climbed into bed, weary with fatigue, but her brain was going at a hundred miles an hour, and when her phone bleeped a text she jumped up, wondering if it was the hospital, hoping it was James, and then felt a little guilty when she saw that it was Evie, because she'd completely forgotten about Finn.

Finn out of Theatre and Recovery and now on ICU.

Way too early to say how it went but thankfully operation over.

It was a group text, Ava knew that. She'd sent one of her own to their family and friends when James had been returned to the ward. As nice as it was that people were thinking of them, the multitude of replies and questions had been somewhat overwhelming, so Ava did Evie a favour and didn't reply.

Just closed her eyes, relieved for Finn, scared for Finn.

Relieved for James, scared for James.

Scared for herself too.

CHAPTER SIX

JAMES texted in the morning and asked if she could bring up a coffee when she picked him up, so she stopped at the kiosk and waited while it was being made and noticed that her hand was shaking as she handed over the money.

She was nervous about seeing him and she didn't want to be.

'Oh, hi, Tom.' She turned as someone came up beside her, and because Tom was blind Ava introduced herself. 'It's Ava.'

'Ava!' Tom smiled. 'I've just come over to have coffee with Hayley—and to bring Sasha to see her mum. Hayley's on call all weekend.'

She glanced over to where Hayley, who was a surgeon, sat engrossed in her baby.

'How are you?' Tom asked.

'Good.' Ava said, because Tom must be the only person who didn't know, but he worked over at the university, and she simply didn't have the energy to talk about it today, and they seemed to be taking for ever to froth the coffee. *Oh, please,* Ava thought, *just hurry up.*

'And James?' Tom added, because he couldn't see the desperation in her eyes.

'Yeah, he's not bad,' Ava said, and did her best to keep her voice light and smiled as the cashier handed her her change, except she dropped all the coins on the floor. 'Sorry.'

She scrabbled to the floor and saw Tom's dog, Baxter, and wanted to weep onto him as she picked up her change. Instead, when she'd collected the coins she stayed kneeling for a moment and stroked his beautiful head.

'Ava.' Tom's voice came from a long way off. 'You can't pat Baxter.'

'Of course. Sorry.' She pulled her hand away and stood.

'While he's got his harness on, he's not to be patted,' Tom explained, and he was right, of course. Baxter was working, she'd simply forgotten, and Tom was only being nice, only saying what he must have to about a hundred times a day, yet it felt like a snub. Of course it wasn't a snub, but she was so prickly and raw that everything hurt a little more.

'I'll bring your coffees over, Tom,' the cashier said when she took his order, and Ava said goodbye as he headed back to his family. A little later as she took her coffee she saw Hayley speaking with Tom, saw Tom wince, knew that now Hayley was telling him.

Blake was there with James when she got up to the ward and so too was Lily. She looked tired today, but she was all smiles when Ava came in as Blake finished off giving his discharge instructions. Ava stood there as Lily hauled over a wheelchair and Ava wondered what on earth she was doing working. Her husband was a consultant after all…

And then she stopped herself, because so was hers and she'd worked, she believed in women working. She was just being horrible, jealous and vile and bitter, and— She didn't know how she felt.

'And Lily has given you all the after-care instructions.' Blake finished up as Ava struggled to concentrate on what was being said.

'I've got everything,' James broke in. 'And I'm not being wheeled down.'

'No choice.' Lily beamed. 'It's a long way to the foyer.'

As James took a reluctant seat Ava handed him his coffee.

'Thanks,' he said.

'Thanks, Blake,' Ava said. It felt strange to be speaking with him in this way—normally she only saw Blake at social events, sometimes when he came with his wife, Joan, to the apartment for dinner. 'I guess we now just have to wait till we get the results.'

'Yes.' James was clearly itching to get out of the hospital. 'Give me a ring as soon as you get *my* results.'

'Of course,' Blake said, and as his eyes briefly met Ava's, she felt a dull flush spread up her cheeks and it refused to go. There were tears at the back of her eyes too as the porter wheeled James down, Lily walking alongside. That blasted flush stayed on her cheeks as she went and got the car, and as she realised she'd forgotten her swipe card to get out of the staff car park the tears started trickling.

But she'd got into the car park, she told herself, so it had to be here, and she rummaged through her bag to look for it. She settled for a tissue instead and wept into it for a moment.

'Stop it, Ava.' She said it about four times. She should have done this at home, last night. 'Not here.'

And she dragged in a breath and rubbed some powder on her face and found her stupid swipe card and drove to where James was waiting with Lily, who was chatting easily with him.

And she knew how she felt then.

Knew the word she'd been searching for these past days.

Excluded.

Excluded from everything.

'I can manage.' He refused her help, just climbed into the passenger side, and he would have driven himself home if he'd been allowed to, Ava realised.

'Thanks.' She tried to smile at Lily, except her mouth wouldn't move.

'You're welcome.' Lily patted her arm. 'We'll catch up soon, Ava.'

They hardly said a word during the short drive home, and there was Veronica waiting at the door as he limped out of the lift.

Excluded.

That was how she felt as Veronica made James's lunch and suggested Ava go to the store and get some more ice for James's ice packs.

And he was the last mummy's boy on earth, but he did love his mum enough to *let* her look after him.

He slept for most of the afternoon then got up and had some dinner, cooked by Veronica, then stood up and declared he was going back to bed.

'Thanks.' He gave Veronica a kiss. 'Go home, Mum.'

'You're sure?'

'I just want to go to bed. Thanks for everything.'

Ava saw her out and then headed back to the lounge but James had already gone to the bedroom and was pulling back the sheets.

'Did you need anything?'

'I just want to go to sleep.'

'Sure,' Ava said. 'I'll bring you in a fresh ice-pack when I come to bed.' She went to head out, didn't want his words to catch her before she closed the door, but it was as if James had been waiting for them.

'Ava. I really appreciate you giving up *your* bed for a couple of nights.'

'James, please.' Ava swallowed. 'Let me come to bed.'

'You can do what you want, but if you get into this bed I swear I'll get straight out and check into a hotel.'

'James, I don't want you in a hotel.' She didn't and she didn't want something else too. 'I don't want a divorce. Can you just listen?'

'No, you listen!' he broke in. 'It was *your* miscarriages, *your* babies, *your* grief, you made it that way—well, it's *my* cancer. And do you know what I don't need now? I don't need to be one of your clients in this, I don't want you telling me that you can't feel the difference in my balls, or your patronising understanding when I'm so scared or drugged up that I can't get it up. Neither do I want sympathy sex, or any of it. The same way I didn't want you in there when I was getting my dressing changed. You didn't want any of it when I was well...'

She couldn't even cry.

'And—' he hadn't finished yet '—I heard you saying to Mum that you had taken a week off. Well, you can untake it, because I won't be able to rest or relax with you in the flat. What was it you used to say when I tried to give you a cuddle or, heaven forbid, a kiss? What was it you used to say when I tried to talk? Oh, I remember: "I need space." In your own words, Ava!'

CHAPTER SEVEN

JAMES was closed.

There might as well have been a sign around his neck—'Not back in five minutes, not open again soon.'

He was completely closed.

He'd done a similar thing when his dad had died, a week after his teeth had been knocked out. He'd just shut her off, only for a couple of days, but by the funeral, when all the bruises had looked brown and yellow, they had been together again, close again, making love again. Not that he'd ever really broken down about his dad—not once in their relationship had James cried, not even when she'd lost the babies. He just didn't do tears, and he wasn't doing them now—if anything, as the weekend passed, more and more he seemed quietly cheered.

He rang friends for chats, he sat on the computer for an hour on Sunday and bought about fifty books for his ereader and then, before he went back to bed, he ordered a pizza.

And, no, Ava noted, he didn't offer her a slice, but, then, why would he when she'd always refused before?

It was incredibly uncomfortable on the sofa and she'd forgotten to put her clothes out the night before, but he didn't wake up as she rummaged through her wardrobe early on Monday morning, neither did he wake up when she showered and did her hair.

Or maybe he was pretending to be asleep.

And then she felt the stab of regret as she qualified it—maybe he was pretending to be asleep, just as she had.

'What are you doing back?' he asked later that day, when she popped back on her lunch break. He was sitting in bed on the phone, but hung up when she came in.

'I just thought I'd check how you were.'

'I'm fine.' He had a computer game on, and if anything seemed to be treating it as a holiday. He hadn't shaved since they'd found the lump, and he was looking like he did whenever they had time off, sort of scruffy and rumpled and actually, impossibly perhaps, happy.

Unlike Ava.

'And there was some news on Finn I thought you might want to hear.'

'Yeah, I heard.' He nodded to the phone on the bed beside him. 'They didn't cut my ears off, Ava.'

And it was so James that if she'd paused for a moment, she might even have laughed, except there was nothing to laugh about today. It wasn't good news about Finn and she ached to speak with James about it. There was shrapnel they hadn't been able to reach and the attempts at removal had made things worse. Right now he was ventilated and in spinal shock. However, she pressed on with a conversation James didn't want.

'It doesn't look good for Finn,' she offered, but James just shrugged and went back to his game.

'Early days,' he said.

'I'll stop and get something nice for dinner,' Ava attempted, 'maybe take-away?'

'If you want,' James said, 'but not for me. I've got a freezer full of stuff from Mum.' And to prove his point he swung his legs out of bed and, much more easily now, walked over to the fridge and grabbed some herbed chicken and stir-fried rice, which was his favourite. Veronica had made loads, of course, and he popped his individual serving, which would feed a horse, into the microwave.

Yet for all his unhealthy eating he looked, and she really shouldn't be noticing such things, fantastic.

He had some bruising down his thigh and had a support on, but over that was new underwear, really sexy, modern underwear—from his shopping trips in Brisbane, Ava reminded herself.

Except she wasn't jealous at the moment, and she wasn't even upset. She was just looking at him, not at his eyes but at his chest and then down to his thigh and that bruise and then up to his flat stomach. Then she met his gaze and he snapped his eyes away, and she didn't know the hows and whys but if it had been another day, another time, they'd have already been on the floor, and she knew he knew it. He sort of grimaced a little bit and moved his support as he walked across the kitchen and his muscles were rippling as he reached into the fridge and pulled out a milk carton, and as if to defy her, because it was one of the few things she really *was* closed-minded on, he drank straight from the carton, then burped and drank again. When the microwave pinged he took his chicken and milk back to the bedroom with him and closed the door.

Maybe it was only she who had wanted to make love, then, Ava conceded.

Maybe he *was* happy it was over.

She stood in the kitchen, and faced the impossible truth.

Maybe he was simply relieved.

She went to walk out, opened the front door and stood a moment, and then closed it, because they had to talk, because, no, he couldn't be happy, he couldn't be relieved. She knew them better than that, knew how good they were, how good they had been. She could not live this a single moment longer so she drew in a breath, tried to gather the strength to just walk in the bedroom and force him to listen, except she could hear the blips as, assuming she'd gone out, he dialled a number on the phone and then came his voice.

'Yeah, sorry, Steph… It's okay, she's gone back to work. Nearly got caught there! Now, where were we?'

CHAPTER EIGHT

'I'M SORRY about this, Donald.'

'It's not a problem,' Donald said as Ava sat on a chair on the other side of his desk, pulling tissues from his box. 'Ginny has cancelled your clients for the afternoon.'

'Thanks.'

His office was so different from hers, his style, his stance the complete opposite of hers, yet *his* patients adored him. His brusque, direct approach was one that appealed to some, though Ava wasn't particularly grateful for it now, not grateful that he tutted and tsked as she poured out a little more of what was going on. 'You shouldn't have come in this week,' Donald said. 'You've got far too much going on to be sensible at work.'

'I know that,' Ava shrilled. 'But James doesn't want me at home. What am I supposed to do, spend the day walking on the beach?'

'You could ask him,' Blake said. 'Ask him if he's seeing someone else.'

'I could,' Ava said. 'And whether you believe me or not, if he didn't have this diagnosis hanging over him

I would.' She held her breath at the impossibility of it all. 'That's a whole lot of arguing to cram in between now and next week when he gets his results. Can I forgive him?' She didn't know. Sometimes she thought she could, sometimes she knew she never could. They needed time, time to thrash things out, but time was the commodity they'd frittered away so foolishly and now suddenly it was running out.

'Maybe check yourself into some hotel like he's threatening to.' Donald smiled. 'Spend the day in bed, getting room service.'

Ava was surprised to find herself smiling back. 'That's worryingly tempting.'

'Do it, then.' Donald shrugged.

'That's no answer.'

'Well, you're probably not getting much rest on that sofa.' He took a breath. 'Ava, you know James will be feeling scared, he'll also be angry...'

'He's not, though.'

'Ava?'

And she closed her eyes and thought about it, because Donald was right, James must be feeling those things, but then Donald pushed things too far. 'And he'll be feeling protective of you.'

'Of me?' Maybe Donald was from another planet after all.

'Of course he is. Even if your relationship was perfect at the moment, he'd still be behaving like this to some extent—he knows what's coming up better than anyone, maybe he doesn't want to put you through it too. Especially—'

'That's ridiculous—'

'Especially,' Donald spoke over her, 'if he thought the marriage was over anyway.'

'So what do I do?'

'What the man said,' Donald said. 'Give him some space. Give yourself some space too. Go home tonight with a take-away for one, and a movie and a pile of work. Let him get his own dinner, he's clearly capable. Buy a carton of milk and write your own name on it.

'But for now I'd suggest you go into that scruffy office of yours, take the phone off the hook, pull down the blinds and have a sleep.'

So she did.

She could hear the noises from the overhead loudspeaker and the murmur of Ginny on the phone, and for the first time since cancer had invaded, for the first time in a very long time, she slept.

And it helped.

And, to Donald's credit, his other suggestions actually helped too.

She shouted hi when she came in from work late, after seven, having stopped at her take-away, and she sat on the couch and ate noodles *with* chopsticks—from the box. James had always found that a bit pretentious. What the hell was the point when you had a drawer of forks and spoons? he would say. Well, James was in his room, so she used her chopsticks but ended up getting a spoon for the sauce at the bottom. She put on a movie, a movie that didn't involve guns, or worlds ending, or murder investigations, so there was no way it was a ploy to get him on the couch, and when he padded out a little bit later, she did hear a small laugh as he opened the fridge and must have seen 'Ava's milk'.

There was a pause.

Just a pause, and for that, after the days she'd had, she was terribly grateful.

CHAPTER NINE

JAMES knew the time lab results came in during the evening.

He knew too that things were being rushed through.

And though he'd told Ava and everyone else not to expect results till the middle of next week, on the Thursday evening after his surgery, just in case, he tried to log in and pull up his file, but Blake had locked him out and the lock remained.

He waited half an hour and then caved in, texted Blake to see if there was any news.

Out with Joan for wedding anniversary—will let you know as soon as I can.

He didn't say no. And James knew then that the next day he would know his results, that decisions would be made for the journey he was about to begin.

'Hi!' Ava walked in as he stood looking out of the window and as he turned to say hi, Ava smiled, but she was giving him the space he'd insisted on because she went straight through to the kitchen and poured herself a drink of water.

How could he put her through all this? James wondered.

He knew what lay ahead—knew as well as anyone who hadn't been through it all what lay ahead.

And for what?

James knew the statistics better than anyone, knew the odds were in his favour, that Donald was right, a future probably awaited him, but what if not?

He'd seen what losing the babies had done to Ava; he'd seen his vibrant, happy wife slowly go downhill to the point where their marriage was over.

A marriage that had, for a very long time, been such a good one.

And instead of staring out of the window, or slumping on to the couch or going back to his bedroom, when Ava went to the kitchen this time he followed her through.

'How was work?'

'Slow!' Ava said, opening the fridge, but there was nothing she fancied and she didn't want another takeaway. 'Two patients cancelled. I'd have come home earlier except I went for a coffee with Evie.' She saw his vague frown as she turned round. 'We've sort of become friends.' And it just sort of underscored how little they spoke, so she asked after him. 'How are you doing?'

'I'm bored,' James said, which wasn't strictly true. His mind had never been so restless, but he wanted distraction very badly. 'I can't stand another week of this. I think I'm going to go back to work next week.'

'You haven't even been out of the flat,' Ava pointed

out. 'You could go for a walk.' She said. 'Or we could, it's a nice—'

'I have been going for walks.' James said, and he sort of, almost, smiled. 'There was no choice, given there wasn't any milk.'

'There is milk…' Ava started, and then she sort of almost smiled too. 'If you want to get out a bit further than the corner shop, I could drive you to the beach.' She knew he'd say no, knew he'd just shake his head and head back to the bedroom that was his this week, except he didn't give the answer she was expecting. Instead, he nodded and walked out of the kitchen. 'I'll just get changed.'

She knew that James hated being driven so Ava was a little bit surprised, as they approached their local beach, when James suggested they drive on a bit further.

'How about the other beach?' James suggested. 'We haven't been there for a while.'

It had been their regular beach many years ago. James had been renting a large house along with some fellow students just a few hundred metres or so from the beach when she had first met him and as they drove past the house she saw James crane his neck for a glimpse of the house he had once lived in and the one she had also moved into.

'It still looks like a bombsite,' James said. It really was a renovator's delight, or maybe the whole thing would be better pulled down because from the front gate to the chimney work needed to be done, but they had known so many good times there. 'Its probably still being rented out to students.'

Ava parked the car as close as they could get to the beach and headed down the once familiar route. The sun was low on the water and the beach busy, with joggers and teenagers and couples like them, or people walking alone, just taking time to indulge, and the silence wasn't awkward, more pensive. It was James that broke it.

'Thanks for this. I think I was getting cabin fever.'

'It's nice to get out,' Ava agreed, because it really was. 'We used to go walking in the evenings a lot.' She gave him a nudge. 'Before you got all important.'

She was talking about his promotion a couple of years ago and instead of snapping back a smart retort as to how home hadn't actually been a bundle of laughs to race back to, James was silent for a moment as he walked on and thought about what she had said, because it was all so much more complicated than that. Feelings and events were so intricately intertwined that it was almost impossible to separate them, but on a night like tonight—when tomorrow everything changed—James did.

'Sorry about that.' She glanced over at his unexpected apology. 'I don't like rushing people,' James continued. 'I tried to put the difficult patients towards the end of the day, so I wasn't putting everyone else behind. You try and juggle it, to get the balance right.' He'd never really tried to explain it before. 'Like last week, when I found the lump, Blake moved his whole morning. And when my results come back I won't want just a ten-minute consultation.' Then he gave a wry laugh. 'Well, I might.'

He wanted a ten-minute incredulous apology from Blake actually, for Blake to tell him that they'd got it all completely wrong, that pathology had found nothing, nothing at all, and the blood tests were a complete mix-up, and Ava even smiled when he told her.

'I just hate pushing people through. I know I can't always take the time I'd like to, but seeing them later in the day…' He gave an uncomfortable shrug. 'It cost us, though, didn't it?'

'It wasn't just that,' Ava said, because they could have worked around that had things been better between them, then she saw him grimace. 'Are you okay?'

'Walking on the sand is harder than I thought,' James said, and he looked on ahead to a place that had once been theirs, where a much younger James and Ava had found out just how much they liked each other one night after a student party. But it was a place that seemed just a little bit too far away to get to this evening and as they turned and walked back towards the car, Ava wondered if James even remembered.

'Are you looking forward to the summer break?' James had asked.

They had wandered away from the party, the excuse being that it was too noisy to talk. Exams had finished and the summer had stretched ahead. Ava had lied when she'd answered him—after all, she couldn't really admit that she couldn't stand the thought of nearly three months of not seeing him. She'd had a crush on him for ages, they had spoken a couple of times, but now, just when they were really talking, just when it seemed things were starting to move on, she wouldn't see him for ages.

But of course she hadn't told him that. Instead she'd said that, yes, she was looking forward to it.

Then he'd asked, 'What plans have you got?'

'Well, it's my birthday in January and Mum and Dad have offered to get me a flight up to Queensland to go and visit my cousin.'

'A return flight, I hope?'

'I should check that, actually.' Ava had smiled as they'd sat down. 'I wouldn't put it past them.'

And she halted, because she really didn't want to talk about her parents, about how really every holiday for as long as she could remember she had been sent away, either to an auntie's or grandparent's, and now that she was older, the supposed gift was just another way to ensure she didn't get in her parents' way.

'I think I'll just ask them for the money instead. I'm going to be looking for a flat...' She really didn't fancy flat-sharing, but living at home wasn't working, and on her waitressing wage it was all she could afford.

'What about you?' Ava asked. 'Are you looking forward to it?'

'That depends,' James said, 'on whether or not I've got your phone number.'

Her breath seemed to burn in her lungs as he voiced what she had been thinking and her face was on fire as he moved towards her. And at eighteen, close to nineteen, she had her first kiss. Not that he knew it was her first, she hoped, and it certainly wasn't his, because James's mouth knew exactly what to do.

He stroked her lips with his and she felt his hand steady her head as he increased the pressure, as she tried to work out how to breathe with the man she had been thinking so much about finally close, and he simply didn't let her be clumsy or awkward, he just kissed her nervous lips till they gave in to the bliss, and just as her mouth accustomed to another on hers there was the shock of her first taste of tongue and another layer of bliss was exposed to her by him.

She struggled to contain it, to not simply melt beneath him as his lips pressed her down towards the sand. She was about to halt him, to stop him, except her mind asked her why, when it felt so nice with him over her.

His lips dragged from her mouth, to her cheeks, to her ear, and the feel of his hot breath there should surely not be so nice, or was it the words that had her unfurl?

'Don't go to Queensland,' James breathed. 'Spend the summer here.'

She could spend for ever here in his arms being kissed. Then there was a bombardment of new sensations, his hand moving up from her waist, warm fingers sliding up beneath her T-shirt, and she knew she should halt him, that perhaps she was giving him the wrong idea about where this was leading.

She could feel the solid press of him against her sand-dusted thigh, and still, dangerously, she kissed him back, and as his hand found her breast she wanted it to stay there. James knew that, for she moaned into his mouth and then she pulled back from him, looked up at him, and he felt her sudden tension—her hands on his shoulders and a flash of uncertainty in her eyes—and James removed his hand and went back to simply kissing her.

All he'd done that night was kiss her. He'd spent the entire summer gradually taking each barrier down, dismantling each insecurity, taking things slowly, acting patiently as she drove him wild.

And he wondered if she even remembered.

'It doesn't look good for Finn,' James said as they headed back to the car, and they spoke for a bit about Finn, about how hard it was on Evie.

'She's still working,' Ava said. 'But any minute she's not she's either with him on ICU or asleep on the on-call room there.'

'Finn wouldn't want that,' James said.

'Well, while Finn's got a tube down his throat, he doesn't exactly have much say in things.'

And James wouldn't want that either, and he tried not to think of a time when it might be Ava catching some shut-eye in a camp bed by his side. Ava spoon-feeding him, Ava running herself ragged through the 'Till death us do part' bit. He was being ridiculous, he tried to tell himself for the hundredth time this evening because, yes, the statistics were good.

But the glass was resolutely stuck on half-empty—he simply couldn't get it to half-full.

They got back to the car and once there he looked up

at the house he had once lived in, looked at the room that had once been his, had been theirs, but it ached to remember that time, so he climbed into the car and they drove the length of the beach that they had used to come to so often. He didn't want it to be tomorrow, didn't want to get his results, even though he was desperate to hear them. He knew too much about what lay ahead, knew how hard it would be not just on him but also on them. All that he would put Ava through, and for what?

He looked over at Ava. Her face was pale from the strain of the last few days but, then again, it had been pale the day he'd come home from Brisbane. The strain of the last two years was taking its toll—he'd promised to make her happy and clearly hadn't been doing a very good job.

'Do you want to get something to eat?' James suggested. 'Maybe go to Pete's?'

'Sure,' Ava said, a little taken back at his suggestion. 'I hope I'm not banned.'

'Banned?'

And she told him, well, not all of it, but about how she'd been upset and had dashed off without paying for her wine.

'They'll have your photo up at the bar.' James smiled, but it was a pale one—he'd been trying to get her to go to Pete's for the last two years, but now that he had cancer his wish was her command. Suddenly everybody was treating him just a little bit differently—as they walked into the bar they ran into Lexi and Sam, casual friends from the hospital, but the conversation was forcibly jovial and he wanted things the way they had been before.

'That was awkward,' James said as he steered Ava to their regular spot by the window.

'Lexi has got a lot on her mind,' Ava said. 'She's probably really worried about Evie.' Lexi was one of Evie's sisters and even if they hadn't been so friendly then, Ava recalled when their younger sister, Bella, had had a lung transplant and how neither she nor James had known how to broach it in conversation. It was hard being in the medical profession at times like this, when you knew perhaps more than a friend should.

'Remember how awkward it was when Bella had her surgery? We didn't know what to say to Lexi then.'

'I guess.' James shrugged as he looked through the menu 'I might get pizza,' James said, only it wasn't to annoy her this time. It was what they used to share when they had first moved here, a family-sized mozzarella, and he'd have far more than half of it. 'And a beer,' he added, because no matter what these results were tomorrow, he was going on a health kick. Good news or bad, he was going to take a lot better care of himself from now on, he just needed this one last night.

'I'm going to have a steak.' Ava was suddenly hungry.

'You need to add a glass of wine to the bill.' James smiled as the waiter came over and he relayed their orders, adding 'medium-rare' to her steak and salad when the waiter asked what her side order was, because he knew how she liked things. 'She has a tendency to run off without paying.'

And as it turned out, the waiter did remember her, and he laughed as he told her that the other couple had picked up her bill.

It was actually a really nice evening. Ava couldn't quite work out James's mood, but they chatted a lot about old times and they certainly weren't maudlin. Well, maybe a little bit, because they were at their old table and by mistake, about half an hour into their time there, the waiter brought over a bottle of champagne they hadn't ordered.

'Sorry!' He smiled when James said with a slightly wry note that they weren't celebrating. 'Wrong table.'

And they sat for a moment and neither said a word to each other. In fact, both looked away, but both surely remembered.

'I can't drink!'

They'd been almost deranged with excitement at the prospect of being parents, their hair still wet from the showers because as soon as she'd told him they'd started kissing and then ended up making love, and afterwards they'd decided to go out to Pete's to celebrate.

'You can have one glass.'

'No.' She'd been adamant, and so too had he, because he'd gone ahead and ordered a bottle and they'd sat holding hands and just grinning at their secret.

'When can we tell people?' James had asked.

'Twelve weeks,' Ava had said.

'That's ages,' James had moaned. 'Then again…'

he'd rolled his eyes '…my mum is going to go crazy, you do know that? She's been waiting years for this.'

James would have had children straight away as soon as they were married had Ava wanted to. He adored kids, was a favourite with the children in his extended family. He couldn't wait for a family of his own, but Ava had really wanted to be established in her career first. Sexual dysfunction had never been her intended specialty—in fact, she had intended to be a GP—but somehow she had drifted towards that area, and it had only been when she'd got to thirty that she'd felt ready to make that commitment, but once ready she'd embraced it wholeheartedly.

The waiter popped the champagne and poured it.

'To twins.' James grinned.

'Please, no!' Ava said, and she did have a tiny taste as they clinked their glasses and said 'Cheers'.

It had been their last perfect night, really, and the last time she'd tasted champagne.

By the next morning she hadn't been pregnant any more.

James suggested they leave the car where it was parked outside Pete's and instead walk the short distance home. She wished he'd at least take her hand, longed for the days when he'd kissed her against a wall or all the way up in the lift were long gone now.

She wanted them back, so badly she wanted them back.

When they got home James put on a movie, not a crime show for once, and neither was it one Ava would have chosen. In fact, it was science fiction, of all things, with subtitles. It was a movie she'd didn't even know that they had.

'I've seen this before, I think.'

'I found it at the second-hand market,' James said, and he sat on the sofa beside her, just not close enough to touch.

She was sure she had seen it, or maybe not. It was the maddest film, but there was a certain sense of déjà vu to it, or at least there was for a little while, but half-way through she was lost.

'No.' Ava shook her head. 'I haven't seen this.' And then she frowned because she'd been quite sure she had.

She never had found a flat before the start of her first semester. She had arrived one night at the house, in tears after her parents had had a blistering row. James had been on his way out with his housemates, but had waved them off and they had stayed behind and gone where they'd always gone—to his room. And though they had done an awful lot of things, they hadn't quite done that.

'I'm sorry about this.'

'Sorry about what?' James had asked. They'd been lying on the bed just talking and kissing, they'd given up trying to make sense of her parents, of trying to work out if her mother actually was leaving her father this time.

'You were going out.'

'Now I'm staying in.' His hand crept up her leg and she didn't wriggle away. Instead her hands found him and more and more she moved him closer to where he stroked her with his fingers, and they almost had a few times before, and he wasn't sure he could play that game again, except he wasn't stroking her now with his fingers, and her hands were up at his shoulders and he was almost there and it killed to not be inside her.

'Ava?'

She looked up into green eyes and there was not a doubt in her mind and she nodded, resumed their kiss because she'd made up her mind.

'Hold on.' He went to get a condom, sure she'd insist on it—she'd even made him have blood tests and things, and only for Ava would he do that—but as she so often did, she surprised him. 'I've gone on the Pill.'

'Yeah, but…' He almost shrank from the responsibility, for about one tenth of a second, and then her hands slid over his back and down to his buttocks and he felt her mouth on his shoulder as he lowered himself and edged his way in, and she sobbed out at the delicious agony and there was a nip of her teeth on his shoulder that almost took him over the edge and then he met Ava, the real Ava that he'd unleashed, her kisses fervent, her words enticing, and his kisses and words were too.

It was sex that was worth waiting for. It was more than just sex that night in his bed.

'God, Ava…'

She heard him moan and she had to come, she could feel the urgency. She could not believe then the noise and the passion and the feel of him inside her, and she knew she'd take for ever, knew because she always had, except he was thrusting inside her, his entire body suddenly rigid, and she was the one uncoiled beneath him. She could hear her own moans, her own shouts, her own collapse into silence, and then back to the real world.

She lay in his arms, watching some strange foreign science fiction film on his television that had started, neither wanting to get up from their haven, happy to read the subtitles, at least until his mouth found her shoulder again.

They never had got to see the end…

''Night, Ava.'

He yawned and stood up at about halfway through the movie, and tonight James did bend to kiss her, not her mouth, but the top of her head, and she felt his fingers in her hair and for a second they lingered, but even as she turned her head to him, he lifted his and headed to bed, and as she heard the door click closed behind him she knew what had happened, thought about it quite logically for a moment, and then she cried.

That walk on the beach, the trip to Pete's and now the film.

He'd been saying goodbye.

CHAPTER TEN

'It's your mother on the phone.' Ginny had rung through.

Ava was about to tell Ginny that she was in with a client, but instead she asked that she be put through. 'You might as well go now, Ginny. I've just got a quick phone consultation and then I'm heading home,' Ava said, then took a breath and took the call from her mum.

'Hi, there,' Ava said.

'Hi, Ava.' Fleur wasn't really one for chatting. 'Any news on James?'

'Nothing yet,' Ava said, because they weren't expecting the results till next week and she wasn't sure that they were even going to make it to next week. She had been on the edge of tears between every patient, had the most appalling feeling in her stomach and all she wanted was to go home.

'Well, let your father and I know when you hear.' There was a slight pause. 'How are you?'

'I've been better,' Ava admitted. 'Actually, Mum...' And then she stopped herself because she was not going to discuss this with her mother and, anyway, Fleur wouldn't understand—her parents' marriage was so liberal and open, she could never understand what Ava was grappling with, aside from James's illness.

Still, maybe she could do with a dose of liberality, Ava thought, maybe she could try talking with her mum. Her mum wouldn't turn a hair if she told her she thought James had had an affair, was still having one.

Turn a blind eye would be her mother's advice. It was strange really, everyone thought Ava was so open-minded, so liberal, except she only was with James. She really did believe in love and was so proud of the couples that came to see her and worked through things. Yes, maybe she did need some of her mum's rather more open views. 'I was thinking I might come over and see you this weekend.'

'Oh!' She could hear the surprise in her mother's voice. 'Is he up and about, then?'

'Not with James,' Ava said. Perish the thought, James didn't exactly like her parents, had said in some rows how they'd messed her up, and the thought of them together with tensions so high didn't particularly appeal. 'Just me. I'll see how the next couple of days go and let you know.'

'Well, ring first,' Fleur warned. 'I don't want you driving all that way if I'm out.'

She was thoughtful like that, Ava refelected darkly, putting down the phone and resting her head in her hands. For all Veronica irritated her at times, at least she was there. All the Carmichael clan had been around and had it been Ava they would have done the same. Well, maybe it would be a slightly diluted version and maybe the fridge would be more full so that James wouldn't starve while she was incapacitated, but at least they would have stepped up.

Her mother hadn't so much as sent a card or even spoken to James.

Ava had never been close to her mother, or her father. The only person in her life she'd been really close to had been James.

'Ava.' There was a knock at the door and she looked up at his voice. Oh, God, he was wearing those grey linen pants and that black shirt and he'd shaved and he had on that cologne and he looked more beautiful than he ever had, more beautiful than the man she had married even, and she was gripped tighter with the fear that was ever-present these days. Because he couldn't be sick, he just couldn't be, and Ava knew why he was there but she asked just the same.

'What are you doing here?'

'Blake got my results in.'

'Already? That is really quick. When are you seeing him…?' Her voice trailed off, knew it was pointless, knew that James wasn't there to ask her to come along with him to find out the news.

'It's good news,' James said, and he went a bit technical for a moment. Yes, it was good news, it just wasn't quite as good as he had hoped, not quite as contained, but it was still stage one. As he explained, her mind couldn't keep up with him and he toned it down. 'I've gone through it all with Blake and I'm going to have a course of chemo. I want to know that it's gone.'

It wasn't a discussion, but that was fair enough, it was James's field after all. 'I'll still be working, I'll just have to schedule around it…' And he spoke a little more about what was involved and there was thin relief because the news could have been so much worse. But there was also a sense of fear of the unknown too, because so much had changed in such a short space of time.

'We'll get through it,' Ava said.

And he shook his head and she knew, really knew, why he was there, and a fear of the known closed in.

She'd known since last night that this was coming.

'I'm moving out.' He said it just like that. 'I'm going round to Mum's now to give her the results and to tell her that I've walked out.'

'Please, don't.' She knew that he meant it, knew he had made up his mind, could feel him slipping away, or rather that he had been slipping away for ages but now, at this moment, he was completely out of her grasp. 'James, please. This isn't the time to be making these sorts of decisions.'

'It's done,' James said. 'I've got a serviced apartment; I've just been and picked up the keys.'

'You're not supposed to be driving.'

'Yeah, well, I was looking on the internet and I found out that there were these yellow things called taxis…'

She hated it when he did this, when he just blocked her out.

'I want to be with you. I want to help you get through it.'

Except she'd blocked him out too, and he told her as much. 'Do you think I didn't want to be with you?' James said. 'Relationships are supposed to be a two-way street, but not ours. Your grief was too private, too deep to share with me—well, you can't just suddenly decide now that you want to be all open and touchy-feely.'

And she stood in her office where she fixed and she healed, where she let couples discuss and say the words that hurt to hear but needed to be said. Except with James it was final. James didn't want to be in here. Unlike her couples, James didn't want it fixed.

'I've taken what I need for now. I'll sort out the study and stuff when I can lift and things, but I'll arrange a time that's suitable with you.' He walked over and put his key on the table and he made it sound so terribly simple, except it was far from that. And then he took off his ring.

Well, she wasn't taking off hers.

'I'm not getting a lawyer,' Ava said. 'I don't want a divorce.'

'Of course you don't,' James said. 'It would be a bit of a stupid thing to do now.'

'Sorry?'

'All the life insurance and everything.'

'Oh, for God's sake…' She was so angry. 'You can be such a bastard.'

And he didn't try and stop the row this time, neither did he lean over to kiss her. He just headed for the door.

'You could go to your mum's.' She was frantic. Anything was better than a serviced apartment. She couldn't stand for him to go through this alone, but she knew him too well, knew his answer almost before it came.

'I don't want to go to my mum's. I don't want anyone near. I want the dignity to puke in private.'

CHAPTER ELEVEN

'How are you doing, James?'

It was two weeks later and he was sitting in a reclining chair, rather than standing beside it, as Harriet, one of the nurses he knew well, ran through the forms.

James hated paperwork, completely loathed it, but it had never dawned on him that the patients felt the same. He'd answered the same questions over and over, five minutes apart at times.

And always the answers had been the same.

Today, though, a few were different and as he skimmed through the form with Harriet, before he had his first round of treatment, he paused.

'My emergency contact has changed.'

'Oh.'

'It's Veronica Carmichael—my mother.' He made a thin joke. 'But only ring her if I'm dead—she worries a lot.'

And he had to change his home address too and delete his home phone number to bit by bit extract himself from Ava's life.

He'd seen Harriet many times all gloved and gowned

up, but it felt very different to be sitting a reclining chair, getting his treatment. She'd done his obs diligently throughout and had chatted a little, but things *were* different. He found it very hard to pinpoint—his patients had spoken to him often about it and now he fully understood. There was this air of sympathy, of forced normality in almost every exchange he had these days, and James couldn't stand it. Sure, he preferred that Harriet wasn't flirting now, it had been awkward at times, but it wasn't about Harriet, it was about everyone. Well, almost everyone. There were still some people with whom he could relax.

'When you said you'd be beside me, whatever I decide…' James turned at the sound of Richard's—his teenage patient's—voice and gave a wry smile as he chatted on. 'This really is going above and beyond the call of duty.'

'I do my best,' James quipped back. 'Well, I guess you got your answer as to what I'd do if it was me.' He smiled at his patient and peer. 'Sorry I missed your appointment.' He really was. He knew how disappointed Richard would have been.

'No problem,' Richard said. 'I actually came back a couple of days after we spoke. I'd decided that I couldn't stand just waiting to see what happened. Blake said you weren't well—he didn't say what was wrong.' Richard looked him right in the eye. 'I'm really sorry.'

And they spoke about their results and their treatments.

'This is your second?' James glanced up to the bag

that was dripping its contents into Richard's arm. 'How was it?'

Richard pulled a face. 'Not as bad as I thought,' Richard said, 'but I've heard it gets worse.'

They spoke for a bit then Richard put his headphones on and listened to some music and when James got sick of the nurses chatting behind the glass—first about him. Did they know he and Ava had broken up? Later about Finn, how much he'd improved, but his arm was practically numb and there was some weakness in one of his legs. But he was insisting on being discharged apparently. He watched a DVD, a war one because he was sick of all the inspirational ones that people kept pressing on him. Still, even if it was a good movie, he couldn't really concentrate and instead he thought about many things as he tried not to think about Ava.

The cleaner was coming to the apartment today, but he'd told her not to come for the next three. He'd had his hair cut really short, because he didn't want to scare her when it all fell out. He thought about the gym and how pleased he was that he was a bit fitter than if it had happened a few months ago, but he wished too he'd eaten better. He'd ordered some frozen meals, healthy ones, the ones that got delivered—but he felt like a fighter pilot scrambling when it was already too late.

'James!' Cleo, the charge nurse, had come in for her late shift and the second she saw him she was over as Harriet removed his IV. 'How are you doing?'

'I'm fine. Just about ready to go home.'

He didn't feel fine, actually. He knew everyone reacted differently but, in fact, for the first time since he'd found that lump he felt ill, as if they'd administered an IV labelled fatigue straight into him.

He had some tea and sandwiches and was ready now to go home, or rather to return to the serviced apartment, but he couldn't stop thinking about the apartment at Kirribilli, about the fridge there that made ice cubes and the bed that was his, and he was still trying not to think about Ava.

'Did you want me to ring through to Ava and tell her you're ready for the off?' Cleo asked, and he saw Harriet's cheeks pink up

'No.' James shook his head. 'I just rang my mum and she's picking me up.' He'd had his anti-emetics, all the drugs dispensed, and he just wanted this over with.

'Ava and I broke up, Cleo.'

'Oh!' He watched as she struggled for a response. 'But you're at your mum's tonight?'

He didn't need a babysitter and they didn't need to know.

'Here she is.' James stood as Veronica entered. He saw the frantic look that had been on his mother's face since he'd first broken the news and he hated that he had put it there. 'Hey, Mum. Ready to go?'

Ava's mum wasn't worried. 'I'm not with you, Ava!' She'd done what she had said she never would and had gone to her mum's one lunchtime in the hope of advice. 'Ava, you haven't been sleeping together, you've been living separate lives, and now you're "devastated" that it's over?'

'You don't understand.'

'It's guilt, Ava.' Fleur was adamant. 'James had his chemo today and the martyr in you feels you ought to be there.'

And Ava listened, but not really, because her mum, she realised, just didn't do love.

'And whatever you do,' her mum said as she saw her to the car, 'don't even think about getting a divorce. No, don't look at me like that, Ava. I'm just being practical—you'd be mad to divorce him now, wouldn't you?'

Ava knew James had chemo today, and the day had stretched for ever, which was maybe why she had gone to her mum's. Sometimes she saw him at work, not often, but she'd started to have lunch in the canteen because so too had James. He'd had his hair cut short, in anticipation of the drug side effects, no doubt, but for now he looked as if he was brimming with health. He ignored her whenever he saw her, and one time she'd seen him sitting chatting with one of the nurses. Previously, she'd have just walked right on over, but instead she'd sat brittle and jealous, bobbing around in limbo—separated not divorced. Married but apart.

She walked through the car park, tried to focus her mind back on work, but really she would have preferred to go home and to bed and just pull the covers over her head. She had never felt more tired in her life.

It had been two weeks since he'd left her, and in those weeks Ava had grimly continued on as if it hadn't happened, as if James hadn't left. Desperately trying to convince herself that telling others would be premature—that any day now James would change his mind, that he'd ring and say he was on his way back home, or that she'd come out of the lift to find him waiting at the front door.

Apart from her mother this lunchtime, Ava hadn't told anybody. Amazingly for SHH, whose grapevine was legendary, word didn't seem to have got out yet. People were still asking her how James was doing, and after all she was still wearing her ring, and maybe James hadn't told anyone either. Maybe he was going to come back to her.

Ava forced herself to keep busy. She swam in the morning and rode most evenings, her time on the horse the only time her head felt calm, and then it was back to the flat that was too empty without him and a night spent resisting the urge to call.

Tonight would be even harder. She could not stand that he would be going through this treatment without her, and then she saw him, at the other end of the corridor and walking towards her. He looked the same as he had the last time she'd glimpsed him. Only Ava could see his exhaustion as James and Veronica neared. It was the first time in all of this that he actually looked unwell, or was it stress that marred his features? She truly didn't know.

At first he pretended not to have noticed her and Ava did the same, walking towards him with her heart hammering in her chest, pretending to check her phone, wondering how she should greet him. Veronica didn't look so well either—she seemed to have aged a decade since James had found the lump.

'Ava.' He nodded by way of a greeting, and she opened her mouth to speak to him to ask him how it had been, how he was feeling, except James wasn't in the mood for conversation and had already walked on.

'Hi, there, Ava.' Ginny gave her a smile as she walked past the desk and with supreme effort she gave her one back. 'Is everything okay?' Ginny asked. 'You're ever so pale.'

'I'm fine,' Ava said when she felt like screaming, and somehow she made it to her office.

Somehow she made it through the afternoon, but for once her mind could not quite focus on her patients. She did her best, of course, maybe they didn't notice, but in truth her mind was with James and her body ached to sleep.

She should be in bed this minute beside him, for she knew that that was where he would have headed, and it was as if her body was insisting, as if it was demanding that that be where she should be too.

'See you, Ginny.' For once she left on the stroke of five, hitched up her bag and said goodnight.

'Oh!' Ginny looked up from whatever she was doing. 'See you, Ava…' Except it was Ginny who forced the smile this time and Ava knew then that she knew.

That word was out.

That James and Ava's marriage was over.

Yes, there was guilt, but it was only a part of how

she felt as she headed for home, as she stood in the lift, which was working tonight, then let herself in the door.

Even if she'd lived alone for three months, it had still been James's home. There had still been the *chance* that he'd come home, but now it just felt empty.

Now would come the appalling silence from friends while they worked out what best to say. She and James had been guilty of that when Donna and Neil had split up.

'Ring him,' Ava had pushed.

'Ring her,' James had pushed.

They'd worried so much as to whom to ring first, in the end she'd gone into the bedroom and James to his study and they'd both rung at the same time on their mobiles and then met back in the lounge for a good old gossip.

She wasn't ready yet to smile at the memory. Smiling felt a long way off—at least in her personal life—and she knew it was pathetic to hope when there was a knock at the door, except she did.

'Oh, Ava.' It was Evie at her door

'You've heard the happy news, then.' She pulled the door open and let Evie in.

'I don't know what to say,' Evie admitted. 'I've been banging on about my problems and all this time…'

'Don't worry about that,' Ava said. 'It's nice of you to come over—it's been pretty chilly at the hospital this afternoon.' She made them both a drink, this time, though, it was for Ava to compose herself for a moment.

'So what's the gossip?' Ava asked when they were both sitting down. 'What's everyone saying?'

'Just that you two have split up. I actually heard something last week, but I just ignored it. I mean I know how hap—' She halted herself. 'I thought you two were so happy, it's just assumed that you are really,' Evie said. 'And what with James being sick, it seemed ridiculous. I knew you'd never...' She felt Evie glance at her wedding-ring finger, the ring still firmly there.

'He left me,' Ava said, but she knew that probably wasn't what was being said. 'Anyway, I don't have to defend myself.'

'Of course you don't.'

'I don't mean to you.' Ava shook her head, couldn't believe the mess her life was. 'We've been having problems for a long time.' Ava let out a little of what for so long she had been holding in. 'It isn't completely out of the blue. It just feels that way, though,' Ava admitted. It was actually nice to have Evie over, she was far easier to talk to than her own mother, and it was a relief to find out a bit about James.

'He's taking the next couple of days off, I think,' Evie said. 'The courses of chemo are three weeks apart, well, that's what I've heard.'

'I don't know anything,' Ava admitted. 'I don't know how bad it's going to be.' They chatted for a while about James and then Ava warmed them both a frozen meal for one and she asked after Finn.

'It doesn't look great,' Evie said. 'Not that I'm allowed to know.'

'He's still not letting you visit?'

'He's not letting anyone visit,' Evie said. 'You know he had some swelling after the operation and that's subsided, but...' Ava felt as if she were looking in a mirror. She could see the lines of tension around Evie's eyes, see the set of her lips as she struggled to stay positive. 'Well, things aren't great, but he's going home tomorrow and there's talk of scheduling another operation...'

They both stopped as they heard noises from above, like an angry ghost of Finn, because they were talking about him, but then Evie laughed.

'That's Luke and Lily,' Evie said. 'Luke prised his key off him and they're sorting out things there tonight, you know, fitting a shower chair and things...' Ava could see the sparkle of tears in Evie's eyes. 'He'll hate that.'

'Better than a wheelchair,' Ava said.

'I think Luke's gone and got another key cut so he can keep an eye on him, and they're stocking up the fridge,' Evie said, 'hiding the Scotch.'

Ava glanced up at the almost full bottle still sitting on the bench and thought about that night. For all they said about Finn's reckless ways, he could be very sensible too. 'He'll just bribe Gladys if he wants some.' Ava smiled. 'Finn's gong to be okay.'

'You don't know that,' Evie said.

But she did. Somewhere deep inside, she just felt that Finn would be okay. She just wished she had the same feeling about James.

Evie went up to help Lily and Luke, but Ava simply couldn't handle any more company or sympathy tonight and after she said farewell to Evie she took a long shower. She was too tired to blow-dry her hair so instead she did the hardest thing.

Took off her ring for the first time in seven years.

She'd felt Evie looking at her ring finger and now she thought about it, Ginny had too. She felt like the relatives days after an earthquake, still insisting the emergency workers keep looking, still demanding there was hope, when it had all but faded. Except she couldn't leave it there by the sink, so she added it to the chain she wore around her neck and she crawled into bed and lay there wondering how he was feeling tonight.

She didn't even try not to think about James.

The first wave of nausea hit at 5:00 a.m.

Just this violent wave, the type that jolted you awake and propelled you out of bed, and then a frantic dash to the bathroom and the chill of cold sweat as you knelt in the dark because you didn't have time to switch on the light.

Ava clung to the toilet bowl and held on for dear life, wondering if she was having sympathy nausea with James, because she hadn't vomited since...

She closed her eyes as another wave hit and then she started to cry because she simply couldn't be pregnant. They'd had sex once, for God's sake. She was on the Pill, except she hadn't taken it the morning they found the lump, and perhaps not the morning after that too.

Ava was terrified she was pregnant.

Refused to be.

She had gastric flu, she decided, and for the first time in a very long time she rang in at eight and used some of her sick leave, made a cup of tea and went back to bed.

Then she woke up at ten-thirty and couldn't dress quickly enough in her haste to find out. She walked down to the chemist, which had once been her regular walk—a monthly walk where she'd buy two pregnancy kits that each contained two pregnancy tests, because if it was negative she'd want to do it again the next morning and the morning after that too, and if it was positive, she'd be taking the test again and again just to be sure.

She bought one that morning.

One single one and then walked back to the flat, cursing her timing because there were Luke and Lily trying to hold back as a very thin and dishevelled Finn dragged himself on a cane towards the lift, his arm hanging limp and useless beside him.

'Morning.' She gave Lily and Luke an attempt at a smile and was completely ignored by Finn.

She felt as if they had X-ray vision and could see through the paper bag she was holding but knew that, in truth, they were thinking of Finn.

'Ava.' Lily returned her smile. 'I was going to call you.' She was just a little bit awkward and who could blame her? 'We should catch up…'

'Sure,' Ava replied, relieved when the lift door opened and she let herself into the flat and raced to the loo. She waited, desperate for the first time for the result to be negative.

She couldn't do this again.

Not now.

Not alone.

And how could she put James through it too?

She cried so hard when she saw that cross and she truly didn't know what to do. Except he had to know, he deserved to know, surely. And now there was a legitimate reason to see him too.

She drove to his serviced apartment and knocked on the door, bracing herself to be honest, to talk it out as she told all her clients, except it was Veronica who answered the door and her face was savage.

'What the hell do you want?'

'My husband,' Ava said.

'He's been up all night, ill,' Veronica said. 'He's told me that if you come to the door that you're not to be allowed in.'

'Look, Veronica.' Ava tried to keep her voice even. 'I need to speak to him.'

'Well, James doesn't need to speak to you, he doesn't need the stress…' Veronica said, and then she took her out into the hall and closed the door behind her. 'What sort of woman would leave her husband at a time like this?'

'He left me!' Ava reminded her, but she knew it was hopeless, knew the gossip around the hospital, and it was the same here—she was the shrew who couldn't stand by her man, who had got out when the going got tough.

'He stood by you through all those miscarriages,'

Veronica hissed. 'Whatever your problems were, could you not have put them on hold?'

'I just need to talk to him.'

'Well, the last thing he needs right now is you,' Veronica said. 'And I mean it, Ava. I bought him some DVDs and we've just been watching them. The best thing, they say, is to stay positive—James needs to be concentrating on himself not trying to repair a marriage that's been over for more than a year.' She must have seen Ava's already pale face turn to chalk. 'Just let him concentrate on himself.'

And she had to put it on hold, Ava realised, not just the marriage but the pregnancy too—she could not add to the pressure that James was under right now.

What was she supposed to tell him? *Oh, darling, I'm pregnant!* She knew the hell that would cause him, the confusion and fear, that James would know what she was going through, that somehow he would feel that he had to support her too as he did his best to get through his treatment.

And how could she tell him tomorrow or next week or next month that she'd lost it? How could she add to it all?

'If I were you—' Veronica broke into her trance '—if you care about him at all, you will just leave him well enough alone.'

CHAPTER TWELVE

IT WAS hell to see him suffer from a distance.

He dragged himself to work, and over the weeks he lost weight, of course, but actually bald suited him. He carried right on working and sometimes she saw him laughing and chatting with colleagues, but only once did he meet her eyes. She was buying a coffee in the canteen and looked up to his and he didn't tear them away. Instead, he made his way over.

'I need to get a few things.'

'Sure.' She felt as if everyone in the canteen was watching them. 'When did you want to come over?'

'Tonight,' James said. 'Unless you're busy?'

'Tonight's fine.'

And, though tonight might be the time to tell him, she knew she wouldn't, for while it *was* hell to see him suffer from a distance, there was also a sense of relief too.

He had enough to deal with and it was better that he wasn't burdened with the worry about the pregnancy, that he wasn't walking on eggshells and worrying about her and how she'd be if she lost it. It actually felt easier for Ava, too, because she wasn't worrying about how disappointed he'd be when she did.

Except she didn't.

And it was starting to show.

So she pulled on leggings and a big sloppy jumper, not that she was really showing, but she was rounding out a bit and she worried he might notice.

He came over as arranged at eight.

Ava had wondered if it would be four mates and a truck, but it was just James.

'It's just mainly books that I came for,' James said, noting her attire, just a little bit annoyed that she hadn't made any effort at all. 'And clothes...' His were hanging off him. 'I've got some jeans from before I put on weight.'

'I threw them out.'

'Well, that didn't take long.'

'I threw them out years ago,' Ava said. 'You couldn't have worn them anyway—they would be totally out of fashion!' She hauled open the wardrobes and found some of his old black jeans that were a couple of sizes smaller and James took some T-shirts and then he went to the study.

'Do you want something to eat?' Ava offered.

'No, don't go to any trouble,' he called.

'It's no trouble,' Ava called back as she walked to the study. 'I could ring out for pizza.'

Except he'd given up pizza, was trying so hard to stick to the promises he'd made to himself deep into the night.

'No, really, I'm fine.'

'Coffee, then?'

She'd laugh if he told her he was drinking green tea.

'A glass of water would be great.' And she thought he was snubbing her while he thought of the fridge that pumped cold water and the sound of ice cubes as they hit the glass and wondered if he'd be pushing things if he asked for custody of the fridge.

'Here.' She handed him the glass and as he drank it down she forced conversation. 'How have you been doing?'

'Oh, you know,' James said. 'Chemo has its fun side.'

'Such as?'

'I can't think right now.' He was at his sarcastic best. 'How annoying is that? Oh, but it's right there on the tip of my tongue.'

'That bad, then?'

He just shrugged and carried on filling a box, and then he was done and their wedding photo was still sitting on the study desk. He hadn't added that to the mix.

'Donna came over,' Ava said. 'She rang for a chat last weekend and then got annoyed that I hadn't told her.' Ava rolled her eyes. 'Honestly, I need a to-do list!'

'Neil rang,' James said. 'Donna must have told him. I think he thought we'd be hitting the clubs together, he wasn't too impressed when he found out about the cancer.' Then he looked over. 'How was Donna?'

'Still talking about Neil.' Somehow they laughed. 'Still *moaning* about Neil. I wanted to put my hand up and stop her,' Ava said. 'I wanted to say, er, my marriage *just* broke up, yours ended years ago...'

And it shouldn't concern him, it was none of his business really, but he did want to know. 'How did your parents take it?'

'Oh,' Ava answered. 'Mum suggested I moved into my old bedroom so she could mother me a bit, you know...' And he stood and he looked because she didn't need to say she was being sarcastic, and even if his own mum drove him crazy at times he couldn't stand the way Ava's family were with her. It would be so easy now to wrap his arms around her, to stay, to just give in, but pride was a wall he couldn't get through.

'I think that's everything.'

He walked out into the living room and he could see the hospital and see the harbour and the view he knew and it smelt like home and he didn't want to go back to the serviced apartment and to sheets that smelt vaguely of bleach. He wanted to go right now and lie down in the bedroom that had once been theirs and just close his eyes, or even just rest on the sofa, except he had another treatment due soon, and it didn't exactly make for tender reunions. And, after all, she hadn't wanted him when he was well.

'If there's anything else you want...?'

'The fridge,' James said.

'Ha, ha.' She tried to laugh as he walked to the door and then she said what was true. 'I miss you.'

And he couldn't not ask. 'How are you doing?'

'I don't know,' Ava admitted. She truly didn't know.

She wasn't teary any more, she was glad he wasn't worrying about her and the pregnancy on top everything else. And she only thought about his cancer for fifty-five minutes of every hour now, which was an improvement on the previous week. It was funny how with James she could sometimes be her most honest. 'I'm tired,' Ava said. 'I'm the most tired I've ever been.'

'And me.'

He was, and always had been the only person who could ever really comfort her, not all the time, of course, because too often she hadn't let him, but tonight she did. He put down the box and he pulled her into his arms and let her rest there for a little while, and he rested there too.

'Come back, James,' she said to his chest.

'I can't,' James said to her hair that smelt of lavender and somehow, in the hallway, not looking, just holding, he was able to be honest, the most honest he had been with anyone since he'd found that lump. He knew that he was too proud for his own good, knew that he could be stubborn at times, but he felt as if he'd been given a golden ticket. Only it was one he didn't want, one that excused all previous behaviour, resolved all rows, that now he was sick, only now was he wanted. And he didn't want a marriage built on her guilt, didn't want to drag her along for the appalling ride when they'd already been about to get off.

'I can't come back, Ava. Let me do this myself.' But, yes, so badly he missed her and it wasn't just pride that stopped him. There was something else too. His mortality had been rammed home to him, and while the statistics were good…

Better to lose him this way, the dark nights told him.

Better that she get over him now, because surely Ava did not deserve another loss. And he found himself kissing her and she kissed him back. A deep, lingering kiss that neither of them wanted to end because then they'd have to confront it, so they just carried on kissing and let their mouths speak a language that was safer than words at the moment. When it ended she put her face back against his chest, a bit embarrassed and confused at the want that was still in them.

'I've got to go,' James said, still holding her.

And she didn't fight it, because she understood that he did.

But it was nice to hold on to each other for a moment.

CHAPTER THIRTEEN

SOMETIMES, Ava now realised, talking *was* impossible.

In fact, as the weeks went on she revised one of her well-worn theories, not just for herself but for her patients too.

'It's good to see you again,' she said as she stepped into the waiting room to call her next patients in.

It really was a joy to see George and Elise—to see all of her patients, in fact. She loved her work, no matter how Veronica or others might sniff or nudge; she loved seeing the difference she made.

Today it was a visible difference as she stepped out into her waiting room and saw Elise smiling and George walking into her office, of course a little awkward, but she'd heard them talking and laughing as she'd gone for their file. She knew before they had even sat down how much better things were for them—it was evident in their body language, in the smiles that greeted her.

And during the consultation she found out she was right.

Right in several ways, in fact!

'I just wish we'd come to see you sooner,' Elise said.

'Well, a lot of couples say that,' Ava admitted. 'They struggle on their own for a very long time, not realising that there's help available.'

'I just wish George had told me all he was going through. I could have helped...'

'Maybe George needed to do that by himself,' Ava said gently. 'Maybe he needed to work things out on his own.'

'But you say we should talk...'

'I know I do,' Ava said, 'but sometimes, when talking doesn't help, all you can rely on is time to heal and your history to hold you together while things sort themselves out. George had a lot of things to deal with, a lot of things to get straight in his own mind before he was able to share. And now look at you—your relationship seems better than it was even before the accident.' And it seemed strange that from something so terrible any good could come, but with George and Elise it had. 'I'd like to see you both again in three months. I also just want to check your medication, George, and I do want to see you again on your own, say, in another month?'

George nodded. He was going back to work in a couple of months, and Ava wanted to make sure he was ready for it.

'Well, it's been lovely to see you both again.' Ava saw them to the door.

'It's been lovely to see you too, Ava!' Elise gave her a smile, a knowing smile perhaps? 'You're looking very well.'

'Thank you.' Ava went a bit pink and she felt as if Elise knew.

Maybe Elise did. After all Ava had a white shirt on that was straining just a little at the top buttons, her waist was getting thicker, and just this morning she hadn't been able to do up her skirt. There was certainly a roundness there, and her bottom was a bit bigger too— the first subtle changes of pregnancy becoming more evident now. She was also further on than she had ever been, which was bizarre. She was swimming, working, stressing, crying, she hadn't even seen a doctor—after all, it hadn't helped in the past, but now… Ava knew that she ought to. She was taking vitamins, looking after herself, but she really ought to get checked.

Her phone rang and she was about to let it go to messages and get some lunch, but she reached for it instead.

'Ava Carmichael.'

'Ava, this is Marco, I am working today in outpatients.' A rich Italian accent came down the phone as he introduced himself—but of course she knew who he was. The dashing Italian obstetrician who was married to Emily, a midwife here. Serendipity, Ava thought with a wry smile, but of course he was ringing to discuss a patient.

'She is four months pregnant through IVF, her husband is paraplegic—they are the most delightful couple, but on speaking to them today, I feel there is not enough information for them. They are both from the country so there is not much help available. Could I arrange for you to see them, or one of your colleagues?

Of course I will write a referral, but I worry that if I make them wait…'

'Strike while the iron's hot, you mean?'

'Scusi?'

Ava smiled. He clearly didn't understand what she was saying. 'I'll come over now.'

After meeting with the young couple, she was actually thrilled that Marco had phoned her and a bit appalled at the lack of information the pair had been struggling with. Barry's accident had happened when he was twelve and there was a whole lot he hadn't been informed about. A shy couple, they had at first been terribly reluctant to speak—but once they had started, a full hour had flown by, and she rang Ginny to make an appointment to coincide with their next antenatal visit, delighted to have been able to help.

'Ava!' She smiled when she saw Bella in the waiting room.

'Look at you!' Ava said, because Bella was looking very glamorous. 'How's the studying going?'

'I'm wearing it today,' Bella said. She was studying fashion and looked gorgeous and happy, having recently married. 'So what are you doing here?' Bella nudged.

'Working!' Ava grinned. 'What about you.'

'Just here to find out a few things. I'm waiting for Charlie but I got here a bit early.' She gave a little blush. 'We're thinking of starting a family and given all my medications and things, we just need to find stuff out. So please don't go gossiping!'

'As if!' Ava rolled her eyes.

'I heard about you and James,' Bella said. 'Felt sick when I heard.'

'Thanks,' Ava said, because she felt sick about it too. 'Anyway, I've got to go, I just need to pop in and thank Marco, but you take very good care of yourself. I hope today goes well.'

'You take care of yourself too, Ava,' Bella said, and as Ava headed to Marco's room and saw the door open she knew that Bella was right, and she knocked and popped in and introduced herself.

'Marco, hi, it's Ava, from the sexual dysfunction clinic.'

'Ah, Ava.' He gave her a very nice smile.

'Thank you for the referral. I've had a long talk with them and I'll be seeing them again. I think it's been really helpful.'

'No. Thank you,' Marco said. 'I was very pleased to have this resource, it was very confident of them to speak.'

He meant courageous, but confidence, courage, it was all the same in a way and it was exactly what she needed to summon now.

'Can I speak to you?' She stepped into the office, closing the door behind her. 'About me.'

'Of course.'

'Off the record?'

Marco gave a nod.

'Your wife's a midwife here.'

'Your husband is an oncologist who is undergoing

chemotherapy.' Marco said. 'I know what this place is like and you can rest assured that you are speaking only with me.'

'I'm pregnant,' Ava said, and it was a relief to say it. 'But the thing is…' she swallowed '…my husband doesn't know—we're separated.'

'It's his?' Marco checked.

'Oh, yes.' Ava nodded. 'And I know I should have told him—it's just that I've had four miscarriages and it's been hell. We were already separated when I found out and I couldn't stand to do it to him again when I knew it was going to end up the same way…'

'But it hasn't?'

'No.'

And she explained about her previous pregnancies and the investigations that had taken place. 'There was nothing to explain it—all the tests came back as NAD…'

'How far along did you get?'

'Ten weeks was the longest.' Ava said. 'We decided, or rather I decided, that I didn't want to get pregnant again. It was just too hard to go through.' It was such a relief to talk and Marco didn't rush her. 'It put an incredible strain on our marriage…'

'I can imagine.'

'I thought that by going on the Pill…' She could feel tears welling, and really she didn't want to start crying but was grateful when he peeled off some tissues and handed them to her.

'I'm sorry.'

'Please don't be—I see many tears here every day. Do you know how far along you are?

She gave him the date of her last period and he checked on his calendar.

'That puts you at fourteen weeks,' Marco said. 'Into your second trimester. Let's have a look, shall we?'

She went over to the examination table and he took her blood pressure and then he took it again. 'It's at the higher end of normal.' Marco gave her the numbers.

'I'm a bit tense.'

'Of course, and I've taken that into consideration, but I'd like to keep an eye on that. I don't want it going any higher if we can help it.' Then Marco felt her bump and she had a bump, not a big one but certainly there was a small bump.

And then he put a disc into the scanner. 'Let's make a recording.'

And she looked and wished so badly that James was here, because there was their baby on the screen and it really was a baby and she was very scared to look because she knew she'd fall in love.

'It looks every bit as good as I could hope,' Marco said. 'The placenta is nice and high, the measurements are spot on and the heart rate is good.' He went through everything as she lay there, not really sure how she felt, and then he helped her up and she went and sat down at his desk. They spoke for a few minutes about antenatal care and she confessed to two swigs of whisky and a glass of wine and horse riding before she'd found out, but Marco just smiled.

'I don't recommend women take up horse riding when pregnant, but if you are a competent rider, many women ride all the way through, and if it relaxes you…' He reached for his pen. 'We should do some bloods too.'

'Can they wait?' Ava said, and maybe she was being paranoid but she didn't want it documented till she had shared things with James.

'Of course,' Marco said. 'But can I suggest you don't wait too long.'

'I've been taking vitamins—'

'Ava,' Marco interrupted, 'I'm not worried about your bloods at the moment. The fact is, maybe I am a little more perceptive about these things than most men, but I knew you were pregnant as soon as you walked in—your husband will be perceptive in this too. He'll see for himself in a week or two.'

And then he spoke some more and he mentioned something that James had on several occasions, something she had baulked at, something that had caused the most terrible rows.

'I haven't been depressed,' Ava insisted. 'I've just been dealing with a lot.'

'Of course—you have been dealing with many things,' Marco said. 'But depression is something I like to speak openly about, especially with women who have suffered losses.'

Ava nodded in all the right places and then thanked him for his care and told him that soon she would be in to see him formally, then headed down to the canteen, still clutching the DVD Marco had made for her.

She bought her lunch and then saw James walking in.

She watched as he moved his tray along the counter, and felt as if the world was watching as he sat at a table far from her. He looked better than he had for a while, but that only meant he had a treatment due soon then, because just as he seemed to pick up and get some colour, he was soon wiped out again.

How did she tell him?

She had the DVD on the table beside her. Maybe she should just walk over now, maybe she'd just give it to him and let him watch it in private. Let him work out himself how he felt, just as she was trying to do.

She watched as a nurse went and sat with him.

That cow, Ava thought, when things like that had never once troubled her.

'Hi, there.' Ava looked up at a smiling Lily.

'Mind if I join you?' Lily asked.

'Sure.' Ava gave an awkward smile. Lily was rather more pregnant than the last time she'd seen her. She was glowing, in fact, and Ava felt awful for her horrible thoughts on the day of James's operation. Not that Lily would know.

'How are you?' Lily asked.

'I've been better,' Ava admitted. 'I just feel as if everybody's watching us, everybody's wondering how I can not be with James as he goes through this.'

'Nobody's thinking that,' Lily said. 'If anybody's saying anything, it's just how awful it must be—for both of you.'

'Thanks,' Ava said, not that she really believed it—

oh, maybe their friends thought that, but gossip could be so vicious and Ava hated it. 'And, Lily, I have to apologise—I wasn't very nice to you when James had his surgery.'

'What?' Lily clearly had no idea what Ava was talking about.

'I wasn't very friendly.'

Lily just laughed. 'I'm sure you had far more on your mind than worrying about being friendly to the nurse.'

'I know.' Ava shook her head. She should just let it go, but Lily was being so nice and she wanted to apologise properly. 'I was just in a horrible place that day. I was jealous that James had clearly spoken to you about his pain and…' she gave an awkward shrug '…that he had told you he wanted to stay in hospital rather than go home.' Lily said nothing, neither confirmed nor denied, just leant over and gave Ava's hand a squeeze.

'It was just everything—and with you being pregnant as well. I knew my marriage was over and the thing is, we lost some babies…' She was starting to tell people, but it was still so difficult. 'Hard to explain.'

'Easy to understand,' Lily said, and Ava gave a smile of thanks, grateful for Lily's kind words. 'You should come out to the farm, get away from everything for a bit,' Lily suggested.

Ava was about to shake her head, to decline as she always did these days. She was just too low to talk to anyone and too scared that if she did, she might reveal her secret before she told James, except getting away for a bit sounded so tempting. Lily and Luke had a gorgeous farm less than an hour away, she'd been to their wedding there and it had been glorious, and it was terribly tempting, and they had always said they should catch up.

'Luke's on call so it will just be us. Come for the weekend if you want.'

She wouldn't go for the weekend, Ava decided, but she did go over the next day.

First, though, she stopped by at Finn's.

She was sick of ignoring him, sick of pretending they'd never talked, so she bought a fresh filled roll from the baker's and two chocolate éclairs and then headed up to him.

'Finn.' She knocked at the door. 'It's Ava.' She knocked again, feeling awkward because clearly he didn't want to see her, or maybe he was out, maybe he was over at Evie's, so she ate the roll and packed up the éclairs, made the forty-minute drive to Luke and Lily's. It was so nice to get away from the hospital and the lonely flat.

Lily had made a picnic—a huge chicken, avocado and mango salad—and then packed it all into a basket with sparkling water and Ava's éclairs. They walked for a while and then sat down and basked in the lovely sunshine as they ate lunch. Lily was marvellous, just let her ramble a bit, because she'd found out that James *did* have another round of treatment on Monday and, of course, she was worried about that. As much as they talked, the two women said nothing at times too—just lay back on the grass after lunch. Lily's eyes closed, her lovely bump moving, and Ava's eyes open, wondering if she'd ever have a bump that moved too, wondering how James would take it when she told him.

But she couldn't now, could she?

Couldn't land this on him when he had a round of chemo booked.

'Do you want to walk?' Ava was suddenly panicked, but Lily just grinned and said sure, and they walked in the sun. Ava calmed a little and, yes, it was good to get away. 'Luke's uncle Tom has a property over there...' Lily pointed out the landmarks as they walked around late afternoon. 'He's wonderful.'

They turned into the stables and it was surely the most beautiful place on God's earth, because just the sounds and the smells had Ava relaxing.

'You've met Glenfiddich,' Lily said, and Ava stroked his mane. He was absolutely beautiful. 'He's the one I rode for the wedding.'

'He's gorgeous.'

'Luke thinks he's too spirited, but he's a baby really. We could go riding,' Lily suggested.

'You're still riding?' Ava asked, because Lily must be seven months pregnant now.

'I'd go mad if I didn't,' Lily said as they walked to the next stable. 'I've had all the lectures from Luke but I've told him that riding keeps my blood pressure down.

'This is Checkers.' Lily gave the old boy a kiss. He was huge—big and black with a white blaze—and Lily told her he had been Luke's when he was a kid. 'He's such a gentle old thing,' Lily said. 'We had some children visiting the other day who had never seen a horse before and Luke put one of them on him. He'd never startle—would you, Checkers?' And though she hadn't said, somehow Ava knew that Lily knew too. 'It's a privilege to ride you, isn't it, baby?' Lily crooned to Checkers.

'Can I?' Ava asked.

It didn't feel brave or risky to be back in the saddle—it felt right. In fact, Ava was quite sure that had there been a blood-pressure cuff attached to her arm now, the numbers would be tumbling down—she felt her heels push down and her pelvis move, felt the strength and the trust in the horse beneath her, and they walked on, mostly in silence, as Checkers did what horses did for Ava—cleared her head.

And she *did* end up staying the night. She and Lily watched a girly movie and ate chocolate as only two pregnant women really could. And they went riding again early in the morning and she cleared her head further still. Finally Ava was ready—to go home.

To think.

To be honest.

Not with James. First she had to be honest with herself.

James had been right and Marco too had been right to flag it.

Depression was such a cloaked thing and, no, she hadn't wanted to have it, hadn't wanted to face it, had refuted it when James had suggested she might be, had got angry when he had insisted she was.

And then she'd given up.

She'd given up so many things. They'd even eaten different meals, hers rich in folate and no raw fish or soft cheese, *just in case*, and she'd hated it when he'd shoved a Camembert in the oven and eaten it all melted. He'd done it the night after her last miscarriage, the night she'd thrown him out of her bed, the night he'd taken residence on the sofa and there he had stayed.

And she looked at those times through his eyes now.

He'd been trying to comfort her, making her a food that she loved, that they could cuddle up on the sofa and share. He just hadn't got how much it had hurt, how unpregnant that cheese had made her feel that night.

She looked through their wedding photos and through loads of albums, watched as her smile disappeared, oh, not in public, of course, but there were little clues in the images. James with his arm around her there at Lily and Luke's wedding. She was just so rigid beside him, and as she sat on the sofa, she recalled the terrible row of the night before. And she'd been so awkward that day because Finn had been best man and the miscarriage had happened just a few weeks before.

And there was Mia and Luca, so clearly besotted with each other as she and James stood slightly apart. She turned the pages and every one was a fresh memory. There she was with Hayley and Tom, and Ava actually smiled when she saw the photo, because he'd told her that day too not to pat the dog, and yet it hadn't felt like a snub then.

And there was Teo and Zoe's wedding photo, taken

on the beach in Samoa, Teo so proud of his bride and loving Zoe's daughter as if she were his own.

James had tried to talk to her about fostering, adoption, but she'd been too scared of being let down.

She looked at her friends, saw Lexi and Sam unashamedly kissing. Those days had long since gone for James and herself.

She'd made it that way.

Ava knew that.

She'd refused to do the one thing she always told her patients they should.

To talk, to be honest, to get help if required. But then, James hadn't been honest either. James had kept it all in too, he'd just been this rock when she'd wanted his pain, and he'd hated it so much when she'd wept. He was an oncologist, for God's sake. He should be used to grief, used to pain.

Not hers, though…

She saw it then, that just as she wasn't the fabulous sex therapist at home, like everybody assumed, James was a different person at work too.

They knew what they were doing at work—it was the relationship part where they'd got lost.

And she wanted him home.

So badly.

Wanted to ring him, but didn't know what to say, didn't know where to start, wondered if he was in bed now, having his mind taken off things by this mysterious Steph woman, if she'd flown down from Brisbane…

She truly wondered if she'd left it too late.

There was a frantic thumping at the door and she ran to it. There was urgency in the knock, need, she was sure he could feel it, sure that finally it was James.

'Ava…' It was Gladys, the cleaner, her face ashen. 'I need help. It's Finn, I've just found him on the floor.'

CHAPTER FOURTEEN

GLADYS was too slow to wait for and Ava charged up the stairs.

She knew Gladys dropped in on Finn a lot and especially since he'd been out of the hospital.

'Oh, Finn.' She was appalled by what she saw—his breathing was terrible, rasping and rapid, and as she rolled him onto his side she could feel the heat from his clammy skin, saw the scar down his neck was angry and infected. How long had he been lying here? She cursed herself for yesterday morning. She should have kept knocking, or maybe rung Luke, but that was ridiculous. The last thing Finn wanted was a caretaker.

'Have you called an ambulance, Gladys?' Ava checked as the old lady puffed in.

'I didn't know what to do so I came and got you.'

'Okay, well, pass me the phone.'

Some doctor she was! She punched in the numbers and spoke to the operator. She didn't even have a bag, well, not one with anything that would help Finn at this moment! He was severely dehydrated and very, very ill, and the wait for the ambulance was interminable, especially with the hospital so close.

'I rang him earlier,' Gladys said. 'I'd made a nice roast and I thought I'd bring some for him, he's been losing so much weight.' She was beside herself. 'He didn't answer and I got all worried. I was nervous to let myself in…'

'Thank God that you did,' Ava said.

'What do you think is wrong with him?'

'He's got a wound infection,' Ava said. 'And a chest infection too by the sound of it.' She was furious with Finn, angry with this stubborn, proud man who just refused all help. 'There's nothing we can do till the ambulance gets here. Go down and get the lift ready for them.'

She thought of Evie, thought of how terrible it would be for her to have Finn come in in this condition if she was on duty tonight, and she used the phone again and asked to be put through to Emergency and then to the nurse in charge.

'No, I need to speak to the nurse in charge now.' She pulled rank. 'It's Dr Carmichael and it's about a patient that's being brought in.'

And the charge nurse, when she came to the phone, was lovely, she got it completely when Ava told her that the patient coming in soon was Finn.

'We'll get set up for him and I'll go and speak to Evie now,' the charge nurse said. 'Thanks so much for letting me know.'

The paramedics were marvellous. They put in two

drips and poured fluids into him and gave him oxygen too, and by the time they had moved him down and the cool night air hit, Finn was coming around just a little. She sat in the back of the ambulance with him for the short trip to SHH.

'Evie…' She knew he was worrying about the same thing as she had.

'She knows, Finn.' She'd never tried to be soft with him and she wouldn't start now, and anyway he wouldn't appreciate it. So she didn't hold his hand and make soothing noises. Instead she watched through the darkened window as the ambulance sped through the night and she was cross with Finn, so, so cross with him, and when he was better she'd tell him—in trying to save Evie from the burden, he'd just hurt her a whole lot more, Ava could see that.

Could see many things as they turned in to the approach for the hospital.

No matter how difficult it might make things, James really did need to know now.

She went to James's apartment straight from the hospital.

Finn was already improving, but Ava still felt faint at the thought of him lying on that floor all night because had Gladys not dropped in, he simply might not have been holding on by morning.

She wanted James, not just to tell him about the baby, not just to fight for them, but because tonight had been horrible and James was the only person who would understand the fright she'd had. She wasn't used to dealing with acute patients. It had been awful to feel so helpless.

Except he wasn't home, and she thought about ringing him, but sometimes you just needed face to face, so she waited it out all night and then in the morning she headed up to the oncology floor, prepared to wait in his office if she had to. To just close the door and have this out. But as she walked along the corridors she saw Evie. She didn't want to stop, but Evie clearly did.

'Ava! Thank you for last night.'

'It's no problem. Thank God for Gladys…'

Ava went to move on but Evie was still talking. She didn't want to hear about Finn, she wanted James. 'He's been treating the wound infection at home, can you believe it?' Evie was furious. 'Hasn't told anyone.' She let out a hiss of frustration as on and on she went when all Ava wanted was James. 'He's refusing to see anyone. Hayley wants to take him to Theatre for debridement, but he's refusing and he's told them to cancel the next operation. He wants to lecture instead of operate—'

'Evie…' Ava interrupted. She didn't want to hear about anyone else, she just wanted James. 'I'm sorry but I have to go.' She was almost running. She just wanted to see her husband. She took the lift to Oncology, except the lift let her out on the wrong floor, on the surgical ward, and just as she was about to go back in when she changed her mind because as desperately as she wanted to see James, there was something about the lifts not working and Finn, something inside her that made her feel brave, made her angry, made her right.

'Can you tell me where Finn is?'

'He's not taking visitors.' The nurse looked up as Ava strode over.

'He's taking this one!' Ava said, and she looked the nurse straight in the eye.

'Sorry, he's made it very clear...'

Ava turned to Hayley, who walked over, and asked again, but Hayley shook her head.

'Ava, he's not seeing anyone.'

'Go and tell him that Ava Carmichael is here and that if he refuses to see me then I'll tell everybody exactly what went on between us in the stairwell the night before his surgery.'

She stood there, cheeks flaming as she was the victim of yet more curious looks. The whole ward seemed to have stopped, even the domestic had stopped mopping, but actually Ava's cheeks were flaming in anger. She was past caring what the lot of them thought as she waited till Hayley returned.

'Has he said that he will see me?' Ava asked.

'Unfortunately, yes.' Hayley smiled. 'I was dying to find out what happened! Room four. Go on through.' Hayley caught Ava's arm as she walked past and then her voice was serious. 'Good luck.'

'Well, here she is!' Finn was at his most toxic—unshaven, the curtains drawn, he jeered as she walked into the room. 'The woman who left her husband in the middle of chemotherapy, her one-balled husband,' Finn added. 'The woman who had drunken sex in the stairwell...' Ava just stood there as he insulted her, just knew, as Evie did, that it wasn't really Finn. 'That's what they'll all be saying now, you realise.'

'I don't care what they're saying.'

'Did we?' Finn asked. 'I've had so many drugs since admission, you know, I can't really remember that night.'

'Oh, you can remember,' Ava said. 'You can remember how scared you were and how badly you wanted Evie. You just don't want to remember, you just don't want to admit it. Well, here's a bit of advice, Finn— you can push people away, you can shut them out, you can deal with everything on your own, and then one day you might have to live with the consequences.' She faced him.

'I'm aware of the consequences, thank you.'

'Are you?' Ava asked. 'Are you quite sure about that? Because one day you might find out that Evie needs you, one day it might be her that's sitting on the oncology ward with a bag of poison going into her arm, and you've pushed so far, you've left it so long, that *he's* dealing with things on his own...'

'I thought you were here to see me...not talk about James.'

'I'm talking about you,' she shouted back—and she was.

Sort of.

'I'm talking about us both, but I'm *telling* you, one day something might happen and you might find yourself the one locked out of Evie's life—when, wheelchair or not, you could've been supporting her. Think about that as you wallow in your self-pity.'

'Get out!' he roared.

'I'm leaving already.'

She did. She had too much adrenaline and was far too angry to take the lift. She ran up the stairs and onto the oncology floor and, when he wasn't in his office, she found out where he was and spoke for several moments with a nurse, the one she'd seen him with in the canteen, in fact, before donning a gown and gloves and being allowed in.

James didn't look up.

He'd been dreading this morning, had made a grim joke to Harriet that he'd considered ringing in sick, and then she'd told him that Richard had, and in all honesty, James didn't blame him. And then he'd heard the nurses start talking.

'What's this about you and Finn on the stairwell?' He was flicking the remote for a DVD.

'Well, that didn't take long.' Ava rolled her eyes.

'Someone really ought to tell the nurses that that glass they stand behind isn't soundproof. Though don't,' James quickly added. 'I kind of like hearing what's going on.'

'Nothing happened between Finn and I except for a long conversation.'

'It's not my concern.'

'Maybe not,' Ava said. 'The same way I understand if you've been seeing someone…' She loved him so much that she spoke the truth. 'I know that I've been hell to live with. I promise you, I understand if there was some-one else, but I'm not giving up on us without a fight.'

'Someone else? Er...' He gave her a very strange look. 'I'm not exactly living the single life at the mo-ment.'

'I meant before,' Ava said, 'before we broke up.'

'I was never unfaithful.'

'Oh, please,' Ava said. 'I'm not stupid—we hadn't slept together in more than a year.'

'I know that,' James said, 'but there wasn't anybody else.'

'Don't lie about this, James,' she begged. 'We can't start again if we lie.'

'Ava, why would I sleep around when I'd been try-ing to save us?'

'So who were you ringing after your operation? I came back to talk and you were on the phone.' She could hear her jealousy, but she swallowed it down and misquoted him. '"Sorry about that, she's gone back to work now—we were nearly caught! Now where were we, Steph?"'

'I was trying to sort out the serviced apartment.' He had the audacity to laugh. 'Steph was very helpful, she's used to men planning on moving out and not tell-ing their wives—though my situation was a touch more complicated. I wanted an end apartment, with the toilet furthest away from the adjoining wall...' She shook her head in impatience at his detail. 'Didn't want to upset the other guests.' He went back to his TV.

'So who were the linen trousers for? The posh new

cologne? I mean it, James. I don't care… I mean, I understand if you…'

'They were for you.' He turned his head and there was so much anger in his green eyes she almost believed him.

Almost, but she knew him too well and he knew her too well too.

'Liar,' she said. 'You know I don't care about things like that.'

'I told the marriage counsellor the same thing.' Ava couldn't believe what she was hearing.

'You went to a marriage counsellor?'

'When I was in Brisbane. Three months of it, telling her everything, and she still didn't get it—I mean, how do you explain us?'

'I don't know,' Ava admitted.

'Like I told her that you eat healthily and that you moaned about the way I ate and she said that maybe I'd let myself go a bit.'

'That wasn't what upset me,' Ava said. 'I just want you to take care of yourself.'

'Well, she said that maybe you wanted me to make more of an effort…'

'No!' She laughed. 'Well, you did look nice.'

'It was for you,' James said, and her heart seemed to squeeze in her chest. 'I joined a gym. I was out running every morning, bought new clothes, shaved, put on cologne, hell…' She could see the hurt and rejection right there on his face, and she winced at the recall of her reaction to him, or rather her complete lack of it. 'And I came home and you didn't give me a second glance.'

'I thought…' Oh, God, she really had thought it was for someone else. 'I thought you'd done it for someone else. And then I got the flowers. I thought you felt guilty, you never send me flowers.'

'Yeah, well, I did feel guilty. I was having a session with the counsellor when you rang, I got all flustered.' Guilty eyes looked up at her. 'I'd just told her we hadn't had sex in, like, for ever, and then you rang. It was as if you knew I was talking about us.'

'Oh, James.'

'She heard what I said, that I'd call you back, and she said that I handled the conversation all wrong, that I should send flowers. I said you didn't appreciate them. Still, it was worth a go…' She could not believe it, that James, her James, would sit and pour his heart out to a stranger, and she told him so. 'Two hundred dollars a week.' James was incredulous. 'The appointments had to be after hours, so it was two hundred dollars! What a damn waste.'

'It wasn't a waste.' She looked at him and could not believe all he had done to save them—how hard he had worked. And what had she done?

'Come home.' She saw him close his eyes. 'I want you home.'

'Ava.' He was so tired, too tired to fight and too tired to refuse, but also too tired to hurdle over this huge mound of pride. 'You don't have to feel sorry for me. I've only got a couple more rounds to go.'

'I don't want you back because I feel sorry for you. I want you back because I love you, because I can't stand us being apart. James, I do know how you feel.'

'No, Ava, you don't.'

'You think that I want to be there for all the wrong reasons. That if we get back together it will be because we have to rather than we want to? Well, guess what? I feel the same too.' She saw him frown. 'Watch this,' she said, handing him a DVD.

'Not more feel-good schmaltz,' James groaned. 'I don't need a single bit more inspiration...'

Ava said nothing as she put the DVD in. She watched his expression as he watched it.

'I'm fourteen weeks pregnant, James. Actually...' she did the maths '...I'm nearly fifteen.' And she watched him frown, watched him try to take it in. 'And in case you do ever wonder, nothing happened on the stairwell.'

'I know that,' James said, and he looked at his wife. 'Because I know you'd tell me if it did.'

'I would,' Ava said. 'And I don't have to because it didn't. We shared some whisky, spoke about Evie and I came inside and then I called you.'

He looked back at the screen, at their baby, and he rewound it and played it again.

'You should have told me.' She knew he wasn't talking about Finn. 'How could you not tell me?' Now he was angry. 'You didn't even try.'

And she opened her mouth to speak, to defend herself, to say that she had been to the serviced apartment to try, but she halted, because this was about them and nobody else needed to be included.

'How could I?' she asked, and it was up to him whether or not he would forgive her for keeping quiet. 'I might lose it,' Ava said. 'But I promise you this, if I do I will cry and I will sob, but I will grieve with you this time, and you will cry too, if you want to, and then I promise you that I will move on, because whatever happens I am so grateful because this baby make me see sense…'

He still wouldn't give in, so she told him the truth. Was as direct with James as she'd been with Finn. 'That's your daughter or son there, and if this pregnancy does last…' They'd let things go so far, she just didn't know if they could claw back from it—but they had to.

'Do you just want access visits, James? Alternate weekends?' And it must have hit him somewhere inside, because he put his hand up to stop her, but she continued. 'I'll have Christmas mornings, please, and then you can take it to your mum's for lunch, or to your girlfriend's, or whatever…'

'Stop it.'

'No!' She would not stop. 'Because that's how it will be.'

'No.' And she watched her proud, strong man start crying, and it was the first time she had ever seen him cry, not held-back tears, not angry tears, just tears, and he was too tired to even wipe them away. He just sat in the chair so, so defeated, and she could see him bald and thin and yet still so proud and just perhaps the most honest and beautiful she had ever seen James, and she couldn't simply hold him and kiss away his tears, so instead she stood in gown and gloves and she stayed strong.

'Or you can come back to me today and I'll never really know if you're just coming back for the baby. I've got the golden ticket, haven't I?'

And she thought the same as he did, James realised, felt the same as he did, was simply a part of him. 'I've got the reason for you to come back...'

'Ava, all I want is to be with you, baby or no baby, that's all I ever wanted.' And she was scared to believe him too.

'Should you be here?' She smiled when he said it, when he looked up at the drip, because he was as terrified as her. 'I mean, with the chemo...'

'I spoke to the nurse when I came in. I have to be careful with your body fluids for the next forty-eight hours, but I'm upping it to seventy-two hours...' She gave him a little wink, but she was terrified of that part too—of chemo and the effects on the baby—but she couldn't live like that any longer, couldn't kill her marriage again.

'I've had whisky, though of course I didn't know I was pregnant then and Marco said not to worry, I probably needed a bit of sedation that night. And I'm swimming...' she looked at him '...and riding.'

'Before you found out?' James said, because he knew how she was.

'No.' She shook her head. 'Yesterday I went horse

riding and I went riding the day before too and for the first time since you found that lump, for a couple of hours I felt great, and the baby is still here and holding on...'

'Are we?'

'Yes,' she said. 'Yes.' She said it again and she was crying now too, and because she couldn't kiss him, instead she took that weary face she loved so much into her gloved hands. She hadn't touched his face in so long—it was relief, sheer relief to hold him, and the relief was mixed with frustration because she could only wipe away his tears through the rubber gloves.

And Ava, once practical, the moment she held him again believed, in kindred spirits and angels and a love that was meant to be. And James, who thought you just died and were buried, believed just a little too as he held her again, because it felt like nothing he could explain.

Not stir-fried rice and chicken and unconditional love, but this danger that came with the woman in his arms. And yet there was a sense of safety too.

She knew him.

She was the only person he wanted to be with and he didn't want to do this alone any more.

'I know you won't believe me,' James said, 'I know you think I'm just saying it, but that morning before I found it, I was thinking about you, I wanted you to come into the shower with me but I thought that might be pushing it so I was going to come out and talk. I wanted us to maybe try again.'

'James.' She didn't care about the nurses behind the

glass partition. Let them hear, she thought, let them see, because she loved him so much she was fine if the whole world knew it. 'What did you think I was coming into the shower for?' She saw him frown and she started to laugh, because the truth was so obvious now. 'I could hear you, you big idiot. You're not exactly quiet when you get it on!'

She saw him smile, she could hear her baby's heartbeat on the screen as the two of them remembered the night that it was made, and she told him her truth, a truth that had been lost in the pain of these past weeks.

'What do you think I was coming into the bathroom for, James? I was coming in to be with you.'

CHAPTER FIFTEEN

AND they tumbled into bed.

Except it didn't happen.

She wanted that.

Knew he did too.

Except it was more private than that for both of them. More difficult than, even in her job capacity, she had ever understood.

He puked his way through the first three days after chemo and she tried not to hover at the door, and he shouted to her once not to come in when she went to, because he didn't want her holding his head, but he did love the endless flannels she soaked in ice, and he conceded and drank her protein shakes when he could keep things down and ate Brazil nuts because Ava believed they would help.

She cooked for two.

Different sorts of meals from before, but this time they ate the same—because she'd been trawling the internet and was obsessed with his diet now instead of hers. And she got now how Veronica had needed to cook, needed to feed him, needed to do something, and she smiled and chatted much more graciously when Veronica came round. They had a baby to talk about so that made things easier too. Then, one evening James was called in for a patient. 'Richard,' he told Ava, because he told her more about his work now. Richard had come back for his treatment yesterday but had been admitted because he was febrile and James, of course, was straight out of the door. Instead of scuttling off, Veronica actually hung around and they chatted awkwardly for a moment and then Ava made tea.

'That time you came around…' Ava's hand was shaking as she pulled out the teabag as Veronica asked the question… 'Did you know you were pregnant then?'

'I'd just found out,' Ava said.

'You'd come to tell him?' Veronica swallowed as Ava nodded. 'James would never forgive me if he found out.'

'And he never will find out,' Ava said. 'And you're wrong, James would forgive you.'

'Can you?'

'I did ages ago,' Ava said, because she'd done an awful lot of thinking—about how hard it must be for Veronica at times to be the one left to carry on. 'It didn't feel like it at the time, but being apart…' She closed her eyes for a moment because it was so hard to explain it and she never wanted to be apart from him again, but just as she had said to George and Elise, from something so awful good things had come. She'd been with James since she was eighteen, had only ever been with James, and had relied on his love perhaps a little too much. Now she knew that if she had to she could make it on her own and so could James. And in their uncertain worlds it brought them both comfort, and Ava knew also that she would never take his love for granted again. 'We're stronger for it.'

And the two women just tried harder, because they had one thing in common at least—they both loved James.

And he loved Ava, so he let her add the blueberries to his oat bran and he cut down on carbs, but he still insisted on sugar in his coffee, and at night they cuddled sometimes and other times slept on their own sides of the bed, and for the next couple of weeks they sort of learned how to share their lives again.

Just not that part.

Oh, they were sharing a bed now and sometimes she woke up in his arms, but they just hadn't got to where they fell asleep like that. She lay in bed this morning and all she wanted was a kiss. They'd had a couple, but sort of awkward ones, and she stared up at the dark and went through her faults.

Yes, she was practical at work but completely neurotic at home, and then she thought some more, went over their rows before they'd got back together, went over the one where he'd admitted that he was scared, and she grimaced as she recalled his words.

I'm patronising. She groaned in her head.

I am—she reluctantly concluded—*he was completely right.* If they had been together when he'd been diagnosed she'd have been terribly efficient about sex and so, so annoyingly understanding.

She actually made herself laugh as she thought about it, just lay in the dark and let out a giggle because, yes, at times she could be a right royal pain.

Maybe she should get up and have a shower.

Except she'd run out of conditioner *again*, but she'd bought some last week, she was quite sure of it.

'Don't look at me,' James said when she'd accused him last night of pinching her expensive stuff. 'What would I need conditioner for?'

She was disorganised too, Ava decided.

And then she felt something—something she'd been chasing, something that it felt like she'd been waiting for for ever, and it came the moment it wasn't on her mind.

This flutter in her stomach.

So fleeting, so vague, and of course it must be wind.

Except she felt it again.

Like a tiny mouse scratching from the inside.

'It moved.'

Her fifth pregnancy and she'd never felt her baby move, and she was now completely certain that it was.

'What?' Already woken by her mad, morning laughter James rolled over to face her on his side.

'The baby...'

He put her hand to her stomach and of course he couldn't feel the little mouse scratching.

'I felt it.'

'I know,' James said, because, well, Ava didn't say things that hadn't happened—she was far too practical with her body for that. So he held his hand on her tummy for a full sixty seconds and, no, he couldn't feel

it, and got a bit bored maybe waiting, because all by itself his hand wandered…

It just did.

Over a body that was changing, and his hand traced
her stomach and then dusted down—it said hello to
her thighs, but didn't greet her knees before it worked
its way back up.

She felt each stroke and then she felt his caution, the
wait for her to say no, or for her to say she was tired, or
needed space, or a panicked reminder about the *baby*!
But instead she felt his mouth on her breast and, God,
she loved his mouth, and she let her thighs relax and
felt his fingers explore, and as controlling as she was,
it was his fingers that controlled her then.

'Ava…'

He slipped his fingers in where she lay, loose-legged,
and the very solid nudge of him every now and then
told her that he was just as fine as she was. She lay
there and didn't think about saline balls, or chemo, or
that he was bald, or that she had a baby on board and a
womb that could collapse at a moment's notice. She just
thought about the lovely things he was doing to her and
the lovely things she was doing to him too.

And she listened to their noise.

And James was usually noisy, but this morning it
was she, moaning and groaning and giving Kirribilli
Views their wake-up call of old.

'I'm going to come.' She said it in panic, because
she should surely be the calm, reassuring one, insisting
on taking things nice and slowly, except she couldn't.

'Come,' he said as his fingers brought her closer. 'I want to watch.'

And her books went out of the window; she should be so much more laid back, so much more...*thoughtful*.

Except she wanted him. Was she terrible that that was all she wanted?

'Come inside me!'

He was inside her in a minute.

He moved over her, split her apart with his thighs and there he was on top, her hands grabbing at shoulders, thinner than she remembered at uni but so much stronger their union now, and this was their glorious moment, because eyes never changed.

Green eyes gazed at her.

Loving her as together they came.

James.

Ava.

Worth fighting for.

EPILOGUE

'YOU'D turned them off.'

James gave a wry smile as he walked into the room.

Right at the end of her labour, when things had suddenly become tense, Ava had remembered that she might have left her hair straighteners on. Actually, she was quite sure she had, because she'd been straightening her hair for her antenatal appointment when all the drama had started, trying to tell herself that the contractions she was having were nothing to get excited about, they were probably Braxton-Hicks. Marco had warned her that her baby was a big one, and was today going to talk about inducing her, or even recommend she consider a Caesarean, which Ava definitely didn't want. Except that as she'd stood there pondering how soon he might induce her, and just how much bigger she could possibly get, her waters had broken and things had moved surprisingly quickly from then on.

'James?'

He'd heard her voice from the bathroom and even before he'd walked in there he'd known.

And he'd known how terrified she was too.

And he had been terrified as well, but not for a moment had he shown it, especially when by ten minutes later she was already two heavy contractions in, and four heavy contractions in by the time he'd been put through to Maternity to tell them they were on their way.

'Ring your mum!' Ava had ordered as they'd headed for the door, because Veronica had asked to be kept up to date with all news.

'She'll want to come,' James had said as she'd doubled up at the door. 'We'll ring her afterwards.'

'By the time she gets there,' Ava gritted, 'it will be afterwards.'

She was almost right.

There was something about Finn and lifts because as they stepped inside he was on his way down, dressed in a suit and on his way to work, his last day at work before his operation next week.

And after a brief good morning he suitably ignored them, because there were certain times you didn't want to be seen—except the lift wasn't moving and it was James rather frantically pushing the buttons and then there was nothing prim about Ava, Finn noted as she cursed like a navvy and pressed the buttons herself, because she was not going down by the stairwell and she was not having her baby here. But thankfully the lift started moving and as Finn got out at the ground floor while they headed down for the car in the basement, he had the decency to simply step out.

Emily, who was quite pregnant herself, examined her on arrival.

'We might just see about getting the doctor down.' She'd given Ava the nicest smile and had called out to a colleague and then quietly set up for delivery as Ava bore down.

'It's too fast...' Ava begged, because her mind couldn't catch up with the speed of things, and it was then she remembered the hair straighteners and that she might have left them on.

Marco, when she said it again, had told her to forget such things.

'Ava, don't worry about that now.' He said it very calmly. In fact, had she not been his wife, Emily might not have noted the slight tension in his voice, and she looked down to where the head that was almost out, and then it retracted. It was called 'turtle sign' and indicative of shoulder dystocia. Emily noted that James was a big guy, with very broad shoulders, and she saw James watching too, saw the dart of nervousness in his eyes, and Emily took a calming breath as Ava ranted about the hair straighteners, and her patient did not need to know what was happening yet, she was terrified enough.

'Nice slow breath, Ava,' Emily said. 'Let that thought go. Your baby's nearly here and then James can go home and check on those straighteners for you. Now, let's bring your legs right up.' She took one leg and James the other to open up the pelvis some more, and James told her that, yes, soon he'd go home, that she could stop worrying about that now.

And that helped her to stop terrifying herself, convincing herself, in fact, that as she laboured on, the flat was burning down, which meant the contracts wouldn't go through on the house they had bought.

Yes, they had a house.

The one she'd imagined James walking into, with kids hanging off him and clearly at peace with his saline ball, except she hadn't been walking past with frozen meals and vegetables and cat food. Instead, she had been sitting on the veranda, watching her family be.

And it was the house of her dreams. She simply hadn't recognised it then. It was the house where they had first made love. It had come onto the market three weeks after they'd got back together and everyone had said they were crazy, that they had far too much on their plates without buying an old bomb.

Except they'd fallen in love with it.

And Ava had co-ordinated the renovators and now, if not quite finished, they were ready to move in and the contracts for the flat were going through this week.

It would be there that they brought home their baby.

'You're doing great, Ava,' James said, his voice strong and calm, even though fear ripped through him at the potential precariousness of the situation as he watched his baby struggle to be born. Just for a second he wondered why things had to be so hard for them, wondered just how much more they could take, and then almost instantly he shoved that thought aside because life, too, had been wonderful to them and they could take whatever it sent them.

'Just relax a moment before the next one, Ava.' And she did as he said and relaxed just a little, just breathed for a moment, and the rest of the room breathed too as her pelvis opened that necessary fraction more, and then in a moment her new family was there, her baby being lifted onto her stomach, and there was this breeze of joy and relief and love that swept into the room.

James cut the cord and shook hands with Marco and nothing was said—because today she really didn't need to know, but, yes, if there were to be any more baby Carmichaels then it would be a Caesarean next time.

No, today Ava didn't need to know what a close call it had been for a moment.

Today she just had to concentrate on being a mum.

And so, after they'd cuddled their son and just marvelled at him, they had opened the door to Veronica, and there had been cuddles and kisses all around. Ava thought it was nice to have her there, nice to share the joy, nice to be happy but a little bit wistful too.

'I wish your dad was here.'

'So do I,' James admitted, and again Ava understood Veronica a bit more.

'What did your parents say?' Veronica asked. 'They must be beside themselves.

'They will be when they pick up their voicemail,' Ava said, understanding her own parents a little less, and she felt James's hand squeeze her shoulder just a bit tighter. And just as she was being moved to her room,

James had felt her tense and in the end had given her a kiss and popped home to check that she had turned the straighteners off.

And, yes, just as they hadn't at the start of their relationship, no longer did those sorts of things annoy him.

Well, maybe very occasionally, but they knew what was important now.

'I'm going to buy you the sort that turn off themselves,' Veronica offered when James came back and gave the inevitable all-clear.

'Well, can you buy her an iron that turns itself off as well, then,' James said. 'Oh, and an oven that turns itself off when you close the front door...' He looked at their new surroundings. 'Nice room.'

It was a wonderful room, with an amazing view—a view that so often had soothed her, a view that was there patiently waiting to see her through good times and bad, and she was infinitely grateful for it.

'Here!'

He handed her flowers.

Pale flowers with hardly a trace of scent. Iceberg roses from the bushes she had planted in their new garden.

Her very favourite kind.

'Teo's just giving him the once-over,' Ava said, as the paediatrician turned and gave James a smile.

'He's perfect.' Teo finished examining him and handed Baby Carmichel to James. 'Welcome to the sleepless-nights club,' he said.

'Yep,' James shook his hand while with the other he held his son. 'I hear you're a recent member.'

'Zoe came home yesterday.'

And when Teo had gone and the lunches were being brought out, Veronica did the most amazing thing.

'Well, I'm going to head home.' Ava nearly fell off the bed.

'Stay!' she offered, and peered at a very unappetising beef stroganoff. 'James can go out and get something nice for lunch…'

'That rabbit food you two eat?' Veronica frowned. 'No, thanks.' But then she did give Ava a smile because, after all, James was doing very well on it—even if Ava was convinced he was cheating an awful lot of the time. 'Anyway, I've got a lot of phone calls to make. I'll come in this evening, though—if that's okay?'

'That'd be great.'

'Do you need anything? Anything you want me to bring in?'

'Some of your chicken and fried rice maybe?' Ava said, because they'd cheat together tonight. 'And champagne.' She grinned.

'Already in the fridge,' Veronica said, and gave her grandson just one more cuddle before she was gone.

Not that they were alone for long.

Word had got out and the gift shop must be running hot because the domestic kept ferrying in balloons and bunches of flowers

'We take them out at night,' she assured them.

Well, they weren't taking out her iceberg roses, Ava decided.

And James read the cards out to her as she fed their son.

George was in to see Donald and we heard the
news!
So happy for you both.
George and Elise
(Playing lots of Scrabble) xxx

'Who are George and Elise and why are they play-ing lots of Scrabble?' James frowned and then stopped frowning as he got it, because sometimes now she did bring her work home with her, even if he didn't know it, and they were playing lots of Scrabble too—and walk-ing on the beach and, yes, lots of talking and, yes, things would remain fine.

They'd both see to it.

'Oh, and I texted Richard with the news…' James said, because, given all they had been through, Richard had become far more than a patient, 'He rang straight back, he's thrilled, and,' James added, 'he's got some news of his own. We've got an engagement party to go to in a few weeks.'

And then he went to read out another one but he just stopped and laughed.

'Who's it from?' Ava asked.

'Guess.' James grinned.

Welcome to Baby Carmichael
Remembering the stairwell fondly,
Finn (Actually it's Evie, he'd never think to send
flowers) xxx

'Well, that's going to silence the rumour mill.' James laughed and then it faded, because the gift shop was going to be extra-busy in the next few days too. 'I hope his surgery goes well for him.'

'It will,' Ava said.

'You don't know that,' James said, because now he did stress a little, well, he always had, as it turned out, he'd just not told her.

And now he did.

'It's a big gamble,' James said. 'All or nothing this time…'

'Well, whatever the outcome, Finn will deal with it,' Ava said. 'And we'll all be there for him—whether the grumpy old goat wants it or not.'

And she looked down at her son, whose eyes seemed to reach into her heart.

'He's huge.' He had a squashed-up face like a boxer's and was sucking hungrily on his fist despite having been fed twice, and somehow he reminded her so much of his dad that it made her laugh.

'If there is a next time, I'm having a Caesarean.' She caught his eyes and he knew that she knew, but sometimes you didn't need to go over things.

'Yes, Ava,' James said. 'You are.'

And then she looked back at her baby and couldn't quite believe he was here. She peeled off the little beanie that was on his head and tufted the pale brown hair. 'He's got more hair than you.'

'Not for long,' James said, because it was growing

back, and he looked at his wife and climbed up on the bed beside her.

'He looks like an Eddie,' Ava said, and James looked at his son who looked like him, and he thought of his own dad and he smiled.

'Text your mum his name,' Ava said, 'so she can tell everyone.'

And James did, texted a photo of his son to his mother, so she could forward the image of Edward James Carmichael to the people she couldn't wait to tell.

And then the Emily stopped by on her way home and told her how well she had done.

'Thanks so much,' Ava said. 'And Marco too—you were both great.'

'I'm on in the morning.' Emily smiled. 'I'll come in and we can go through your labour,' she said, because by tomorrow or maybe the next day Ava would want to, but for now she needed to rest, just as her son was.

'Do you want me to put him in his crib?' Emily offered, and when Ava nodded she took a not so little Eddie and popped him in his crib and then suggested she could close the curtains and turn the lights down and, given the traffic from the gift shop, maybe a 'no visitors' sign on the door.

'Please,' Ava said, because she loved them all and everything, but there would be time for that tonight, time to share their good news with everyone. She just wanted to be with her husband now and, yes, the view was to die for, but it would still be there when she needed it. She needed some time with James more.

He was clean-shaven, wearing those grey linen trousers and he smelt just a little of cologne as he pulled her into him, and it was all for her.

'Fancy a second honeymoon?' James said. 'Just us three?'

'Yes, please.'

'Beach?'

Ava closed her eyes and shook her head.

'Mountains?' She shook her head again.

'Home,' she said. 'Let's honeymoon at home.' And she thought of their house and their garden that was waiting and the man who lay beside her and just how far the two of them had come, how much deeper their love now was, and she simply couldn't be happier.

'Let's enjoy every precious day.'

* * * * *

HOW TO MEND
A BROKEN HEART

BY
AMY ANDREWS

For Carita. Who knows.

All the characters in this book have no existence outside the imagination of the author, and have no relation whatsoever to anyone bearing the same name or names. They are not even distantly inspired by any individual known or unknown to the author, and all the incidents are pure invention.

First published in Great Britain 2012
by Mills & Boon, an imprint of Harlequin (UK) Limited.
Harlequin (UK) Limited, Eton House, 18-24 Paradise Road,
Richmond, Surrey TW9 1SR

© Alison Ahearn 2012

ISBN: 978 0 263 89188 1

Harlequin (UK) policy is to use papers that are natural, renewable and recyclable products and made from wood grown in sustainable forests. The logging and manufacturing process conform to the legal environmental regulations of the country of origin.

Printed and bound in Spain
by Blackprint CPI, Barcelona

Dear Reader,

The subject matter of this book is a difficult one. The death of a child and the often paralysing grief that comes with it aren't exactly ripe for a romance novel. But in my line of work, I have unfortunately seen many couples go through this harrowing experience and I so often wonder how they fare when they leave the surrealness of the hospital setting and have to get on with their lives without the little person that completed it so utterly. From this Tess and Fletch were born, two people whose profound grief had driven them apart despite their love for each other.

My life has been charmed until recently, with no bereavements or tragedies to speak of. Then half way through 2011 I lost my mother quite unexpectedly. Needless to say I now have more than a passing acquaintance with grief. It's not the loss of a child but grief doesn't discriminate and it's been a long, hard road to trudge.

Giving Tess and Fletch their HEA, even a decade after the tragic events that had marked theirs lives, was vital for me on many fronts.

I hope you root for them as I did during their journey back to each other.

Regards,

Amy

CHAPTER ONE

THICK grass spiked at Tessa King's bare knees as she sank to the ground beside the tiny, immaculately kept grave. Large trees shaded the cemetery and birdsong was the only noise that broke the drowsy afternoon serenity as she laid the bright yellow daffodils near the miniature marble statue of a kneeling angel.

Grief bloomed in her chest, sharp and fresh, rising in her throat, threatening to choke her. She squeezed her eyes shut and sucked in a breath, reaching for the headstone as the tsunamilike wave of emotion unbalanced her.

She let some tears escape. Just a few.

No more.

Even on the anniversary of his death she rationed her grief. It was ten years to the day since Ryan had died. Ten years of living life in greyscale.

The memories struggled for release but not even on this day did she allow herself the luxury of remembering too much. She rationed the memories too. His little body squirming against hers, his boyish giggle and that perfect little bow mouth.

The double cowlick that had refused to be tamed.
It was enough.

Tess opened her eyes, the simple inscription she knew as intimately as she knew her own heartbeat, blurring in front of her.

Ryan King.
Aged 18 months.
Gone, and a cloud in our hearts.

She reached for the letters, the smooth marble cool beneath her fingertips. She didn't let them linger. She wiped at her cheeks, blinked the remaining moisture away.
Enough.

Fletcher King ground his heels into the luxurious carpet of grass, resisting the urge to go to her as she sagged against the headstone. His butt stayed stubbornly planted against the bonnet of his Jag. She'd made it perfectly clear when they'd separated that it had to be a clean break. That she didn't want to see him or talk to him, and every overture he'd made the first year to keep in touch, to check on her, had been resoundingly rebuffed.

Frankly, after nine years of watching this ritual from afar, he didn't even know how to approach her. She seemed as distant today as she had for that awful year after Ryan's death when their marriage had slowly shrivelled and died.

He hadn't been able to bridge the gap back then and

he doubted almost a decade of distance would have improved things.

It didn't mean he was immune to her grief. Even from this distance the weight of her despair punched him square in the solar plexus. Took him right back to the dreadful day as they'd frantically tried to revive their son, hoping against hope, trying to ignore the portent of doom that had settled over him like a leaden cloak.

His frantic *'Come on, Ryan, come on!'* still echoed in his dreams all these years later.

A lump rose in his throat, tears needled and stung his eyes and he squeezed them tightly shut. He'd already cried a river or two; hell, he was probably up to an ocean by now, but he couldn't afford to succumb today.

He was here on a mission.

He needed his wife back.

Tess put one foot in front of the other on autopilot as she made her way to her car. Whether it was because of the dark swirl of emotions or the jet-lag, she didn't see him or at least register the identity of the tall, broad man leaning against the car parked in front of her rental until she was two metres away.

Then, as her belly did that almost forgotten somersault and her breath hitched in the same way it used to, she wondered why the hell not. She may not have been interested in a man in ten years but she obviously wasn't totally dead inside.

And Fletcher King in dark trousers and a business

shirt that had been rolled up to the elbows and undone at the throat was still an incredibly impressive man.

In fact, if anything, the years had honed him into an even more spectacular specimen.

He looked broader across the shoulders. Leaner at the hips. There were streaks of grey at his temples and where his dark, wavy hair met sculpted cheekbones. His three-day growth, black as midnight last time she'd seen it, was lightly peppered with salt. There were interesting lines around his tired-looking eyes, which were the silvery-green colour of wattle leaves.

Did he, too, still have trouble sleeping?

The indentations around his mouth, which became dimples when he laughed, were deeper. Even his mouth seemed fuller—sexier. His lips parted slightly and she caught a glimpse of his still-perfect teeth.

'Hello, Tessa.'

Tess was surprised by the prickle of awareness as his soft voice rumbled across the void between them. The latent attraction was unexpected. She was so used to locking down anything that had an emotional impact on her she was amazed she could still feel a pull at all.

But this *was* Fletch.

'Fletcher.' So much lay unsaid between them she didn't know where to start. 'It's been a long time.'

Fletch nodded, stifled by their formality. 'How have you been?'

She shrugged. 'Fine.'

Fletch suppressed a snort. *Hardly*. Each year she seemed to have faded away a little more. Gone were those curves that had driven him to distraction. There were only angles now. The legs sticking out of her above-knee, cargo-style pants were slender, her collar bones visible through the V-opening of her modest T-shirt were like coat hangers.

'You've got very thin.'

She shrugged again. 'Yes.' Tess ate as a matter of survival. Her pleasure in it had been sucked away with all the other things that had once brought her joy.

He regarded her for a moment. She was still a striking woman despite the angles. And the uber-short hairstyle. She'd cut it some time in that first year after they'd separated. She'd once had long white-blonde hair that had flowed down her back and formed a perfect curtain around them when they'd been making love. He'd spent hours stroking it, wrapping it around his hands and watching the light turn it incandescent as it had slowly sifted through his fingers.

It was darker blonde now, more honey than snow—a direct consequence of moving far away from the sunshine of Brisbane to the drizzly English countryside. It was cropped closely to her head, the back and sides razored severely in. The slightly longer locks on top were brushed over from a side parting, blending in with the jagged edges.

His sister had called it minimalist. He'd preferred the term butchered.

It did, however, draw attention to her amber eyes. They sat large in her spare, make-up-less face, dominating prominent cheekbones that fell away to catwalk-model hollows. They looked at him now, shadows playing in their sherry depths.

Her composure reached across the space between them and squeezed his gut hard. She projected calm detachment but he knew her well enough, despite their time apart, to see beyond. There was a fragility about her he'd have not thought possible a decade ago.

The impact of it rattled the shackles around his heart.

Tess weathered his probing gaze, waiting for him to say something more. Finally she could bear the silence no longer. She cleared her throat. 'I have to go.'

Fletch's gaze was drawn to her mouth. Her wide, full lips were devoid of any cosmetic enhancement, just as he remembered them. The same mouth he must have kissed a thousand times. That had travelled over every inch of his body. The same mouth that had desperately tried to breathe life into Ryan, that had begged a God she'd never believed in to spare their son.

Tess took a step towards her car. 'I have to go,' she repeated.

Fletch blocked her path, gently snagging her wrist. 'Could we talk?'

Tessa recoiled from his hold as if she'd been zapped, crossing her arms across her chest. 'There's nothing to talk about.'

'It's been nine years, Tess. You think we have nothing to say to each other?'

Tess bit her lip. *Nothing that hadn't been said already—ad nauseam.*

Fletch glanced at her white-knuckled grip as her fingernails dug into the flesh of her bare biceps. Her wedding ring, *his grandmother's ring*, snagged his attention. 'You still wear your wedding ring.'

Tess, surprised by the sudden direction the conversation had taken, looked down at it. The rose-gold band with its engraved floral pattern, thinned with age and wear, hung loosely on her finger, only her knuckle preventing it from sliding off. She absently twisted it around with her thumb a few times before returning her attention to him.

'Yes.' She wasn't going to tell him it was her deterrent against unwanted advances from men. She glanced at his bare left hand. 'You don't.'

Fletcher glanced at his hand. It had taken a year after the divorce to take it off yet sometimes he was still surprised by its absence. The white tan line that had remained after he'd removed it had long since faded.

'No.' It had got to the stage where he hadn't been able to bear the memories it had evoked.

Tess nodded. What had she expected? That he would choose to hide behind his as she had hers? That grief would torpedo his libido as it had hers?

Tess dropped her arms to her sides. 'I really have to go.'

Fletch held up his hands. 'I just need a minute, please.'

She felt exasperation bubble in her chest. In less than twenty-four hours she'd be back on a plane heading to London. The same as last year. The same as the last nine years. Why had he chosen to complicate things now?

'What do you want, Fletch?' What could he possibly want to say to her after all this time? After all these years of silence? Silence they'd *both* agreed on despite his lapses early in their separation.

Fletch blinked as her familiar name for him finally slipped from her lips to claw at his gut. 'It's my mother...she's unwell. She's been asking for you.'

Tess felt her stomach drop as concern for her ex-mother-in-law caused her heart to leap in her chest. Fletch looked so grim. 'Is she...? What's wrong with her? What happened?'

'She has Alzheimer's.'

Tessa gasped, her hand coming up to cover her mouth. 'Oh, Fletch...' She took a step towards him, their baggage momentarily forgotten, her other hand reaching for him.

'That's terrible.' Her hand settled against his arm, her fingers on the sleeve of his business shirt, her palm against the corded muscles of his tanned forearm. 'Is it... Is she bad?'

Jean King was one of the sharpest women Tess had ever met. She was funny, witty, insightful and super-smart. Tess's mother had died when she'd been eight and Jean had filled a very deep void. They'd been close right from the get-go and Jean had been her anchor—their anchor—in the dreadful months that had followed Ryan's death. Even when she and Fletch had separated and then divorced, Jean had been there for her.

Fletch nodded. 'She's deteriorated in the last couple of months.'

'When... How long has she had it for?'

Tess had dropped in on Jean on her yearly pilgrimage home those first two years after she'd moved to the UK. But it had been too hard on both of them. Jean had wanted to talk about Ryan and Tess hadn't been able to bear it. So she'd stopped going.

Fletch, aware of her nearness, of her faint passion-fruit fragrance, of her hand on his arm, waged a war within himself. Tess looked as devastated as he felt and it was as if the intervening years had never happened. As if he could walk right into her arms and seek the solace he so desperately craved.

It was a dangerous illusion.

He couldn't hope to execute what he'd come here for if he let emotion take over. He just hadn't been prepared for how hard it would be, seeing her again, talking to her again. He'd foolishly thought it would be easy.

Well...easier.

He gave himself a mental shake and rubbed the back of his neck. 'She was first diagnosed five years ago. She's been living with Trish for the last two years.'

'Five years?' she gasped. Tess couldn't even begin to comprehend a world where Jean King was anything less than her larger-than-life self. 'Why...why didn't you tell me?'

Fletch raised an eyebrow. 'Seriously, Tess? I rang you practically every day for a year after you went to England.... You made it pretty clear that no correspondence would be entered into. Anyway, what were you going to do?' he asked, surprised at the bitterness in his tone. 'Come home?'

Tess bit her lip. He was right. She had been ruthless with her no-contact request. 'I'm sorry...'

She searched his silvery-green gaze and saw apprehension and worry and for one crazy moment almost took another step forward to embrace him. But a decade of denial slammed the door shut and she dropped her hand from his arm, shocked at the strength of the impulse.

She shook her head. 'It's just so wrong. Your mum has always been as fit as a fiddle…'

Fletch felt her withdrawal from their intimacy as keenly as if it had been ten years ago.

Damn it.

Did she really think because she hadn't moved on that things weren't going to change around her? 'She's seventy-four, Tess. She's getting old. Did you think she was just always going to be here, frozen in time, waiting for you to come around?'

Tess recoiled as if he had slapped her, colour draining from her face. 'I doubt your mother has been sitting around waiting on me,' she retaliated.

'You're like a second daughter to her, Tess,' he dismissed impatiently. 'She's missed you every day.'

I've missed you every day.

Fletch blinked at the thought. *He had.* Standing here in front of her, talking to her for the first time in nine years, he realised just how deeply he had missed her.

Tess felt the truth of his starkly delivered words wrap around her heart and squeeze. She wanted to deny them but she couldn't. He was right. They had been close. And Jean *was* getting older.

Fletch sighed as Tess gnawed on her bottom lip, looking utterly wretched. He raised his hands in a half-surrender.

'I'm sorry, I didn't mean to…' To what? Get angry

with her? Make her feel guilty? 'Will you, please, just come and see her? She gets anxious easily these days and you're the one she wants to see the most.'

Tess was torn. She'd love to see Jean again. Had missed her wise counsel and warm hugs over the years. And if it helped ease some of her mother-in-law's anxiety to see her then that was the least Tess could do. But would it be Jean? And would it build an expectation, make it harder to walk away?

Because she was getting on that plane tomorrow. Just like she did every year.

And most importantly, what if Jean wanted to talk about Ryan? What if she didn't remember he was dead? Talked about him as if he was alive and just down for a nap?

Tess looked at Fletcher. 'What about…?' She cleared her throat as a lump formed there. Even just saying it was beyond difficult. 'What does she remember from…?'

Fletcher watched the shimmer of emotion in Tess's amber gaze as she struggled with her words. He shook his head. 'She doesn't remember him at all, Tess.'

It had been a particularly difficult thing for Fletch to cope with. After Tess had refused to hear his name, his mother had been the only person he'd been able to talk openly with about Ryan.

Now it was as if his son had never existed.

'Her memory seems to stretch to about a year after we were married. As far as she's concerned, we've just got back from Bora Bora.'

Fletch had taken Tess to the tropical paradise for

a surprise first wedding anniversary present. They'd lazed in their over-water bungalow all day. Making love, drinking cocktails and watching the multitude of colourful fish swim by their glass floor.

He shrugged. 'There's an occasional recall of an event beyond that but it's rare.'

For a brief moment Tess envied Jean. The thought of forgetting how Ryan had felt in her arms or at her breast, forgetting the way his hair had stuck up in the middle from his double cowlick and how his giggle had filled the whole room. Forgetting that gut-wrenching day and all the empty days that had followed since.

It sounded like bliss.

The fantasy was shocking, wrong on so many levels, and she quickly moved to erase it from her mind. Jean was suffering from a debilitating disease that was ravaging her brain and would rob her of her most basic functions.

There was no upside to that.

And no justice in this world.

Although she already knew that more intimately than most.

Tess nodded. 'Okay.'

Fletch blinked at her easy capitulation. 'Really?'

'Sure.' She frowned, his disbelief irksome. 'For Jean.' He should know she'd do anything for his mother. 'Did you think I wouldn't?'

He shrugged. 'Yes.'

His bluntness hurt but she pushed it aside—it was, after all, a fair statement. She *had* been sneaking into the country once a year for the last nine years with only two paltry visits to Jean to defend herself against his conviction.

But they'd agreed on a clean break.

And she'd stuck to it.

Eventually, so had he.

She gave him a measured look. 'It's Jean.'

Fletch nodded as the husky note in her voice didn't mask her meaning. She wasn't doing it for him.

And that was certainly what he was counting on now.

'Thank you.' He gestured to his car. 'Do you want to follow me?'

Tess shook her head. 'She's at Trish's, right? They still live in Indooroopilly?'

Fletch shook his head. 'No, she's at my place for the moment.'

Tess blinked. 'You have a place in Brisbane?'

Since their separation Fletch had moved to Canada, where he'd been heavily involved in research and travelling the world lecturing. Or at least the last time she'd heard, that had been where he'd been. It was suddenly weird having absolutely no idea where he lived—or any of the details of his life for the last nine years.

She honestly hadn't cared until today but it somehow seemed wrong now to know so little about someone whose life had been so closely entwined with hers for so long they may as well have been conjoined.

When she thought about him, which she still did with uncomfortable regularity, it was always against the backdrop of their marital home. The ninety-year-old worker's cottage they'd renovated together.

Polished the floorboards, painted the walls, built the pergola.

The house they'd brought Ryan home to as a newborn.

'I'm renting an apartment on the river.'

'Oh. Okay.'

Tess tamped down on her surprise. Fletch had always despised apartment living. Had loved the freedom of large living spaces and a back yard.

But, then, a lot of things had changed over the last ten years.

'Right,' she said. 'I'll follow you.'

Fletch nodded. 'It's only about a ten-minute drive. See you soon.'

'Sure,' Tess murmured, then walked on shaky legs to her car.

Nine minutes later they drove into the underground car park of a swanky apartment block. She pulled her cheap hire car in beside his Jag in his guest car space. They didn't talk as he ushered her to the lifts or while they waited for one to arrive.

Tess stared at the floor, the doors, the ugly concrete walls of the chilly underground car park—what did one say, how did one act around one's ex? An ex she'd deliberately put at a fifteen-thousand-kilometre distance?

A lift arrived, promptly derailing her line of thought. He indicated for her to precede him, which she did, and then stood back as Fletch pushed the button for the nineteenth floor. More silence followed. Surely at least they could indulge in inane conversation for the duration of their time together?

A sudden thought occurred to her and she looked at him leaning against the opposite wall. 'How did you know I was going to be there today?'

Fletch returned her look. 'Because you're there every year on the anniversary.'

Tess blinked at his calm steady gaze. 'How do you know that?'

'Because I watch you.'

Another silence descended between them as her brain tried to compute what he'd just said. 'You *watch* me?'

He nodded. 'Nine years ago you were leaving as I was arriving.' He remembered how close he'd come to calling her name. 'I thought you might come back the next year. You did. And the year after that. So now I… wait for you.'

The lift dinged. The doors opened. Neither of them moved. The doors started to close and Fletch shot an arm out to push them open again. 'After you,' he murmured.

Tess couldn't move for a moment. She stared at him. 'Why?'

'I know you think that your grief is deeper than mine but he was my son too, Tess. I also like to visit on the anniversary.'

Tessa flinched at the bitterness in his voice. And then again when the lift doors started beeping, protesting their prolonged open state. She walked out, dazed, conscious of Fletch slipping past her, leading the way down a long plush hallway with trendy inkspot carpeting. She followed slowly, still trying to get her head around Fletch's revelation.

She drew level with him, glancing up from the floor. 'I meant why wait for me? Why not just visit for a while and leave?'

Like she did.

Fletch wished he knew the answer to that question. It was the same thing he told himself every year as he set out for the cemetery. Go, talk with Ryan for a bit, then leave.

But he didn't. He'd sit in his car and wait for her. Watch her kneel beside Ryan's grave.

Torture himself just a little bit more.

He shrugged. 'To see you.'

CHAPTER TWO

'Mum, we're home,' Fletch called as he opened the door, checking behind him to see if Tess was following or still standing in the hallway like a stunned mullet.

He wasn't sure why he'd said what he'd said. Except it was the truth. He just hadn't realised it until right that moment. He'd kidded himself that it was to check up on her but now he knew it was more.

That there was part of him, no matter how hard he'd tried to move on, that just hadn't.

He walked into the apartment, throwing his keys on the hallstand. 'Mother?'

A voice came from the direction of the bathroom. 'I'm in here, darling, there's no need to shout.' Jean appeared a moment later with a spray pack in one hand and a mop in the other.

'Mum, you don't have to clean the apartment,' Fletch said, trying to keep the exasperation and relief out of his voice as he unburdened her of her load.

He didn't like to leave his mother alone for too long these days. She seemed so frail and unsteady on her feet and he worried she might fall and injure herself while he was out.

Especially if she was mopping floors.

'I have a cleaning lady for that.'

'Nonsense, darling, I have to make myself useful somehow. Now, is Tess working late or shall I put something on for tea for her tonight?'

Tess stepped out of the shadow of the entranceway where she'd been frozen since Jean had entered the room. Jean, who had once been a towering Amazon of a woman and was now white-haired and stooped and looked like a puff of wind would blow her over.

She sucked in a breath at the absurd urge to cry. 'No, Jean, I'm here.'

Jean looked over her son's shoulder and smiled. 'Oh, Tess! There you are!' She hurried forward and pulled Tess into an effusive hug. 'Goodness, you're getting so skinny,' Jean tutted, pulling back to look at her daughter-in-law. 'And your hair! Did you have that done today? I love it!'

Tess swallowed hard at the shimmer of moisture in Jean's eyes as her mother-in-law wrapped her in another hug. She shut her eyes as she was sucked into a bizarre time warp where the last decade and all its horrible events just didn't exist. She held tight to Jean's bony shoulders.

Her mother-in-law had become an old woman while she'd been away. Guilt clawed at her.

'How about a cuppa?' Jean said, finally letting Tess go.

'Great idea, Mum,' Fletch agreed. 'Why don't you take Tess through and I'll get the tea?'

Jean smiled and nodded. She turned to go then

stopped, her smile dying as a look of confusion clouded her gaze. She looked at her son blankly.

'Over there,' Fletch murmured gently as he pointed to the corner of the open-plan living space where a leather three-piece suite, a coffee table and a large-screen television formed a lounge area.

Jean's gaze followed the direction of Fletch's finger. It took a moment or two for the set-up to register. 'Of course.' She shook her head. 'Come on, Tess. Tell me all about work today.'

Tess moved off with Jean but not before her gaze locked with Fletch's. She saw his despair and felt an answering flicker. No wonder Fletch had looked tired earlier—this had to be killing him.

Jean patted the cushion beside her and asked, 'How was the unit today, dear? Busy as usual?'

Tess sat beside Jean, bringing her thoughts back to order. 'I…' She glanced at Fletch for direction.

Since moving to England Tess had changed her speciality to geriatrics so nursing Alzheimer's patients was part and parcel of what she did every day. But each patient was individual and responded differently to having their misstatements corrected.

He nodded his head encouragingly, which didn't really tell her very much. 'I didn't go to work today,' she sidestepped. 'It was my day off and I had…some business to attend to.'

'Ah, well, no doubt Fletch will know. Fletch?'

'It wasn't too bad, Mum,' Fletch said as he placed a tray with three steaming mugs on the coffee table and apportioned them. He sat on the nearby single-seater.

'Still a lot of kids with the last of the winter bugs getting themselves into a pickle.'

Tess picked up her mug and absently blew on it. So they were validating Jean's false sense of reality? At this stage of her disease it was probably all that was left to do. Too many dementia patients became confused and distressed when confronted with their memory loss, and to what end? They were too far gone to realise what was happening to them.

Jean sighed and looked from one to the other. 'I'm so proud of both of you. It can't be easy going to work each day looking after such sick little kiddies.'

Tess squeezed Jean's hand in response. What else could she do? She and Fletch hadn't worked at St Rita's Paediatric Intensive Care Unit together for ten years. Not since Ryan had died there. In fact, she hadn't been able to return to that field of practice at all, hence her move to the other end of the spectrum altogether.

Fletch changed the subject to the weather and they let Jean lead from there, navigating a maze of patchwork conversation—some lucid, some not so lucid. They got on to the spectacular view from the floor-to-ceiling glass doors, with Jean teasing Fletch about his fancy apartment. 'I can't believe you two got this thing. What happened to that gorgeous little cottage you were renovating?'

Fletch smiled at his mother. 'We sold it. Too much hard work.'

'Oh, pish,' Jean said, swatting her hand through the air. 'As if you're afraid of hard work.'

Tess swallowed a lump as Jean, despite the dementia, looked at her son the way she always had, like he could hang the moon. Fletch's father had died when he and his sister, Trish, had both been very young and Fletch had been the man of the house for a long time.

'Gosh, Tess,' Jean remarked, shaking her head. 'Look how skinny you are! And where did that lovely tan go? I can't believe how quickly that gorgeous tan of yours has faded. It hasn't been that long since you've been back from Bora Bora.'

Fletch felt the bleakness inside ratchet up another notch. *The tan had gone to England and never come back!*

Jean held up an imperious finger. 'Hold on a moment.' And she scurried off towards the direction she'd originally come from.

Tess felt exhausted with jet-lag and trying to keep up with Jean's meandering conversation and rapid-fire subject changes. But not as exhausted as Fletch looked. 'What medication is she on?' she asked.

Fletch rattled off a series of the most up-to-date dementia pills on the market. He shrugged. 'They've held it at bay for many years but—'

Jean bustled back in, interrupting them. 'Here it is,' she said, brandishing a book of some description. When she sat down and opened it Tess realised it was a photo album. The one she'd put together all those years ago after their return from Bora Bora.

Fletch frowned as a hundred memories flooded his mind. He shook his head slightly at Tess's questioning look. He'd had no idea his mother had this album. It, along with all the others, had been stored in one of the many boxes that he'd packed their marriage into after he and Tess had separated and she'd run away to the other side of the world.

Maybe when he'd asked his mother to get rid of it all just prior to his move to Canada, she'd decided to keep a few souvenirs? He hadn't really cared at the time how she'd made it disappear, just that it had. God knew, he hadn't been able to bear the thought of going through it all himself, deciding what to keep and what to discard.

Getting rid of it all, holus bolus, had been a much easier option.

And yet here was a part of it, turning up like the proverbial bad penny. A full Technicolor reminder of how happy they'd been.

'See, now look at you here,' Jean said, pointing to Tess in a bikini on the beach. 'Brown as a berry!'

Tessa stared at the photograph, shocked by the sudden yank back into the past. She'd taken three photos from the ruins of their marriage—all of Ryan. Not that she'd been able to bear to look at them. They lived at the back of a cupboard she never opened.

But it had been a long time since she'd seen ones of Fletch and herself.

A stranger stared back at her. Yes, she *was* very tanned. She was also deliriously happy, obviously in love and blissfully unaware of the giant black hole hovering in her future. In fact, the woman in the photograph looked nothing like the woman she was today.

And it had nothing to do with the tan.

For a fleeting second, Tess wished she could jump

into the photo, like Mary Poppins had jumped into that pavement painting, and give herself a good shake.

If only she'd known then what she knew now.

If only…

'I think this is my favourite one,' Jean said, flipping to one of Fletch, towel wrapped around his waist, elbows on the balcony railing, looking back over his shoulder and laughing into the camera, crystal waters behind him.

Tessa stilled as she remembered she'd been fresh from the shower and naked when she'd taken that picture and the series of intimate photos that had followed—ones that had not made it into this album! She remembered making him lie on the bed and loosen his towel, snapping shots of every glorious inch of his body.

Then he'd grappled the camera from her and returned the favour, asking her to pose for him and taking a set of photos a professional photographer would have been proud of. To this day the one on her stomach, looking over her shoulder with her hair flowing down her back, the sheet ruched around her bottom revealing only the slight rise of one cheek, was the best picture ever taken of her.

She remembered being so turned on by their nude photo session they'd made love for hours afterwards, rolling and sighing and moaning to the gentle swish of the waves.

She glanced at Fletch—did he remember?

His gaze locked with hers, turning almost silver as heat flashed like a solar flare. It dropped to her mouth and she watched as his throat bobbed.

'It's my favourite too,' Fletch murmured.

Oh, yeah, he remembered.

Tess sat through the rest of the album, desperately trying to claw back some control of her brain. Bora Bora was in the past—a long time in the past. She hadn't come here to take a walk down memory lane, although she guessed to a degree that had been inevitable. Neither had she come to rekindle the sexual attraction that, prior to Ryan's death, had always raged like an inferno between them.

She'd come for Jean. To alleviate some anxiety and then turn around and go back to her perfectly fulfilling, asexual, far-away existence.

Jean closed the album. 'I think you two need to go back to Bora Bora. You're both too tense.' She patted Tess's hand. 'And pale.'

Before Tess could answer, an alarm blared out and she jumped slightly at the same time Jean clutched at her chest and looked at Fletch anxiously.

'It's okay, Mum,' Fletch reassured her as he reached over and turned off the alarm on the clock that was sitting on the coffee table. 'Remember, that just means your show's about to start.' His mother continued to look at him blankly. 'Wheel of Fortune,' he prompted.

'Oh.' Jean sagged a little and dropped her hand to her lap. 'Oh, yes, oh, I love that show!'

Fletch nodded as he picked up the remote and flicked on the big sleek screen to the channel that played non-stop 1980s television shows. 'There you go, just starting,' he said as the game-show music rang out.

'Tess.' Jean bounced like a little girl on Christmas morning. 'Do you want to watch it with me?'

Fletch watched the play of emotions mirrored in Tess's eyes. She was obviously shocked by the many faces of Jean. 'Actually, we're going to go out on to the deck and have a chat,' he said.

But his mother wasn't listening, engrossed in the show, her invitation to Tess already forgotten. He inclined his head at Tess, indicating they move away, and she eagerly complied, following him to the kitchen.

'Would you like something a little stronger?' he asked as he removed the mug she'd brought with her and placed it in the sink.

Following a period after she'd moved to the UK when she'd drunk a little too often, Tessa didn't drink much these days. But if ever she needed alcohol, it was now. Being with Jean was heartbreaking. And being with Fletch, seeing those pictures, was…disturbing.

'Yes, please.'

Fletch pulled a bottle of chilled white wine out of the fridge and held it up. 'All right?'

Tessa nodded. 'Sure. Thanks.'

He poured them both a glass and handed her hers. Normally he'd clink glasses with someone in this situation but nothing was normal about right now so he took a mouthful then led the way to the deck.

Fletch, conscious of her behind him, put his arms on the railing and inhaled the late-afternoon river breeze. He took another sip of his wine then turned to face her.

'Thank you,' he said.

'I'm so sorry, Fletch,' she murmured. 'It's…it's so unfair.'

Fletch's lips twisted into a bitter smile as his mobile phone rang. 'Since when has life ever been fair?' he asked as he located his phone and answered it.

Tess nodded. *Truer words had never been spoken.*

She moved to the far side of the railing to give Fletch some privacy. She had absolutely no desire to eavesdrop on the conversation but it was hard not to when he was standing two metres from her.

It was Trish and Tess gathered Fletch's little sister was asking after Jean. Then she heard Fletch tell her that he'd been to the cemetery and reassured her three times that he was fine. Like Jean, Trish had been a tremendous support for them after losing Ryan. She'd worried about them, about her brother particularly, like a little mother hen. Tess knew that if Trish had been able to turn back time for them, she would have.

Her name was mentioned and Tess wondered how Trish was taking the news that she was here. They'd been close once, like real sisters, but Trish was loyal to a fault and while she'd been supportive for that horrible year, she'd been angry with Tess over her desertion of Fletch.

It had hurt at the time but blood was thicker than water and it was only right that she should stand by her brother.

Fletch hung up. 'Sorry, that was Trish.'

'So I gathered,' she murmured, swishing the wine in her glass absently. 'How's she and Doug doing these days?'

'Great. Doug started his own computer repair business five years ago. It's thriving. Trish gave up the child-care centre a few years ago to work full time taking care of the books side of things and managing the job schedule. They have Christopher, he's almost two. And she's seven months pregnant with number two.'

Tess stilled, the swirl of the wine coming to a halt. She glanced at Fletch. Trish had a child? A little boy. A little boy only a few months older than Ryan had been when he'd died?

And another on the way?

She and Fletch had been trying for another baby just prior to Ryan's accident.

The ache that was never far from her heart intensified. In a split second she both envied and despised her ex-sister-in-law with shocking intensity.

Fletch watched Tess's face as a string of emotions chased across the taut face, which seemed suddenly paler. 'She always wanted babies, Tess,' he said gently.

Tess breathed in raggedly. She nodded her head vigorously. 'Of course.' Trish had absolutely doted on Ryan. 'That's great,' she said, forcing words past the husky lump lodged in her larynx. 'So, you're an uncle, huh?'

Fletch nodded. 'Yes.'

Of sorts. He hadn't had a lot to do with his nephew given how often he was out of the country. But he was a dear little boy who adored him. And if it was hard at times to hold his wriggly little body and not think of Ryan, not see the similarities between the two cousins, then he erected another layer around his heart and sucked it up.

Tess heard the grimness in his response and knew that it couldn't have been easy for him. She hesitated for a moment, went to take a step towards him until a shout of 'Buy a vowel!' coming from the lounge area halted the reflex before her foot had even moved.

She smiled at him as the sound of Jean's excited clapping drifted out. 'How's Jean with him?'

Fletch felt his answering smile die. 'She doesn't remember him most days. It's hard for Trish. Especially as Mum's been living with them since just before Christopher was born.'

Tess frowned. 'How come she's living with you now? I don't mean to tell you how to manage Jean's condition but I don't think changing her living arrangements at this stage in her disease is such a good thing, Fletch.'

'Trish had problems with her first pregnancy. She went into early labour at twenty-four weeks. They managed to stop it and get the pregnancy through to thirty-four weeks. A month ago she went into early labour again with this one. Which they also managed to stop. But given her history and her age, her obstetrician ordered bed rest and no stress for the remainder of the pregnancy.'

'Ah,' Tess murmured. 'Not very easy when you're looking after a toddler and your high-needs mother.'

Fletch grimaced. 'No.' He rubbed the back of his neck. 'Trish tried day respite but the unfamiliar setting distressed Mum, made her anxious, which flowed on into the nights. Mum stopped sleeping and she started to wander. She had a couple of falls.'

'Oh, no,' Tess gasped.

Fletch shrugged. 'Lucky she has bones made of concrete.'

Tess laughed, remembering the time that Jean had slipped and fallen down a flight of stairs with not even a bruise to show for it. Fletch smiled at her laugh. It was as familiar to him as his own and yet not something he'd heard for a very long time.

Another thing he'd missed with surprising ferocity.

'We got a day nurse in but the same thing happened. An unfamiliar face just aggravated the situation. So...I took a leave of absence from Calgary and came home to step in and do my bit. Look after Mum until after the baby's born.'

Tess understood the conundrum he and Trish faced. The familiar was important to dementia patients, who clung to their repertoire of the familiar even as it shrank at an alarming rate around them. But, still, uprooting yourself from the other side of the world was a big ask.

Although she guessed not for Fletch. He'd always been very family orientated, always taken care of his responsibilities.

'It's a good thing you're doing,' she said softly.

He looked at her. 'It's family, Tess. Family sticks together.'

Tess shied from the intensity of his silver-green eyes. Was there an accusation there? Sure, she'd asked for the divorce but he hadn't exactly put up a fight. In fact, he'd been pretty relieved as far as she could recall. Did he really blame her for wanting to get as far away from it all as possible?

She took a deep breath. She wasn't going to go there. She was finishing her drink. She was going back to her hotel room.

Tomorrow she was getting on a plane.

'So you're not working, then?'

Fletch shook his head. He looked into his drink. 'That was the plan but St Rita's approached me with an interesting proposition and I've accepted a temporary contract…'

Tess blinked as the information sat like a lead sinker in her brain. 'St Rita's? In the…PICU?'

Fletch glanced up into her huge amber eyes, flashing their incredulity like a lighthouse beacon. 'In both the adult and kids' ICUs. They want someone to head up a study on the application of hypothermia in acute brain injury. They've asked me. I didn't come here to work but…how could I refuse? It's a marvellous opportunity.'

Tess was quiet for a moment while she processed the startling information. 'Oh.'

She knew that since their separation and his move to Canada, Fletch had become an authority—*some might call it an obsession*—on cold-water drowning, undertaking several world-renowned studies. In fact, he was probably one of the world's foremost experts on the subject. She'd read everything he'd ever published from the impressive studies to journal articles and every paper he'd ever given at a conference or a symposium.

None of them had brought Ryan back.

'It's part time, only a few hours a day with no real

clinical role. I can do a lot of the work from home, which is perfect, leaves me a lot of time for Mum.'

Tess nodded. It sounded ideal. She just wished she could understand how he could go back there. She knew, although she didn't pretend to comprehend, why he'd chosen that particular field of research but how he could handle the subject matter was beyond her. And how he could enter St Rita's without breaking down she'd never know.

Her eyes sought his. She remembered how he'd told his mother earlier about the kids with the last of the winter bugs. She'd thought he'd been fobbing Jean off but obviously not. 'You've...you've been into the PICU?'

Their gazes locked. 'Yes. Several times. In fact, I called in there on my way to the cemetery.'

Tess let out a shaky breath. 'Right...'

What did she say now? How was it? Have you been into room two? Did it bring back memories? Was Ryan's presence still there or had it been erased by years of other children and hospital antiseptic?

Instead, she said nothing because she really didn't want to know.

Fletch's stare didn't waver. 'It wasn't easy, Tess.'

She looked away. *Had he thought it would be?* Did he expect her sympathy? An embrace? Applause? Some kind of a shared moment where everything was suddenly all right because he'd confronted some ghosts?

A surge of emotions knotted in her belly and she knew she had to leave. Get out. Far away from Fletch and all that reminded her of that dark, dark time.

Denial had been working for her just fine.

She just wanted to go to bed and sleep off the jet-lag and not have to think about any of it.

'Well,' she said, downing the contents of her glass in one long swallow. 'It looks like you have everything worked out.'

'Tess.'

She ignored the reproach in his voice. 'I've gotta go.' She placed the wine glass on the table and headed for the door.

'Tess,' he said, catching her arm lightly as she brushed past him.

Tess stopped. 'Let me go,' she said, staring straight ahead.

'Tess, please, stay for a while.'

She squeezed her eyes shut. 'Fletch.'

'I want to talk to you, Tess.'

'I think we're all talked out.'

'It's about Mum.' He felt her arm strain against his hand. 'Please, Tess, just hear me out. For Jean.'

Tess sighed, and her muscles relaxed, knowing she was defeated.

Damn it.

And damn him.

CHAPTER THREE

Tess sat at the table, staring out over the Brisbane River, while Fletch was in the kitchen fixing them both a top-up of their glasses. A light breeze ruffled her utilitarian locks and she had to shake herself to believe she was actually sitting on her ex-husband's deck, drinking wine.

The whole scene felt surreal. Jean's dementia had dragged her reluctantly into her past. A time when things had been simple and she'd truly believed that love could get a person through everything. It was a strange reality that warred with her present-day situation.

What did he want to talk to her about regarding Jean? Surely he had better access to the medical side of Jean's condition than she did? He probably had half a dozen gerontologists up his sleeve he could talk to. Or maybe he was after practical advice? How to care for his mother on a day-to-day basis? Or a recommendation for a good home-care agency, maybe?

Whatever it was, she hoped he made it snappy because when she got to the bottom of her second glass she was walking away.

Fletch paused by the sliding door, watching Tess's

profile for a moment, and wished he was sure of her. He needed her help. Once upon a time he could have counted on it. But a lot of water had flowed under the bridge since then and she was so very, very skittish.

Plus he wasn't so sure of himself now. His plan had sounded fine in theory but being with her again was confrontational on many levels. He'd thought he could handle it but standing two metres from her he realised it would be physically and emotionally harder than he'd ever imagined.

Still…he was desperate and Tess was perfect.

He took a deep breath and stepped out onto the deck. 'Here you go,' he said, placing her refilled wine glass in front of her.

Tess glanced down at the offering and murmured, 'Thanks.'

She picked it up and took a decent mouthful, the smooth, fruity crispness against her palate not really registering. She placed the wine back down as Fletch sat opposite her, hearing the clink as it met the smoky glass of the tabletop. 'You wanted to talk about Jean?' she prompted.

Fletch sighed. Obviously there wasn't going to be any small talk. Which he'd have preferred. He had no idea how she was going to react to his proposition, although instinct told him it wouldn't be very well…

'I need to get someone in for Mum. Someone who can be here while I'm out. When I accepted the contract I thought I'd be able to juggle it and her. It's only part time and Mum doesn't need constant care and attention. But the truth is I don't feel comfortable leaving her at all. I just don't think she's safe enough and I'd feel a hell of a lot better if she wasn't here by herself.'

'Like a home-care nurse?'

Fletch shook his head. 'No. I'm not after someone to help with her physical needs because she's still capable, so far, of taking care of that. Although having someone who understands Alzheimer's is a definite plus... I'm thinking more like a companion.'

'You mean someone closer to her own age?'

'I mean someone who knows her. She's not great with strangers—they distress her.'

Tess's brow wrinkled. 'That would be ideal, of course. Are you thinking of one of her old friends?'

Fletch didn't take his eyes off her. 'I'm thinking of someone closer than that. Someone she knows really well who has experience with the elderly and with dementia sufferers. The best of both worlds.'

Fletch watched and waited—waited for his meaning to sink in. It didn't take long.

Tess narrowed her eyes. Was Fletch thinking what she thought he was thinking? She shook her head at him. 'No. No way.'

'You're perfect, Tess.'

She shook her head again, mentally recoiling from the plea in his wattle-leaf gaze. 'No.'

'I know this is kind of out of the blue—'

'Kind of?' Tess spluttered.

'I wouldn't ask if I wasn't stuck.'

Tess stared at him, wondering when he was going to grow a second head. 'Putting *everything* else aside, I'm leaving for the UK tomorrow.'

'It's just until after Trish is back on her feet. A couple of months.'

Tess blinked. 'I have a *job,* Fletch.'

Fletch snorted. He'd always thought Tess squandering her critical care skills in a geriatric facility was such a monumental waste of a highly skilled nurse, even if it was to his advantage now.

She glared at him. 'That I love. Where I get an enormous amount of respect and job satisfaction.'

It might just be a little nursing-home in the middle of the Devonshire countryside but people depended on her. The staff and the residents. When she'd needed a place to hide and lick her wounds they'd taken her in and given her a direction for her life. They'd helped her function again.

'I'm sure they'd understand if you explained the circumstances. I can recompense you if it's money you're worried about.'

Tess shook her head at his utter gall. Had he thought she'd just agree? They'd been virtual strangers for the past nine years and he expected her to just…comply? And that splashing some money around would sweeten the pot? Sure, she loved Jean, he knew that. He knew how close they'd been. But it was still a big gamble for him to take—betting the bank on her.

The woman who had already turned her back on his family.

'So this is it?' she demanded. 'This is your brilliant plan? Ask your ex-wife? Who just happens to be here at the same time you need someone to look after your mother? That's crazy! What would you have done if I hadn't been in town?'

'It's not crazy. It makes absolute sense. You're the perfect person to ask. And, yes, the timing has been perfect too but, frankly, Tess, I would have gone to England to get you.'

'To *get* me?' Fletch held up his hands in a placatory manner.

'To ask you,' he amended.

Tess wasn't placated. 'How about this, Fletch? How about you give up *your* job and look after *your* mum instead? Trish's been doing it for two years. Surely you can take a lousy couple of months off to do your bit.'

Fletch nodded. 'And I will. If you won't…I will. But studies like this are so important, Tess. The results can help the way we treat acute head injury. What we learn from them can make a real difference to neurological outcomes. This is critical stuff, Tess.'

'Someone else can do it,' she snapped.

'Yes.' He nodded. 'Someone else could…but this is what I do.' He placed his hand on his chest. 'This is my field of expertise.' And his passion—Tess could hear it lacing every syllable. *But chasing after medical rainbows wasn't going to bring Ryan back.* She stood up, the metal chair legs scraping against the terracotta tiles.

'No, Fletcher. I'm sorry about your study, I really am, but I do not want to do this.'

He rose too and opened his mouth to interject and she held up a finger, silencing him. She looked into his determined face, his jaw set, his hand thrust on a hip, and she knew he didn't get it. Didn't understand why she'd be rejecting his perfectly rational plan.

He didn't understand how just being around them—him and Jean—would be like a hot knife to her chest every day. How the reminders of Ryan that she was able to keep rigorously at bay on the other side of the world would be torturous.

It was suddenly vitally important that he understand. Vitally.

'I get by, okay? I make it through each day and I sleep at night and my life is on an even keel. It may not seem very exciting to you—I'm not setting the world on fire with my cutting-edge research, but it took a while to reach this place and it works for me, Fletch. I don't want to undo it.'

Fletch felt his breath catch as the fierce glow of her amber eyes beseeched him. He held her gaze, ignoring the anguish he saw there. 'I came home the other day to a blaring alarm and smoke pouring out of the oven. She'd baked some biscuits and forgotten about them.'

He refused to look away, refused to back down. His mother was his priority and Tess was the answer. He needed her.

Whatever the emotional impact.

He was pushing her, he knew that, but listening to her talk had him thinking that maybe this was exactly what Tess needed also. Maybe she needed to start living a life where she more than just *got by*.

It was criminal that she was living this half-life stashed away in the English countryside where no-body knew her past and she could eke out an existence by pretending nothing had happened. That her whole world hadn't come crashing down and sucked her into the deepest, darkest despair.

Maybe it was time for both of them to confront the past and deal with it. To talk and grieve together instead of separately. He'd let her deny and avoid all those years ago because her sorrow had been all-consuming and he'd been walking through a minefield he'd had no idea how to navigate whilst suffering his own debilitating grief.

He hadn't pushed her back then.

But maybe it was finally time to push.

Tess swallowed as his intense look seemed to bore a hole right through her middle. It made her feel ill thinking about Jean almost burning the place down but her ex-mother-in-law wasn't her responsibility.

She was ex for a reason.

And she didn't want to get sucked back into lives that were too closely entwined with the tragic events that had defined all their lives since.

It just would be too hard.

She shook her head and turned away. 'Goodbye, Fletcher.'

Fletch shut his eyes as she whirled away, heading for the door. *Damn it!* He'd felt sure he'd be able to convince her. He opened his eyes, resigned to letting it go. He'd tried. But he had to respect her decision.

Tess stalked into the apartment. *Wheel of Fortune* had finished, the show's theme song blaring out. Jean was nowhere to be seen.

'Jean?' Tess called, reaching for the remote. Nothing.

Not that anything could be heard over the roar of the television. 'Jean?' she called again, hitting the mute button.

'Tess?'

Tess walked quickly towards the feeble, panicked voice she could hear coming from the kitchen area. 'Jean?'

'Here…I'm here.'

Tess rounded the bench to find Jean sitting on the floor, her back propped against the fridge, staring down at two raw eggs, one in each hand, the shells crushed, yolk oozing between her fingers. She looked at Tess with red-rimmed, frightened eyes, the papery skin on her cheeks damp.

'I don't know what these are,' she said to Tess, holding them up.

'Oh, Jean…' Tess sank to the floor beside her and put her arm around skinny shoulders. 'It's okay,' she murmured. 'It's going to be okay.'

Jean shook her head, pulled away to look at her daughter-in-law. 'I'm frightened, Tess,' she whispered, and started to tear up again. 'Something's wrong. H-help me, please.' Her voice cracked. 'Please…h-help me.'

Jean dissolved into soft tears and Tess felt her heart swell up with love for this woman who had been like a mother to her as she snuggled her into the crook of her shoulder.

'Shh,' Tess crooned, rocking slightly. 'Shh, now.'

Tess heard footsteps and looked up to find Fletch staring down at her with solemn eyes. He crouched beside them and Tess saw that all-too-familiar look of sadness sheen his eyes to silver. She watched as he reached for his mother's shoulder, placed his long brown fingers over her pale, waxy skin and gently rubbed.

'It's okay, Tess,' he whispered over his mother's bent head. 'I'll fix it.'

Tess shut her eyes as Jean's plea tugged at her. *She was almost out the door, damn it.* She didn't want to be needed like this. Not by Jean. And certainly not by him. *Not fair. So not fair.*

But, as Fletch had only just pointed out, when had life ever been fair?

Could she really turn her back on Jean who had never asked her for anything? Fletch maybe, but Jean?

She opened her eyes. 'Let me see if it can be arranged...'

Fletch felt his heart swell with relief and something else far more primal. He sagged slightly as what seemed to be the weight of the entire world lifted from his shoulders. 'Thank you,' he mouthed. 'Thank you.'

Tess pushed the 'end' button on the phone thirty minutes later. Her boss at Estuary View Nursing Home had been very understanding of Tess's predicament and had urged Tess, her best employee who only ever took the same two weeks off every year, to take as much time as she needed.

So, that was that.

She kept her elbows firmly planted on the balcony railing, staring out over the river darkening to liquid mercury. The city's first lights winked on the polished surface and shimmered in the wake of a City Cat as it fractured the surface. She was surprised at the tide of nostalgia that crept over her.

Brisbane was her home town.

And she'd been away for a long time.

In recent years it had been a place to dread, a place of terrible memories, a heinous pilgrimage. But a sudden strange melancholy infused her bones.

Irritated by the path of her thoughts, Tess turned her back on the river. Through the open doorway she could see Jean sitting happily once again in front of the television, sipping a fresh cup of tea, her incident with the eggs forgotten. Fletch sat beside her, holding her hand, his dark wavy hair a stark contrast to the thin, white wisps of his mother's.

He looked up at her at that moment and for a second they just stared at each other. Tess felt the melancholy sink into her marrow. Then Fletch raised an eyebrow and she nodded at him and he once again mouthed, 'Thank you,' before kissing his mother gently on the head and easing away from her.

Tess moved inside, following Fletch into the kitchen. 'All sorted?'

She nodded. 'Yes.'

They were standing a couple of metres apart and Fletch took a step towards her as a well of gratitude rising inside him propelled him forward. In the old days he would have swept her into his arms. 'I know this is a big ask, Tess…'

Tess shook her head. If he truly knew, he wouldn't have asked. 'You have no idea, Fletch.'

Just looking at his face caused her chest to ache. It

took her back to times she'd spent ten years trying to forget. Ryan had looked so like his father it had been ridiculous. He took another step towards her but she held up her hand to ward him off.

Fletch stopped. 'You think this is any easier for me?' he asked.

Tess dropped her gaze at the honesty in his. It was a horrible situation for them both. 'What time do you want me here in the mornings?'

Tess had no idea where she was going to stay for the next couple of months but she'd figure it out. In the interim she could extend her stay at the hotel. But there was no way her budget could stretch to such luxury for more than a week.

Fletch frowned. 'I don't just want you here in the mornings, Tess, I want you here twenty-four seven.'

Tess's gaze flew back to his face. 'What?' Her heartbeat kicked up a notch as his meaning sank in.

'Mum's wandering more during the night and can become quite agitated when you try and get her back to bed. She's particularly disorientated when she wakes up in the morning since moving from Trish's. She sees me and the first person she asks for in the morning or if she wakes at night is you. It'll be good for her to have you right there when she's so distressed.'

Tess held his gaze. 'And when I go?'

Fletch had always believed in not borrowing trouble. He had it covered for the next two months and that was all he was worried about for now. 'We'll cross that bridge when we get to it,' he said, his expression grim.

'Your mother's condition needs a little more forward planning than that,' she said waspishly.

Dealing with families of dementia sufferers, Tess knew that those who had planned for every contingency coped better with the curve balls the condition threw them.

Fletch nodded. He couldn't agree more. 'Another reason why I need you here. Forward planning.' He looked into her shuttered gaze. 'It makes sense for you to stay here, Tess. And where are you going to find short-term accommodation at such late notice?'

Anywhere but here. 'I have friends in Brisbane…'

'Do you? Do you really, Tess? Kept in contact with the old crowd, have you?'

Tess broke eye contact. He knew she'd severed all links when she'd moved overseas. Before that even, when concerned friends had been too much for her to handle. She'd withdrawn from all her support groups, from her life really, as grief had consumed her utterly.

'I can't pretend happy families with you, Fletch,' she said, the marble surface of the kitchen bench cold beneath her hand. 'Too much has happened. Living with you again…it'll bring too much back.'

Fletch nodded. He knew that. And after only a couple of hours in her company he knew it would be harder than he'd originally thought. But sometimes the greatest gain came at the greatest cost. Ten years ago she'd shut down, shut him out—shut the world out—and he'd let her. With her here and committed to the task she wasn't running away any more and maybe, just maybe, they could face head-on what they hadn't been able to a decade ago.

'You think it's going to matter where you lay your hat each night,' he asked her downcast head, 'when we'll be seeing each other day in and day out?'

Tess knew he was right. It was going to be difficult whether she stayed here or not.

Fletch willed her to look at him. 'We have to prepare ourselves for the fact that this isn't going to be easy, Tess. It *will* bring back painful memories. But if we keep our focus on Mum then I'm sure we'll get through it.' He shrugged. 'Who knows, we might even become friends.' He gave a half-smile. 'I hear that's possible.'

Tess speared him with a look. 'We're not an ordinary divorced couple, Fletch.'

He nodded, acknowledging the truth of her words. 'Still…I never wanted it to be like this between us, Tess.'

Fletch tamped down on the guilt that he kept in a box labelled 'Tess', knowing that ultimately it was he who had severed their relationship. He wished he could go back and undo what he'd done that night nine years ago. That his actions hadn't made their already shaky marriage untenable and guilt hadn't driven him to grab hold of the out she'd given him.

Yes, their relationship breakdown had been multi-factorial and, yes, she had been the one to ask for a divorce, but when it had come to the crunch, he hadn't fought for it.

Or her.

He'd run away—just like she had.

Tess still remembered her surprise at his easy capitulation when she'd asked him for a divorce. 'We don't always get what we want,' she said testily.

He held up his hands in surrender. He didn't want to get into this now. He really didn't.

'This apartment is big enough for all of us, Tess. It would really help Mum and me if you stayed here for the duration.'

Tess would have liked nothing more than to walk away and never see Fletch again. But there was no way she could turn her back on Jean now, and Fletch was right—it was easy and convenient for her to stay here.

She hadn't fought with him nine years ago as they'd calmly ended their marriage—why waste her breath doing so now? She'd do what she had to do then leave—just like she'd done before.

'Fine,' she muttered. 'I'll go and get my stuff.'

An hour later Tess was back from checking out of her hotel and following Fletch as he showed her to her room.

Which looked suspiciously like his room.

'This is your room,' she said bluntly, looking at the signs of his habitation strewn everywhere.

His watch and one of those crime novels he loved to read lay on the bedside table. A desk by the large floor-to-ceiling windows housed a sleek laptop and a tottering pile of papers and medical journals. A tie was thrown over the back of the chair. A pair of socks lay discarded on the thick, expensive-looking carpet.

'Yes. It is.'

Tess stared at him incredulously. 'I am *not* sharing a room with you.'

Fletch clutched his heart in mock injury. 'You wound me.'

'Don't you have another room in this luxury riverside apartment?' She ignored him, crossing her arms. 'And don't you dare lecture me about being adult, about me not having anything you haven't seen before or about keeping the pretence going into the bedroom because this is not negotiable!'

Fletch smiled as her eyes hissed fire at him like a lava flow of molasses. She looked so much like the old Tess for a moment that his breath caught.

Even if he hadn't seen any of what she had in a very, very long time.

'The only other bedroom I have, my mother lives in.'

'This is a two-bedroom apartment? Only two bedrooms?'

Tess hoped that the squeak she could hear in her voice was just being distorted through the layers of confusion in her brain.

'It's okay, Tess. I'll sleep on the couch. It's perfectly comfortable. Probably better with Mum tending to wander during the night anyway.'

Tess felt a wave of relief wash over her as she sagged against the doorjamb. In fact, she felt a little silly at her reaction that could be seen as being slightly over the top. But, honestly, sharing the apartment with Fletch was bad enough—she didn't even want to contemplate sharing a bed with him too.

She already knew how good that was.

And guilt had driven all the good out of her a lot of years ago.

'I think you're going to need to get yourself some clothes,' Fletch said as he plucked her overnight bag from her fingers and strode across his room, dumping it on his bed.

She nodded. 'I hadn't exactly planned on staying. I'll slip down to a department store in the next couple of days and pick up a few outfits.'

His eyes met hers as he tried not to think about the time she'd dragged him into the change room at a department store on a slow Sunday morning and had had her way with him in front of three mirrors.

He failed.

And if the sudden smoulder in her eyes was anything to go by, so had she.

'I'll let you get settled in,' he said, withdrawing quickly—because he knew from bitter experience that down that path lay no good.

Tess was in bed by eight-thirty. The jet-lag, the wine and the tumult of emotions from the day had well and truly caught up with her. She'd tried really hard to stay awake with Jean and Fletch but in vain. Fletch had nudged her awake and ordered her to bed. She hadn't even bothered to shower or change—just kicked out of her cargo pants and collapsed onto the bed in her knickers and T-shirt, barely getting the covers over her before she sank into the blissful depths of dreamless slumber.

She wasn't sure how many hours had passed when she first heard the commotion. It took Tess a while to realise Jean's sobbing wasn't coming from inside her head as it usually did but externally, outside the room somewhere.

And it was actually real this time.

She sat bolt upright as the shackles of heavy slumber fell from her eyes. The clock said two a.m. as she kicked the covers aside and stumbled out of the room, her heart pounding like a gong.

'Jean?' she called as she hurried down the hallway to her mother-in-law's room.

Nothing. *The bed was empty.*

'Jean?' she said again, louder this time as she headed towards the source of human anguish getting louder and louder.

'Out here, Tess,' Fletch called.

Tess entered the lounge area. The lamp near the television threw weak light into the room and she headed to the lounge where Fletch sat comforting his weeping mother.

'Everything okay?'

Fletch nodded over his mother's head as Jean sobbed.

'It's no good, Fletcher,' Jean sobbed. 'No good.'

Tess, her lack of clothing eliminated from her subconscious by nagging fatigue and her pounding heart, crouched down in front of them. 'Hey, Jean, don't cry, sweetie. It's okay.' She rubbed her palms against a pair of bony knees. 'What's the matter?'

Jean turned wet cheeks on Tess. 'You should never let the sun go down on an argument. Never spend a night apart. Fletch's dad and I never spent a night apart.' She grabbed Tess's hand. 'You never know how long you have with each other.'

Tess murmured, 'Of course not,' not entirely sure what was going on.

'I was just telling Mum that I got in late from the hospital and didn't want to disturb you so I collapsed on the couch.'

Ah. Now Tess got the reason for Jean's distress. And it was *acute* distress. She was crying, her movements agitated.

'It's still wrong,' Jean sobbed. 'You don't care about being disturbed, do you, Tess, darling?'

Tess looked at Fletch. He was at his disturbing best. Shirtless and trouserless, his big, bare chest and long, bare, dark-haired legs exuding a masculinity that was almost overwhelming in the intimacy of the little circle they'd formed. He rubbed the back of his neck in a helpless gesture and the lines of worry and tiredness around his eyes and mouth seemed to deepen.

She wished like hell they cancelled out the scruffy sexiness of his tousled hair and unshaven jaw.

'This is how people get divorced,' Jean continued, worrying at the fabric of her nightgown, rolling it between her fingers. She suddenly clutched Tess's arm. 'Oh, no…you're not getting divorced, are you?'

Tess felt her heart sink. Jean's level of anxiety was distressing to watch. As fanciful as it might seem to them, she was worrying herself sick.

And for that there was just one thing she could do.

She took a deep breath and slid her hand onto Fletch's knee and then up a little further to his thigh. 'Of course not, Jean,' Tess murmured, not acknowledging either his harshly indrawn breath or the tensing of his firm, bulky quadriceps. 'Fletch and I are fine, aren't we, darling?'

She looked at him then and smiled, sincerely hoping he could act better than she could.

CHAPTER FOUR

FLETCH was too stunned to say anything for a moment. His body, on the other hand, wasn't as reticent. Her hand searing into his flesh took him back to the days when they hadn't been able to stop touching each other and in an instant he was hard.

A decade ago she'd have sensed his arousal in a flash with that weird sexual ESP they'd shared. She would have smiled at him, moved her hand slowly up his leg and kept going until she'd hit pay dirt.

'Fletch?'

He blinked as Tess's voice yanked him back to the here and now. To the startling reality of the present— Tess hadn't wanted him in a very long time and his mother was sitting right beside him.

His very distressed mother.

Grateful he was sitting down, Fletch grappled with what exactly the question had been.

'We're fine, aren't we?' Tess prompted, squeezing the firm, warm muscle beneath her palm.

Fletch saw the *keep up* look in her amber gaze as he fought against the automatic impulse to shut his eyes.

Her little squeeze had shot straight to his groin like a blast from a taser. God, he was too tired for this. He'd tossed and turned on the couch for hours.

'Of course we are,' he agreed heartily as he picked up the thread of the conversation. He covered Tess's hand with his own. 'I really just didn't want to disturb you, that's all.'

Jean's fretting eased as she patted their joined hands. 'You're such a sweet boy, darling, but, trust me, sleeping on the couch can be the beginning of a slippery slope. Look at Aunty Lynne, she and Joe sleep in different bedrooms now because of his snoring and they can barely stand the sight of each other. That all started at the couch, you know.'

Fletch glanced at Tess, his sexual frustration tempered by his feelings of helplessness. Did he tell his mother that both Lynne, his father's sister, and her husband Joe had died in the last few years?

Tess saw the inadequacy in his gaze and squeezed his thigh again. This could not be easy for him. 'Well, Fletch doesn't snore,' she said, diverting the conversation, 'so I think we'll be fine.' She gave Jean a wry smile. 'Now, how about a mug of nice warm milk?'

'Good idea,' Fletch said, leaping at the opportunity to escape the steady torture of her hand.

He reached for his trousers, desperate for some more cover. Tess's foot anchored one leg to the floor and she stood to release it. But then her bare thighs were at eye level. And even though they were thinner than he remembered—ballerina thin—and skinny wasn't something that had ever really appealed to him, his hard-on didn't seem to care, especially given how a quick flick of his eyes upwards also put her knickers squarely in his line of vision.

He looked down and hurriedly stuffed his feet into the legs of his trousers. He rose quickly, not looking at her, dragging them up his legs and over his hips in one fluid moment, zipping the fly as he took his first stride away.

'I'll make them. Sit down,' he threw over his shoulder as he headed towards the kitchen. And sanity.

Tess felt a blush creep up her cheeks and was grateful for the low light as she sank down next to Jean. She wished she hadn't caught his heated gaze on her thighs or that brief glimpse of the bulge being contained by his underwear—but she had.

He was aroused?

Mugs clattered in the background and Jean chatted away beside her, oblivious to Tess's internal conflict as she grappled with the incident. Had her touch, her completely artificial touch, on his leg done that?

It had been too long surely? Too much had happened between them. Too much angst. Too much sorrow.

Yes, Fletch had always been a very virile man and their sex life had always been firmly in the mind-blowing category. Nothing had seemed to dent it. Not shift work, pregnancy or living with a newborn.

Until Ryan's death anyway.

And then it had all changed. She just…couldn't. She'd barely been able to eat or string a sentence together for so long. Anything beyond that, anything requiring any kind of emotional energy or physical effort, had been too much.

And Fletcher had been understanding and patient.

But in the end it had defeated him.

Or at least she'd thought so. Until now. Seeing the evidence of his arousal had been startling. Was that just a normal male reaction to the proximity of a semi-clad woman or could he still really desire her after all these years?

It was a shocking concept.

A dangerous one.

The microwave dinged behind her and Tess dragged her thoughts away from her ex-husband's libido. It certainly wasn't something she was going to analyse. Now or at any other time.

'Okay, three warm milks coming up,' Fletch announced, placing the beverages on the coffee table.

Tess pushed everything aside as she picked up her mug and pulled her recalcitrant thoughts firmly back to Jean.

After leaving his mother with assurances that he would be returning to the marital bed, Fletch did indeed head to his room. Tess had volunteered to settle Jean back to sleep and he needed a shower.

He hadn't had one earlier as he hadn't wanted to disturb her. Sure, he could have had one in the main bathroom but all his stuff, his toiletries and clothes, were in his bedroom so he'd put it off till morning. But after the events of the night, after his involuntary reaction to her, he was prescribing himself a cold shower.

A quick, cold shower.

In and out before Tess even knew he was there. His mother often took quite some time to settle once she'd been wandering—the darkness exacerbating her dementia—so he should be well and truly clear before Tess came back.

Not that he wanted to be thinking about his ex-wife as he shed his clothes and stepped into the shower. Or what had happened at her tentative touch. Things started to stir again and he turned the cold spray on full bore, sucking in a breath as the icy spray pelted his flesh.

He dunked his head beneath the shower head, squeezing his eyes shut. He absolutely didn't need this.

Whatever the hell this was.

Some latent attraction? A vestige of what they'd once shared? Those endless hours in each other's arms, making love like the world was about to end, like their skin was brushed with crack cocaine and they *just couldn't get enough.*

Fletch shook his head against images that usually only visited him in his dreams. It was dangerous ground.

He turned so the spray drummed hard down his back, hoping it would scour the memories from his pores. Praying they'd sluice off his skin and disappear for ever down the drain hole.

But the drumming in his head mocked even louder.

Tess. Tess. Tess.

Tess sat with Jean for a while after she'd fallen asleep, surprised that her ex-mother-in-law had gone down as easily as she had. Surprised but relieved. Many a night she'd spent with an Alzheimer's patient trying to calm them so they'd sleep and it was rarely an easy task.

Tess was so tired when she entered the bedroom she almost missed the sound of the shower. She blinked as she stared at the closed en suite door.

Fletch?

She didn't move for a moment as a sense of déjà vu swept through her. Walking into their bedroom, the shower running.

Of course, once upon a time she'd have pushed open the door—not that Fletch would have bothered with shutting it—stripped off her clothes and joined him.

Which wasn't an option now.

But what the hell was? This *was* his room.

She was the intruder.

She clutched at her abdomen to allay the funny tightness building there. Her fingers hit warm flesh and she looked down absently at her clothes, or lack of them. She remembered how her bare thighs had burned beneath his gaze earlier. How his body had responded…

Her legs sparked into action. She could at least get into her pyjamas. She opened her carry-on case, which was all she'd thought she'd need for her whistle-stop foray back to Australia, and located the over-sized man's T-shirt she wore to bed. She'd got into the habit of wearing Fletch's T-shirts to bed during their marriage and, out of comfort, had continued the practice.

Not that they belonged to him any longer. Or any other man, for that matter. Her men's shirts these days came to her courtesy of the men's department at a store.

With the shower still obviously running, she whisked off the T-shirt she had on and threw the other one over her head. It came to mid-thigh and she felt infinitely more covered even if it was too broad across the chest, causing it to constantly fall off her shoulder and the V-neck to hang too low on her bra-enhanced cleavage.

She scrambled into the bed—Fletcher's bed—getting under the covers this time, and waited for him, her eyes firmly trained on the en suite door. It didn't matter how tired she was, that her eyes felt like they'd been rolled in shell grit, that the room seemed to tilt precariously every now and then.

Or that something had happened before that had the potential to be a real problem between them.

They needed to talk. About Jean.

Sitting with her before, Tess had come to a decision. A crazy one for sure, but the right one nonetheless. She and Fletch needed to have a conversation—no matter how difficult the subject matter. And the sooner they had it, the sooner she could get to sleep.

All providing she actually could sleep if he agreed to what she had to say.

The door opened suddenly and she took a deep, steadying breath.

Fletch's breath hissed out as he spied Tess sitting up in his bed, looking exhausted but grimly determined and somehow sexy as hell with her huge amber eyes and one shoulder bare except for a narrow bra strap.

'Oh, God, sorry, I thought you'd still be in with Mum...'

Tess didn't drop her gaze to take in her fill of his

bare chest or the long length of his legs not covered by the boxer shorts. But she was uncomfortably aware of them in her peripheral vision.

'It's okay,' she said softly. 'Jean went straight off to sleep. She was exhausted.'

The tension coiling the muscles in Fletch's neck as tight as piano wire eased a little. Already the decision to ask Tess to stay seemed to have paid off. 'Thank you. You're great with her.'

His mother had never settled so quickly for him.

Unfortunately it wasn't enough to fully dissipate the tightness in his neck. And after his reaction to her earlier, he doubted it ever would. Not while they were living under the same roof.

Still, keeping focused on the reason why she was there—his mother—and keeping as much distance as was possible inside the confines of his apartment, Fletch figured he could just about survive it.

Tess pulled the shirt sleeve up onto her shoulder. *That helped.*

It promptly slid off again. *Oh, boy...*

'So...' He hesitated. He didn't know why. 'Goodnight, then...see you in the morning.'

He turned to go but her soft 'Fletcher' pulled him up short. He turned back and quirked an eyebrow. 'Yes?'

'I think you should sleep in here with me.'

Fletch could have sworn he actually heard the synapses in his brain misfire. Certainly for quite a few moments he was struck completely dumb.

Well, this sure blew the distance ploy out of the water.

Tess watched as a range of emotions flitted across her ex-husband's face. Did he think she'd suggest something so out there if she didn't think it was absolutely necessary?

'We can't have a repeat of tonight, Fletch.'

Fletch shrugged. There'd been so many disrupted nights like this since he and his mother had moved into the apartment two weeks before, it seemed normal to him now. Still, the sentiment weighed heavily in his mind.

'She's not going to remember what happened in the morning.'

Tess raised her legs beneath the covers, tenting them as she propped her chin on her knees. 'I know. But do you want her to go through the same distressing anxiety every time she wanders in the middle of the night and finds you on the couch?'

Fletch knew the short answer was no. Of course he didn't. And Tess's solution was, obviously, a quick, simple fix. But nothing had been simple between them for a long time.

They were bereaved, aggrieved and divorced.

That was a whole lot of baggage to take with them to a bed they hadn't shared in nine years.

'If you're not on the couch,' she continued, 'there's no reason for any distress.'

Tess projected a calm, measured professionalism, like she was talking to a relative of a patient, but on the inside the mere thought of what she was suggesting was making her quake. She hadn't seen him in nine years and now she was proposing they share the same bed.

Maybe she'd wake up in the morning and it would have all been a bad dream.

She was used to that.

Fletch hastily diverted his gaze from the bed, mentally sizing up the room. 'I suppose I could sleep on the floor...'

Tess could barely hear him over the thudding of her heart, like a drum in her ears. She knew he was trying to do the right thing but did he really have to look at the bed like it was a viper's nest?

Did he really think *she* wanted to share the thing with *him*?

'Don't be ridiculous, Fletch,' she dismissed impatiently. 'You can't sleep on the floor for two months.'

Fletch lifted his gaze to meet hers. 'So...to be clear. You're suggesting that I sleep in the bed. With you?'

Not a suggestion he'd ever imagined he'd hear coming from her mouth ever again. The tension in his shoulders headed south to grab a stranglehold on his gut.

Tess heard the note of incredulity in his voice and shrugged. 'Will it really be *that* difficult to sleep with me again?'

Fletch swallowed hard, the knowledge of his recent monster erection colouring his reasoning. 'No.' He gave a self-deprecating smile. 'That's what I'm worried about.'

Tess couldn't help but be amused at the absurdity of it all and the rather sceptical look on Fletch's face. He'd always been so decisive, so take-charge, it was a novelty to see him so completely flummoxed.

Her mouth kicked up at one side briefly before returning to a determined line. 'We're not teenagers, Fletch. I'm not proposing reconciliation. We're just two adults making the best out of a less-than-satisfactory situation. I'm sure we can control ourselves.'

Fletch heroically refrained from mentioning that controlling herself when they were in bed together had never been a forte of hers.

Or of his.

Not until after Ryan's death anyway. Her control then had been savage. She'd stopped needing him, stopped wanting him, overnight.

But he'd still needed her. So very, very much. More than that—he'd needed her to need him back.

Fletch stood at the end of the bed, still hesitating as a decade of distance yawned between them. 'I could put a roll or something down the middle of the bed,' he suggested.

Tess surprised herself with her laugh. 'How very Victorian.'

He laughed back. 'I thought a fan of Georgette Heyer would appreciate it.'

Their smiles lit the room briefly then slowly faded. Tess sighed. 'It's almost three in the morning and I'm jet-lagged to hell and back, Fletch. I'm too tired for this conversation. Just get into bed.'

He nodded, coming to a decision. She was right. It *was* half past stupid hour. And they *were* adults. 'Okay. Let me just check everything's locked up one more time.'

Fletch went through his usual pre-bed door-checking routine. It was a particular nightmare of his that his mother would manage to find her way onto the balcony during one of her many night-time walkies and plunge to her death.

Still he lingered over it, his heart pounding loud enough to wake the whole building. Certainly loud enough to wake his mother.

He was about to sleep with his ex-wife. With Tess. And even though it wasn't sexual, he felt like a virgin again, like he was sleeping with a woman for the first time.

Satisfied everything was locked up tight and unable to put it off any longer, Fletch made his way to his bedroom, quickly checking on his mother as he turned appropriately neutral opening sentences over and over in his head.

Something to break the ice.

Decrease the awkwardness that she surely must feel as keenly as him. Something like *What's the weather like in Devonshire at the moment?* Or *How about those English cricketers?*

Fletch stopped in the hallway just shy of his door and allowed an internal groan free rein.

How lame!

But anything was better than *Take all your clothes off and let me make love to you.*

Because a few lousy hours back in her company and the imperative to be with her, to peel off her clothes and bury himself inside her, was raging in his blood like a fever. It was a bad time to discover she was a habit that he'd never managed to shake.

It had been ten years and he wanted her as much now as he ever had.

Guilt, hot and fierce, rose in him and he squeezed his eyes shut to dispel the images of their intertwined bodies.

He didn't deserve her.

He had proved himself unworthy.

He took a deep, steadying breath, shaking off the tug of dark memories and guilt, and stepped into the bedroom. But whatever pithy comment had been on the tip of his tongue died before even a syllable was spoken and he sagged against the jamb as a knot of tension released like the strings of a marionette.

Tess was asleep.

Sound asleep if her soft snore was any indication.

She lay on her side, knees tucked up, sheet anchored beneath her arms. The bedside lamps threw shadows that darkened the hollows of her cheeks and the smudges beneath her eyes. Even in slumber she looked like she carried the weight of the world on her shoulders.

He watched her for a long time, keeping his distance. Knowing he'd do anything to erase her burden. Wishing that he could go back to this day ten years ago and fix the damn lock, take away her migraine, remove the bucket, stop the overnight deluge, make the ambulance come faster.

Feeling again the rage and the helplessness. His complete impotency that when it had counted most, he hadn't been able to protect his family.

He squeezed his eyes shut, pushing his thumb and

forefingers hard into the lids, blocking the images. God, he was tired. So very tired.

He needed perspective.

He needed sleep.

He pushed away from the jamb and drew level with the bed. Slowly he eased himself onto it, being careful not to disturb her, sticking close to the edge and lying as stiff as a centuries-old mummy.

After a moment he slowly turned his head to look at her. Or her back anyway. Once upon a time he would have reached out and stroked his hand down the notches of her spine, drawn her in closer. Instead he turned away and reached for the lamp switch, extinguishing both with one action, plunging the room into darkness.

She stirred and he held his breath. She muttered in her sleep, rolled over, settled again. She was closer now. And facing him. He could feel her breath fanning his shoulder and as his eyes adjusted to the darkness he could make out the outline of her mouth.

Great.

Fletch rolled his head back until he was staring at the ceiling. There weren't that many more hours left in the night. But he had a feeling he was going to see every one of them.

He did finally fall into an exhausted sleep just as dawn was spreading its first blush across a fading night sky. After lying tense and unmoving for a couple of hours, listening to her breathe, his body finally succumbed to its baser dictates and slowly relaxed into the folds of slumber.

Unfortunately, thanks to those baser dictates, it didn't last long. They didn't seem to mind that he'd had less than four hours' sleep all night. All they cared about was that it was morning, something warm, soft and female was snuggled into him, his hand was full of a smooth, clad buttock and a certain part of his anatomy was wide awake.

Fletch's eyes flew open as every muscle contracted in painful unison. His heart pounded in his chest as, for a brief moment, total disorientation reigned.

Then Tess moved a little, readjusting her head against the ball of his shoulder, murmuring something nonsensical, her lips grazing his skin, her hand skating close, too close, to his painfully tight erection.

And he was suddenly one hundred per cent orientated.

His first instinct was to leap out of the bed like the mattress had caught fire. He doubted Tess would appreciate that they didn't have control of their bodily functions while under the influence of sleep and he had no desire to have her accuse him of taking advantage of the situation.

He'd realised yesterday just how hard this was going to be, but with her draped all over him, this was a whole other level of difficult. Too many mornings like this and he might just forget the reason she was there. Forget that this was fake and they were only pretending for his mother's sake.

He had to be careful they didn't cross a line—even in their sleep—because emotionally he didn't think she was up to it.

And he knew for sure he wasn't.

But right at this moment she was hard to resist. Her head was tucked into his shoulder, her breath was warm on his bare pec and she was all soft and supple against him. And his nostrils were full of her—passionfruit, honey and something else distinctly feminine.

He drew in a deep steady breath, sucking her deep into his lungs, savouring her.

Tess had always smelled so good.

So he didn't move. Not yet. He would—soon.

But not yet.

Tess woke slowly through myriad layers of a heavy sleep surrounded by a feeling of heat and solidness, a powerful malaise infecting her bones. She chased the last vestiges of a dream she couldn't quite remember across the fading edges of her sleep like a child would chase the tail of an escaped balloon as it rose in the sky.

She murmured a protest—her dreams were so rarely good and she fought against the sticky fingers that were trying to drag her away from the tail, back into the world of the conscious.

A hand curving around her bottom was comforting and she wriggled into it, bending her knee higher, revelling in the hairy bulk of a leg under it. Her lips brushed against firm, warm skin and an earthy aroma, very male, tickled her nostrils.

Hmm. Fletch had always smelled so good.

Beneath her hand, a solid slab of flat muscle undulated and tensed as if it was agitated. She smoothed it absently, stroking it lightly. Her fingers brushed something hard, something familiar and it twitched against her hand.

She frowned. *Something very familiar.*

The last strand of sleep fell with a loud clang like a metal shackle.

Fletch?

Her hand froze. The breath hitched in her lungs. Her eyes opened with a start. She was instantly awake, instantly aware of her situation.

She pushed away from Fletch abruptly, scrambling back to her side of the bed like an epileptic crab until her back hit the bedhead and she yanked the sheet up to her chin.

'What the hell?' she demanded, glaring at him.

Fletch glared back as he too boosted himself up against the bedhead. Okay, he was guilty of not separating from her earlier but no way was she going to make him the big bad wolf when she was the one draped against him with her fingerprints all over his belly.

'It's the morning,' he said defensively. 'It happens.'

Particularly if a woman is rubbing herself against me like a great big tabby cat.

Tess fought the urge to blush as she remembered how many times his biological wake-up call had led to a little morning glory. He looked so virile with his tousled hair, his big bare chest and his frown but, still, she couldn't believe she'd been…pawing at him. She dropped her gaze.

Fletch wasn't satisfied. 'You were the one touching me,' he reminded her downcast head for good measure.

Tess nodded, mortified at her behaviour. He was right.

They were divorced, for crying out loud!

'Yes.' She looked up at him. 'I'm so sorry, I was… dreaming and… God! Sorry.'

Fletch sighed at her obvious embarrassment. He should have known this was going to happen, that their bodies would naturally gravitate towards each other. That they'd subconsciously seek affection.

He rubbed a hand through his hair. 'No…I'm sorry. It's just… I don't know, Tess. It was probably inevitable. Our bodies were just reverting to type, I guess… in sleep…'

She knew what he was saying was most likely correct but it had still been a shock. She'd known last night when she'd felt the heat of his gaze on her thighs that they were on shaky ground. The fact that he didn't look any happier about it than she helped.

She grimaced. 'Maybe we're going to need that roll between us in the bed after all.'

Fletch was momentarily taken aback by her glum observation. Then he chuckled, tension slowly oozing from his muscles. 'Maybe we just need to realise that we can't control what we do when we're asleep and not get ourselves in a tizz about it when we wake up.'

Tess look affronted, crossing her arms. 'I did not get in a tizz.'

Fletch chuckled again as he threw back the sheet and swung his legs to the floor. 'Oh, you were in a tizz all right.'

'You don't have to leave, Fletch,' she said as he stood

and the mattress shifted a little beneath her. It was *his* bed, for crying out loud. 'I promise no more tizzies in future.'

He looked down at her. 'Are you sure? Because if there's one thing I've learned over the years it's that morning hard-ons are part and parcel of being a man. Are you okay with that or should I buy myself a sleeping bag?'

Tess swallowed. She hadn't had a single sexual urge in a decade. She doubted her libido, weird dreams aside, would be a problem. But he was giving her a choice. Which would be a lot easier to make if it hadn't felt so good being pressed against him just now.

She thought she'd suppressed those feelings a long time ago.

Obviously not.

Still, she couldn't let him sleep on the floor in a sleeping bag when there was enough room for both of them in the bed. She swallowed. 'I'm okay with it.' They just needed to be careful, that's all. 'As long as you keep them on your side of the bed.'

Fletch nodded. *Fair enough.* 'I'll check on Mum.'

Tess watched him go. Watched the strong lines of his bare back as he disappeared out the door. She shook her head to clear it. To try and grasp the rapid events that had led to her being back in her ex's bed.

Yesterday morning her life had been on track. It hadn't been rock-'n'-roll exciting but she liked it that way. Today she'd been sucked back into her baggage-laden past. Not a place she would ever have volunteered to visit.

But she'd told Fletch she'd do it for Jean and she'd meant it. And if that meant she had to be on her guard, even in her sleep, well, she guessed she could hack it for two months.

Determined to divert her thoughts, she sank down into the bed, thinking about her mother-in-law, already planning a schedule and thinking of ways things could be made a little easier.

'Still out to it,' Fletch announced as he re-entered the room a minute or so later. 'She usually sleeps late the morning after a disturbed night.'

Tess nodded. 'I've just been thinking about that,' she mused, surprised to feel the urge to check out his naked chest. 'I may have something that could help.'

'Oh?'

'What does the lease say about pets?'

CHAPTER FIVE

AFTER the embarrassment of their early-morning start, the day flew by. Tess took advantage of Fletch's flexible working hours and went out as soon as the shops opened. Nothing to do with needing some breathing space—*not at all*—and everything to do with needing some clothes.

She spent a couple of hours bargain hunting to extend her meagre wardrobe and did a bit of a grocery shop. Jean had always liked to cook and there was no reason why she still couldn't do so with Tess around to 'help'.

So she brought some basics that were needed for the meal plan she and Fletch had worked out whilst trying to make awkward conversation over breakfast and extras for daily baking, which had always been a particular favourite of Jean's. In fact, Jean had been a champion cake-icer in her day so Tess made sure she included those ingredients in the trolley. Hopefully this skill could be nurtured and retained for as long as possible.

So much about Alzheimer's was focused on what the sufferer couldn't do, couldn't remember, instead of making the most of what they could.

She did not think about Fletch and their early-morning predicament. Or at least every time she did she stopped herself. Denial she was good at.

Denial she'd perfected.

And having to pretend they were happily married was something well worth denying.

When Tess got home Fletch went into St Rita's for a few hours to meet with the ethics committee over the parameters of his study. It wasn't his favourite part of the research process but a very necessary evil that not only protected trial subjects but also himself and the hospital from any potential liability.

When he was done he accompanied Tess and his mother to get the pet Tess assured him would help with Jean's anxiety. He was still sceptical as they entered the animal shelter and were greeted by a cacophony of barking but when Jean's face lit up he had to concede it might have merit.

Jean looked at them. 'What are we doing here?'

'We're getting a kitten,' Fletch said patiently for the tenth time in the last thirty minutes.

Jean beamed at him. 'Really?' She clapped her hands together. 'Can I go and look?'

Tess laughed at Jean's childlike relish, feeling vindicated. It had been a hard sell talking Fletch into flagrantly disregarding the lease agreement but she'd seen with her own eyes how much difference a pet could make in the life of someone suffering from dementia and had refused to be easily deterred.

When presented with the evidence, of which she could quote both anecdotal and scientific verbatim,

Fletch had reluctantly agreed. She would have liked to push for a dog but common sense and apartment living took precedence and she'd suggested a house-trained cat.

'Of course. Go ahead.' Tess grinned. 'We'll just have a quick chat to the attendant and be along in a moment.'

When Tess and Fletch spotted Jean ten minutes later she was crouched down in front of a cage, talking animatedly to the animal inside. 'Oh, look, darling.' Jean waved at her son impatiently to move faster. 'It's Tabby.'

Tess quickened her steps, smiling at Jean's eagerness. It seemed Jean had already chosen her kitten and named it!

'Thank goodness you found her,' Jean told the shelter attendant following closely behind Tess. 'I didn't realise she'd gone missing. Trish would be worried sick if she knew her beloved Tabby dog had wandered away.'

Tess frowned. *Dog?* They drew level with the cage and looked down at a chunky, white-whiskered, ancient golden Labrador.

'You obviously haven't starved while you've been away, have you, girl?' Jean tutted. She poked her bony fingers through the cage wire to stroke the dog's ear. The dog whined appreciatively and angled its head for Jean to reach the sweet spot.

'Tabby?' Tess murmured to Fletch.

'Childhood dog of Trish's. She thought she was getting a cat and already had the name picked out,' he said quietly.

Tess pressed her lips together to suppress a smile, not game to say a word.

'Yes,' he said testily. 'The irony is not lost on me.'

'Come on, then, girl.' Jean gave the yellow-grey head one last scratch and stood. 'Let's get you home.'

Fletch looked askance at the dog. Putting aside that he lived in a nineteenth-floor apartment, the Lab looked like it was going to expire any moment either from old age or a triglyceride-induced heart attack. Maybe both.

He shook his head and muttered, 'Great,' as he sent Tess a *fix this* glare.

A bubble of laughter surged into her chest and Tess bit the side of her cheek to prevent its escape. It felt good to have the spectre of their living arrangements temporarily removed from the forefront of her brain by something so frivolous. 'Er, Jean,' Tess said, gently cupping Jean's elbow and leading her towards the next cage. 'We're here for a kitten, remember? Let's have a look around a bit more first, hey?'

And hopefully forget all about the dog.

Jean dug her feet in and looked at her reproachfully. 'Tessa! We can't leave Tabby here. Trish would be heart-broken. She belongs at home.'

Tess flicked a glance at the dog, which looked at her steadily with those big brown eyes, then at Fletch. He shook his head very firmly from side to side. 'We agreed on a cat,' he murmured in a low voice. Like a rumble of thunder.

Tess rolled her eyes. 'Okay, sure,' she soothed, turning back to Jean. 'We can take her home but how about looking at some cats as well? Look,' she said, pointing to a nearby cage containing a very playful kitten pouncing on a squeaky toy. 'Isn't that little fella cute?'

Jean turned to her son. 'Fletcher,' she admonished, wringing her hands, her voice high and worried. 'It's Tabby. We can't just leave her here!' She sank to the ground in front of the obese, elderly Labrador's cage and rocked slightly on her haunches. 'It's okay, Tabby, I'll get you out of here.'

Tess shrugged at him as Fletch rubbed a hand through his hair. His frustration wafted towards her in almost tangible waves.

'Maybe I can help?' the attendant, a middle-aged woman, intervened. 'I know you had your hearts set on a cat but you came here looking for a companion for your mother who suffers from dementia, right?'

Fletch nodded and she continued.

'Then you really can't go past old Queenie here. She was brought in two days ago after her owner of fourteen years, an elderly lady, died in hospital. Queenie had lain next to her owner, who had taken a fall and broken her hip, all night and into the next day. The lady said that Queenie had refused to leave her side until the community nurse arrived. She'd be a perfect companion for your mother.'

Tess felt goose-bumps prick her skin at the touching story. She watched Jean's agitated movements settle as she stroked Tabby/Queenie's head and murmured to her. What else did they need to make up their minds?

'How did she come to be here?' Tess asked.

'The lady's son brought her in. He travels a lot and doesn't have the time required to care for an arthritic, deaf dog.'

'Deaf?' Fletch shook his head. *Of course*. Queenie was a walking disaster zone.

'Yes.' The attendant smiled. 'She's old and fat. She has arthritic hips and is deaf. She's no pretty young thing, that's for sure. But that just makes her even more ideal for your mum. She's used to being a companion to an elderly lady. She's not young and spritely requiring someone young and spritely to keep up with her. She's content to sit and just be. And she's loyal to a fault.' The woman folded her arms across her chest. 'You won't regret it. Mark my words.'

Tess nodded heartily in agreement, also folding her arms. She turned beseeching eyes on Fletch. He gave her an exasperated look. 'I live on the nineteenth floor.'

'She's fully toilet trained,' the attendant jumped in.

'And exercise is good for Alzheimer sufferers,' Tess added. 'We can go for a few walks a day so Queenie can do her business. It'll be a good routine for Jean as well.'

Fletch looked down at the dog who looked up at him, flopped her head to the side, thumped her tail twice and whined at him, leading him to suspect that she probably wasn't all that deaf.

But three women, four if he counted Queenie, were looking at him like he was lower than a snake's belly, and he knew when he was outgunned.

'Okay, Mum.' He sighed, looking down at her. 'Let's get Qu—Tabby home.' He helped Tess get his mother to her feet and met her sparkling amber gaze above Jean's snowy head. She grinned at him and he growled, 'Smarty pants,' at her.

But as they filled out the paperwork and he watched

his mother sitting in the waiting area, stroking a contented-looking Tabby, he couldn't help but smile. Because despite what his lease said, he could already see how the dog had a calming effect on his mother.

And that was most definitely worth it.

It was midnight when Fletch headed to bed. He'd been working on study paperwork—or at least that was what he'd been telling himself. He hadn't exactly been very productive. Tess had been out on her feet early this evening and he'd ordered her to bed at seven.

It had been hard to think about anything else since. Other than her, *Tess*, in his bed.

And how they'd ended up this morning.

And how they might end up tomorrow morning.

But she'd been asleep for a good five hours now. She should be completely immersed in the land of nod. God knew, he was so tired he could barely see straight.

He looked in on his mother as he passed her room and lingered in the doorway for a moment. She was curled on her side, her snowy hair visible in the moonlight streaming through her window. Her hand rested on Tabby's dozing head. Just then the dog shifted, looked behind her straight at him and again Fletch wondered just how deaf their deaf dog really was.

She gave a quiet whine and Fletch said in a low voice, 'It's okay, Tabby, it's just me. Good girl. You come and let me know if Jean gets out of bed, okay?'

Tabby thumped her tail twice and whined again in what Fletch could only assume, what he hoped, was agreement then laid her head back on the bed. He smiled to himself and continued down the hallway to his bedroom.

Tess was sitting up in bed, reading his detective novel, when he entered. 'Oh...sorry,' he said. 'I thought you were asleep.'

She looked up from the book. 'I was, but you know how jet-lag is. I woke an hour ago like I'd been asleep for a week and I checked on Jean and I tried to go back to sleep but I couldn't so...I thought I'd read.'

'Yeah,' he murmured, trying not to look at her bare shoulder. 'Jet-lag can be a real pain like that.'

Tess nodded. 'It's awful.' Every year it took two weeks to recover from her three-day jaunt to the other side of the world.

Fletch stood for a few more moments as the silence grew between them. 'Anyway, I just came to have a shower and then get back to it.' He resigned himself to another night of little sleep—there was no way he could crawl into bed with her while she was still awake. It was too...happy families.

And they hadn't been that in a very long time.

She nodded. 'Sure.' And dropped her eyes back to the page she was reading.

Tess was aware of him disappearing into the en suite in her peripheral vision and breathed a sigh of relief when he was gone.

It was going to be a long couple of months.

She steadfastly ignored the sound of the shower as she read the same page three times. It was bound to be awkward for a while. Especially being back in bed together. It wasn't easy pushing the memories away as she always did when he was right there beside her, a very painful reminder.

And not just the memories of Ryan, but of them.

Especially after this morning.

But she'd committed to help with Jean. And it wasn't for ever—it would get easier.

Fletch made sure he had a shirt on as well as his boxers before stepping back into the bedroom. Tess, still reading, looked up from the book. He stayed in the doorframe, leaning his shoulder against the jamb, and smiled at her. 'Since when do you read detective novels?'

Tess shrugged. 'It was that or one of those very scintillating medical journals on your desk.'

Fletch chuckled. 'They may have been more conducive to sleep.'

She smiled. 'Actually, I personally find articles on the latest mitochondrial studies and or DNA sequencing real page-turners.'

Fletch threw his head back and gave a deep belly laugh and for a moment Tess couldn't breathe. How long had it been since she'd heard that sexy laugh?

Ten years? Since just before Ryan had died?

The long tanned column of his throat, sprinkled with dark whiskers, drew her gaze. Her nipples tightened as an image of her rising from the bed, crossing the room and kissing it took her by surprise.

What the hell?

She blinked rapidly to dispel it.

'Mum seems very settled tonight with Tabby curled up beside her.'

His calm observation dragged her out of a quagmire of confusion. She nodded absently whilst she sorted through appropriate responses.

'I think we're onto a winner there,' she said as her faculties returned. 'Tabby's stuck really close to Jean. It was great to see them sitting on the couch earlier, watching television together, Tabby's head resting on Jean's knee.'

Fletch nodded. 'It was a little confusing for Trish, though, when Mum rang her to tell her we'd found Tabby and she really needed to take better care of her dog.'

They laughed together this time. Listening to the one-sided telephone call had been comical. Tess was just pleased that Trish had caught on fast and knew enough to go along with her mother's false reality.

'Sorry,' she apologised after her laughter had died away. 'It's awful to laugh at something like this.'

Fletch shrugged. What could they do? This thing was happening to them whether they liked it or not. There was a long row to hoe and they needed some relief from the grim reality of it all.

He knew that better than anyone.

'Gotta laugh or you cry, right?' he said philosophically.

Tess didn't respond. What could she say? She'd made a decision when she'd moved to England to lock her grief away and try and get on with things. And it had worked for her. But there wasn't a whole lot of laughter in her life.

'Anyway, I hope it's a sign of things to come,' Fletch continued. 'Mum being this settled.'

Tess shook herself out of her reverie. 'I'm sure it will be. Studies show there is much less nocturnal wandering where pets are present. And even if the person does wander, the theory is that the pet will wake also and either stay with the person or raise the alarm.'

Fletch snorted. 'Except we got ourselves a deaf dog.'

Tess smiled. 'Dogs sense these things intuitively. I think Tabby's already bonded with your mother. I think she already knows, somehow, that Jean needs looking after.'

Fetch didn't answer and Tess wondered if his thoughts had turned to another dog in another time, as hers had.

Memories of Patch, the little Jack Russell terrier that Ryan had been given for his first birthday, arose unbidden. How he'd tried to alert them to what was happening to Ryan that dreadful day.

How he'd tried to save Ryan.

It still hurt to think about her son's faithful companion, about that day, and how she'd blamed Patch for so long for not doing enough. Not barking earlier. Not trying hard enough. But Ryan had adored his puppy dog and suddenly she needed to know what had happened to him.

'Did you take Patch to Canada with you?' she asked into the silence.

Fletch shook his head. 'Trish took him for me. He died from a snake bite a few years ago.'

'Oh.' Tess's guilt at how she'd shunned Patch flared

to life again. But the little dog had just been one more painful reminder she hadn't been able to bear to look at.

Fletch watched a series of emotions chase shadows across her face. 'He did his best, Tess,' he murmured gently. 'The bucket was wedged into the corner of the sandpit and weighted in the bottom with sand. It was heavy and he was a little dog.'

Fletch remembered it as if it was yesterday. Patch's incessant barking, something different about the tone of it waking him even before he'd heard Tess's frantic 'Fletch!'. Tearing out of the house just behind her into the back yard as a blur of brown and white hurled itself at the bucket over and over, toppling it as they reached him, disgorging water and sand and a pale, blue-lipped Ryan.

Tess shut her eyes, shutting down the images of her shaking Ryan, of the rag-doll feel of him against her chest. 'I know.' She nodded. 'I know.'

Fletch wanted to go to her. But, like at the cemetery for the last nine years, he held himself back. She didn't look any more open to his comfort now than she had all those years ago and he'd been rejected too many times to travel down that road again. So he gripped the jamb and waited for her to regain her composure.

She opened her eyes and grimaced at him. 'Sorry.'

Fletch shook his head. 'Don't be. This is hard for both of us but…thank you. Thank you so much for doing this for me. I know it's not easy being here with us again, reminding you of things you don't want to be reminded of.'

He'd hated it that Tess had shut him out in that year

after Ryan's death. She'd decided the only way to cope had been avoidance and it hadn't mattered that he'd wanted to talk about it.

Had needed to talk about it.

To talk about Ryan.

She hadn't been able to even bear having his name mentioned so he'd stopped trying and internalised everything and they'd grown further and further apart.

So he knew that being here, being confronted by him every day, had to be challenging for her. He just hadn't realised how challenging it was going to be for him as well.

'It's fine, Fletch.'

Dredging up the past was something she'd avoided at all costs and even a small foray into it had left her suddenly weary again. She shut the book. 'Think I might try and get back to sleep again.'

Fletch nodded as she climbed back into her shell. 'Sure.' He pushed off the doorjamb. 'I've got some paperwork to get back to. I'll be in later.'

Just like old times.

Fletch waited another couple of hours and got into bed when she was asleep and that was pretty much the pattern for the following couple of weeks.

They went to bed at separate times, Tess first, he crawling in with her at some time after midnight, turning his back to her lest he do something crazy and reach for her because lying with her again, night after night, had been much harder than he'd ever suspected it would be.

Sure, there'd been other women since their divorce. Not many, but a few. They'd been brief episodes, a handful of dates, a slaking of a thirst more than anything, where he'd given in to the dictates of his body but had kept his heart well and truly out of the equation.

But he couldn't do that with Tess.

Lying in bed with her was a painful reminder of how good it had been between them back at a time where they'd been emotionally free to love each other. And in that strange twilight zone between sleep and waking it was easy to believe that nothing had changed between them.

His heart certainly thought so. After years of keeping it heavily guarded, it refused to buy into the happy-families façade. In those sleeping hours, when he had no conscious control, it knew her.

Knew Tess on a primal level.

Recognised the woman beside him as his mate.

It was only the slow dawning as he became more conscious that things got back under control. As each new day loomed ahead he remembered his place on the page. Days of her constant companionship, of smiling and laughing and pretending that things were fine. Of playing happy families.

No respite from her or the fears and failures of the past. No escape for his poor confused heart.

No escape from the fact that things weren't fine.

The embarrassing mornings didn't help. No matter how scrupulously they maintained distance as they drifted off to sleep, by morning their bodies had subconsciously sought the warmth and comfort neither of them would ask for consciously.

Fletch often woke spooned around her, an erection pressing into the soft cheeks of her bottom. Or on his stomach, one arm flung out, his hand spread possessively on her belly. Or on his side, snuggled up to her, his leg bent at the knee pinning her to the bed.

And then there were the times when he woke and she was spooning him. Or had *her* hand on his belly. Or *her* leg entwined in his.

The only way to cope with their intimate postures had been to get up before her. Untangle himself and get out of the bedroom under the guise of taking Tabby outside for her morning toilet.

Do not stop. Do not look back.

And pretend it hadn't happened.

It certainly hadn't made for easy days despite outward appearances. The trepidation with which he greeted each day was tempered by Tess's academy-award-winning performance as chief organiser, but was there, nonetheless.

He knew it was difficult for her too yet she soldiered on, planning an activity every day to keep his mother, whose night-time wandering had settled dramatically, stimulated. Some days they cooked. Some days they rented classic movies that Jean knew well or visited some of Jean's old friends. Other times they went out to a museum or lunch in the city at a teahouse that had been around for a century.

His mother particularly enjoyed the morning and afternoon walks they took for Tabby's sake. Whether it was just Jean and Tess or he and his mother or the three of them, Jean chatted away happily as they trod the riverside boardwalk.

He knew his mother loved it when they were all together but frankly he preferred it when it was just the two of them. It felt forced with Tess there. Like they were trying too hard to be something that they weren't, that they hadn't been in a long time, that they could never be again, no matter how much their bodies betrayed them in their sleep.

And it felt…dishonest. Even if it was for a good cause.

And he knew she felt it too.

At the beginning of the third week there was a knock on the door as Fletch stacked the dishwasher after lunch. He'd not long got back from the hospital where the first patient in their study, a twenty-six-year-old motorbike accident victim, had been enrolled. 'I'll get it,' he said, waving off Tess who had put her sandwich down and risen from the table.

It was Trish. She was leaning against the door, looking huge and glowing at thirty weeks. Doug stood behind her, holding an excitable Christopher. Fletch's heart contracted at the sight of his nephew, at the features so familiar to him.

Trish kissed her brother's cheek. 'Okay,' she said, advancing into the apartment, 'I'm going stir crazy at home. The doc said I could have a little foray and your apartment was the only place that Doug would agree to take me to. Before you ask, all I've done is sit in a car and walk from my house to the car and from the car to your apartment.'

Fletch's lips twitched as Doug rolled his eyes. 'Okay, then.'

'Unc, unc, unc,' Christopher chanted, squirming in his father's arms, leaning forward and reaching out for Fletch. Just as Ryan had done when he'd come home from being at work for long hours. It was only natural for Fletch to take him and to plant a kiss on the baby-soft cheek.

'I'd kill for a cup of tea, which, by the way,' Trish said, smiling at him sweetly, 'you have to make because I'm not allowed to do anything.'

Fletch laughed. 'Well, come on in, then, and I'll make you one.'

Christopher still in tow, he entered the open lounge area, laughing at something Doug had said. It wasn't until he'd made it to the kitchen and heard an audible gasp that he realised the fuller implications.

He turned. Tess was frozen at the sink, her hands in sudsy water, staring at him. Or more correctly at Christopher.

He took a step towards her. 'Tessa.'

Tess held up her hands to stop him, suds sliding off them into the sink. The ache in her chest, the one that was always there, just smothered under years of pushing all the pain away, intensified.

The little boy in her ex-husband's arms smiled at her. A green-eyed little boy with blond hair that stuck up in the middle from his double cowlick.

A buzzing in her ears became so loud that for a moment she thought she was going to faint.

Ryan?

CHAPTER SIX

FLETCH handed Christopher back to his father. 'Tessa,' he said again, stepping towards her.

She backed up, her hip sliding along the bench. 'It's fine,' she said quickly, shaking her head. She didn't want him to touch her, to comfort her.

She just needed a moment.

There'd been other children in the last nine years. Of course there had been. Granted, they weren't common at the nursing home. But residents' grandchildren would come to visit and she'd coped. Smiled and agreed they were the most beautiful babies in the whole entire world and got on with her job.

But they were on the other side of the globe—not here.

Not in Fletch's arms.

Not looking like a carbon copy of Ryan.

She watched as the three adults looked at her, frozen in their positions, lost for words, waiting for her next move, not daring to even breathe in case she cracked into a thousand pieces. Only Christopher seemed oblivious, bouncing up and down in Doug's arms, making truck noises with his little bow lips.

Just as Ryan had done.

God, she was going to be sick.

'Excuse me for a moment, please,' she gasped as she whirled away from them and hurried to the main bathroom.

She lost her lunch and probably her breakfast too as she heaved into the toilet. A knock sounded on the door. 'Go away,' she yelled, knowing it would be Fletch.

Tears pricked at her eyes and she pressed her lids shut tight, beating them back. She'd cried her yearly allocation of tears at the cemetery a few weeks ago.

They were the boundaries she'd set herself and they'd worked for her.

And if she started now she might never stop.

After a few minutes Tess pulled herself up to sit on the closed lid, psyching herself up to go back out there. She had to do it, she knew that, but her cheeks warmed at the very thought. She'd completely and utterly embarrassed herself. Trish and Doug were guests in Fletch's home, not to mention family, and she'd made them feel uncomfortable.

And then, of course, there was Christopher…

Tess stood and looked at herself in the vanity mirror. She looked even whiter than her usual English pallor.

She looked like she'd seen a ghost.

She grimaced at the irony then turned on the tap, brushing her teeth and scrubbing vigorously at her face with cool water to put some colour back into her cheeks.

She dried off then inspected her face again. Marginally better.

'Go!' she ordered her reflection.

Thankfully her feet obeyed and Tess found herself walking out to join everyone, the thrum of her heartbeat in her ears. They had all joined Jean in the lounge area and were laughing at Christopher, who was patting Tabby.

Fletch, who wasn't really tuned in to the conversation, rose immediately when Tess came into his peripheral vision.

'You okay?' he asked anxiously.

Tess nodded as she drew closer. 'I'm sorry,' she apologised to Trish and Doug, whose attention was now also firmly on her. Thankfully, Jean was preoccupied with her grandson and Tabby. 'It was just a bit of a shock.'

Trish nodded. 'It's okay,' she assured gently. 'It really is quite freaky how similar they are.'

'No.' Tess shook her head. 'It's not okay. It was rude and I'm sorry.'

'Well, let's just agree to disagree on that one.' Fletch's sister grinned. 'Are you going to join us?' she asked.

Tess wanted to say no. To plead a headache or busy herself in the kitchen. But she'd already been unforgivably rude.

'It's fine if you don't want to,' Trish murmured.

'Don't be silly, Trish,' Jean said as her wandering attention came to rest on the byplay. She frowned at her daughter.

'Of course Tess wants to join us.' She patted the empty lounge next to her. 'Come and sit here, darling.

Trish has brought one of the centre's little cherubs over for a visit.'

She squeezed Christopher's cheek and he squealed in delight then she looked at her daughter reproachfully. 'Trish, you know how much Tess adores children, why wouldn't she want to join us?'

Nobody said anything for a moment as Tess realised that Jean didn't have a clue that Christopher was her grandchild. Tess saw the flash of grief in Trish's eyes and noticed Doug's hand slide onto his wife's shoulder and squeeze.

'Of course I'll join you.' Tess smiled at Jean brightly.

Jean smiled back. 'Come and meet…oh, dear.' She turned to her daughter. 'What did you say his name was, Trish?'

Trish gave her mother a wan smile. 'Christopher, Mum.'

'Oh, what a gorgeous name.' Jean clapped her hands a few times. 'Maybe you can call this one…' she tapped Trish's belly '…Christopher if it's a boy? Tess?' She turned back to Tess. 'Did you know Trish was pregnant? You girls are so secretive these days!'

There was no need for a reply as Christopher's giggle distracted them all. Tabby was sniffing the toddler and her whiskers were buzzing the little boy's neck. He looked at his mother excitedly and said, 'Doggy!'

Trish laughed. 'Yes. Tabby. Can you say Tabby?'

Christopher gave another dribbly smile. 'Yabby, yabby, yabby!'

Everyone laughed then. Even Tess. Even though her heart ached just looking at Fletch's nephew.

After half an hour that stretched interminably Doug stood and announced it was time for a yawning Trish to go back to bed. Trish protested but Doug was firm. After a noisy round of goodbyes Jean and Fletch saw the trio to the door.

Tess watched them go, a lump rising in her throat as Christopher, who was grinning at her from over Doug's shoulder, waved madly at her. She'd spent the time they were there scrupulously not looking at him, not touching him, but there was just something about a happy, waving toddler that had her automatically waving back, even if she couldn't raise a corresponding smile.

Ryan had been such a friendly, easygoing little boy too.

It wasn't until she heard the door click closed that Tess finally relaxed.

Fletch crawled into bed just before midnight. It had been an eventful day. He'd tried to engage Tess in some conversation over his sister's unannounced visit but she'd insisted she was fine and didn't want to talk about it.

It was a touch too déjà vu for him but he'd learned ten years ago that Tess was hard to sway when her mind was made up. He lifted the sheet carefully and slowly lowered himself onto the mattress. He'd fallen into the habit of immediately turning his back on her but tonight, try as he may, he just couldn't. He propped himself up on his elbow and watched her for a while.

Her breathing was deep and steady but even in her sleep tonight her eyebrows seemed to be knitted in a frown. He wished he'd had the desire to confront her today about her avoidance issues. To say the things that needed to be said. That should have been said a decade ago.

But this wasn't a do-over of their marriage. This was her doing him a favour for a couple of months. He couldn't change what had happened back then in the aftermath of Ryan's death. The way grief had pushed them apart. And ultimately what he'd done when he'd been at emotional rock bottom.

There were so many things that had come between them. One heaping on top of the other until neither of them had been able to see the other any more.

And that wasn't going to be fixed by any enforced intimacy.

Fletch fell back against the pillows as a familiar rush of disgust enveloped him, his actions that September night still haunting him.

But that too couldn't be changed.

He'd known it the second it had been done. And wishing it was different didn't make it so.

So he did what he'd done every night since she'd been back in his bed, what he'd done for so many nights after Ryan had died and she'd started shutting him out.

He rolled away from her and shut his eyes.

Tess woke to a wet feeling on her hand. Her eyes flew open as if they'd been zapped by a bolt of electricity. She backed up, accidentally nudging a prone Fletch as Tabby's dear old face filled her entire vision and the low, urgent whine went straight to a place deep and dark inside her.

Her heart beating like a runaway train, Tess's thoughts were incoherent for a moment or two.

It was Fletch who said, 'What is it, Tabby? Is Jean okay?' as he climbed out of bed.

Tess followed on autopilot. To Jean's room. The bed was empty. The bathroom—also empty. Then quickly out to the lounge. His laptop occupied the coffee table but there was no Jean. Around the dividing wall into the kitchen, where Jean was muttering to herself as she paced up and down.

Fletcher felt a rush of relief like a slug of tequila swamp him. 'Mum?'

Jean's hair was wild, like that of a mad scientist, as she looked at both of them with crazy eyes. 'Where's Ryan?' she demanded, her voice high with distress, her tone urgent. 'Tess? Where's Ryan? I thought I could hear him crying and I've searched the entire house but he's nowhere.' She put a hand to her mouth and her eyes grew large. 'What if he's been kidnapped?'

Whatever Tess had been expecting, it hadn't been this. She felt as if Jean had punched her in the stomach and she grabbed for the bench top to steady herself. Fletch had assured her that Jean didn't remember Ryan.

Just as she hadn't remembered poor little Christopher.

Tess didn't know what to say. Not after today. Not with Christopher's sweet little face such a poignant reminder of her own little boy. She could barely breathe, let alone form a coherent response.

'He's at Trish's,' Fletch said. 'Having a sleepover.'

Tess flinched as his hand came to rest on her shoulder, just as Doug's had done today with Trish.

'Trish wanted to give us a night off,' he embellished.

Jean seemed to sag as her agitation settled almost immediately. Tabby licked her hand and the transformation was complete. 'Well, why didn't you say so?' she accused mildly. 'I was worried half to death.'

Fletch flicked a glance at Tess. She still hadn't moved. Her distress wasn't as palpable as his mother's had been but he could tell she was rocked to the core. He wanted to go to her but his mother's needs were more immediate.

And a lot easier to fathom!

Jean patted her chest where the lacy yoke of her nightie met bare neck whilst she absently stroked Tabby with her other hand. 'That is so like Trish, though, isn't it?' She shook her head. 'I wish those two would stop wasting time and get pregnant. They'll make such great parents.'

Fletch nodded, his pulse settling. 'Would you like a warm milk, Mum?'

Jean gave him an indulgent smile, the missing Ryan already forgotten. 'That would be lovely, dear. Tess?'

Tess blinked. She could see Jean's lips moving but she couldn't hear any of the words. There was a pain in her chest, right in the centre of her heart, that was expanding rapidly and she could barely breathe.

'Tess?'

Fletch's deep grumbly voice pierced her inertia. She looked at him. What did he want? What had he said?

'Milk?' he prompted in response to her blank look.

Tess shook her head as the pain became a pressure

that built relentlessly. Pushing against her rib cage, clogging her throat, pressing against the backs of her eyes.

She couldn't stay here. And drink milk. She couldn't pretend that her mother-in-law's state tonight hadn't affected her. It may have sprung from Jean's confused condition but to her anything to do with Ryan was absolutely crystal clear.

And sometimes still so very real.

No matter how much she tried to ignore it.

'Tess?' Fletch prompted again, laying his palm over hers.

She pulled away. 'No.' She shook her head. 'Thanks,' she added. 'I think I'm just going to go back to bed. It's late…'

Fletch nodded. 'Of course.' He searched her face, her amber eyes looking huge in her thin, haunted face. 'I'll be in later,' he murmured.

But he doubted she'd heard him as he spoke the words to her retreating back.

Tess lay in the dark, staring at the ceiling, while her body waged a war between sleep and grief. She wanted to sleep. She wanted to be able to shut her eyes and let a black tide wash her away into the embrace of a deep, dreamless slumber. And she wanted to be there before Fletch came back to bed.

But memories of Ryan—memories she'd spent a decade suppressing—refused to be quelled and swept her along on another black tide. A rough-and-tumble ride that left her feeling bruised and battered.

The way his hair had smelled. His delighted little

giggle. His fat pudgy fingers that had wound into her hair as he'd sucked his thumb. His father's silver-green eyes that had lit with mischief or wonder. The way every single discovery had been met with complete awe. The way he'd looked up at her as he'd fed at her breast, with such unconditional love and trust.

Trust that she had destroyed completely as she'd slept that morning ten years ago while her son had drowned.

'Tess?' Fletch approached the bed tentatively half an hour later. His mother was settled back in bed with Tabby, blissfully unaware of the emotional carnage she'd left in her wake. 'Tess?' he said again.

The room was dark and her back was to the door but he knew she was awake. He could sense her turmoil as if it had flashed out at him like a lighthouse beacon.

'I'm sorry, Tess. She hasn't mentioned Ryan in well over a year. It was probably having Christopher here today that triggered latent memories.'

He climbed into bed beside her, sitting up with his back against the headboard. Her shoulder was bare and his fingers itched to touch it. To loan her some comfort.

To seek some comfort.

But he couldn't bear her to flinch at his touch again.

'Tess?'

Tess, her eyes squeezed tight, contemplated continuing to ignore him but it was patently obvious he hadn't bought into her act. She opened her eyes on a huffed-out breath. She rolled onto her back. 'It's fine, Fletch. Go to sleep.'

He looked down at her, her amber gaze glimmering with unshed tears and tightly reined emotions. 'I can't.'

Her eyes, accustomed to the dark, watched him for a moment or two. He looked like someone had knocked the stuffing out of him and she realised that Jean's outburst hadn't been easy for him either. Both the distressing state of her and the subject matter.

She pushed herself up to sit beside him, ensuring there was a decent distance between them, and they sat contemplating the darkness around them for a few moments.

'I'm sorry,' Tess murmured. 'It was… I got a bit of a shock when Jean said… I wasn't expecting it.'

Fletch nodded. 'I know.'

They fell quiet again. 'I miss him,' he said eventually.

Tess squeezed her eyes shut again as the pressure spiked behind her eyeballs. 'Don't, Fletch.'

'He loved her, though, didn't he, my mum? Do you remember how he used to call her Ninny?' He laughed. 'And she used to call him Rinny?'

Tess drew her knees up and shook her head. She didn't want to be sucked back into those days. When their lives had been perfect and nothing had been able to touch them. The pressure became unbearable. 'Fletch.'

Fletch heard the note of warning in her voice underpinned by a tautness that could have strung piano wire. He shoved a hand through his hair. 'Damn it, Tessa, I'm so sick of not talking about him…of not having anyone to talk about him to. Surely after ten years we can reminisce without it being so…fraught?'

His voice may have been low and husky but to Tess

it sounded like a clanging gong in the silence, and the dam holding back her grief started to crack.

Fletch turned to implore her. He just wanted to remember his son for a few minutes with the one person who had loved him with the same intensity and devotion.

Couldn't she give him that at least?

He noticed her hands trembling first against her drawn-up thighs. Then her shoulders shaking. Then a low noise, like a wounded animal. 'Tessa?'

Tess shut her eyes on a sob that broke free from her throat. A tear squeezed out. Then another.

Fletch felt as if a giant hand had grabbed a big loop of his intestine and twisted—hard. Why hadn't he just kept his big trap shut? 'Tess?'

She couldn't respond. Couldn't talk. Daren't open her mouth for fear all her locked-in grief would come spewing out and she'd never survive the fallout.

He turned on his side, reaching out a hand, touching her shoulder, waiting for the flinch, determined this time to push through it and comfort her. But there was only more sobbing.

Not great honking sobs either. Pitiful, muted ones.

Apportioned. Rationed. Kept strictly under control.

But he knew what they'd cost her.

When she'd announced two months after Ryan's death there'd be no tears, she'd been true to her word.

Still, he hadn't meant to upset her. He'd just needed…

What? What had he needed?

Connection.

'I'm sorry,' he murmured, scooting closer. 'God, Tess don't…please.'

He pushed his hands into her hair and swiped at her tears with his thumbs. 'Shh, it's okay, honey, don't.'

Even though he knew if anyone needed to cry it was Tess, her pathetic mewing was so heart-wrenching he couldn't bear it. He leaned in and kissed her forehead. Kissed her eyelids. His lips mingled with her tears. 'Shh,' he crooned as he tasted both their salt and their anguish.

His palms moved down to cradle her face as he followed the tracks of her tears, sipping at them as he went. Down the slopes of her prominent cheekbones. Into the dip of the hollows beneath. Past her nose. To the corner of her mouth.

'Shh,' he murmured against her lips. 'Shh.'

And then the soft butterfly presses became something else. Something different.

Something more.

Tess felt her wretchedness ease as something altogether took over. Something unusual yet familiar. Hesitant yet insistent.

Something separate from her grief.

And she grabbed on for dear life.

Her mouth opened beneath his and the harsh suck of his breath echoed around them. Her tongue reached out tentatively, seeking his, and she felt his deep groan reach right down inside her to places she'd long since forgotten existed.

Places that were coming to life with a roar, not a whimper. Heating and liquefying and pulsating.

Fletch's hand slid from her jaw to the back of her head, angling it so he could deepen the kiss. Tess obliged, letting him in a little more, sighing against his mouth. He slid his hand to her back, gathering her closer, their chests touching, their hips aligned, their legs brushing.

She wound her arms around his neck, the motion squashing her breasts against his chest, and Fletch could feel their softness and the twin points of her aroused nipples that told him more than her sigh ever could.

His head spun, his pulse tripped. Her lips tasted sweet and every time he drew in a breath the aroma of Tess, imprinted on his DNA, filled up his senses.

It was intoxicating. She was intoxicating. And it had been *so damn long*.

He didn't know what was going on but right now he couldn't have cared less. All he knew was that he needed this, needed her, with a gnawing, aching desperation.

Tess could feel her body igniting. From the sealed heat of their mouths, liquid warmth oozed like quicksilver into her marrow. Into every muscle and sinew. Into every cell. Pushing forth into areas that had been shut down for a decade. Where she'd felt cold and bleak for a decade.

She felt Fletch's hand at her breast and she moaned into his mouth, arching her back, pushing herself harder into his palm, her hips moving more intimately against his. She felt the thickness of his arousal and rocked herself into it. The guttural sound he made at the back of his throat fuelled the flames licking through her blood and the urgent hand he clamped against her bottom, where cheek met thigh, pressed her closer. She had no idea what she was doing. All she knew was it felt good. And in the storm of sensations she'd found a new way to reach the oblivion she craved.

Respite from thoughts of Ryan that had been hammering at her skull ever since Jean's clueless ramblings.

Suddenly she wasn't a grieving mother or a failed wife. She was a woman. And she felt whole again.

Whole.

The word was like a glacial hand on her neck and Tess froze in his arms. Since when had she needed a man to feel whole?

Especially this man, whom she'd loved too much and knew too well?

She'd moved to the other side of the world to get away from him, to get the emotional distance she'd needed just to survive. And she hadn't so much as looked at a man in a decade. Yet one touch from Fletch and she was practically climbing on top of him?

Undoing all the hard work. Knocking down all the emotional barriers she'd erected to survive in a world that had been turned upside down.

What was she doing?

She couldn't need Fletch to feel whole again. She just couldn't. She had a life to go back to. A life that worked.

A life without him.

She wasn't here for this. She didn't want this.

She didn't need it.

Fletch realised suddenly that Tess had stopped responding. He drew back, his heart racing, his breath ragged. 'Tess?'

She could see desire turning his silvery-green eyes all smoky. Her chest rose and fell in the same agitated rhythm as his. She pushed against him. 'Let me go.'

Fletch blinked. *Huh?*

She pushed harder. 'I can't do this. Let me go,' she said, more frantic this time.

Fletch felt like the bed had been yanked out from under him as she wrenched away. 'Tess. No.' He grabbed for her but she'd removed herself from the arc of his reach.

She shook her head as she scrambled to the farthest point of the bed from him, her back against the headboard again. She yanked her oversized shirt down over her drawn-up knees until only the tips of her toes were visible.

As a physical deterrent it was fairly flimsy but symbolically it screamed *Keep out* very effectively. She hunched into it. 'I'm sorry,' she whispered. 'I can't.'

Fletch fell back against the mattress, suppressing a roar of frustration. His pulse hammered, his breath rasped, his erection strained.

'It's fine,' he said after a few moments, staring at the ceiling.

Even though it wasn't. Even though déjà vu was pressing him into the mattress with the weight of a hundred bitter memories. Reaching out for her on too many occasions and being rebuffed. Desperate to hold her, to reaffirm their love, all met with stony resistance.

And whilst she may not have flinched away this time,

her sudden change of mind was just as gutting. Because for the first time in a decade she'd needed him.

He'd never been surer of anything.

She'd needed him.

'I don't know what happened,' Tess said.

Fletch's obvious wretchedness added guilt to the mix of her ricocheting emotions. The need to explain herself took her by surprise.

Fletch shut his eyes. 'It's fine,' he dismissed again.

But it wasn't. She didn't want him to think she was playing games. 'I haven't… I don't… It just…took me away. Before I knew it, nothing else existed.'

Fletch shoved a hand through his hair as her meaning sank in and he felt cold all over. So she *had* needed him.

As a distraction.

A sudden surge of anger boiled away the ice.

She'd used him.

Tess realised what she'd said as he rolled out of bed. 'Wait, Fletch…I didn't mean… It's not like that…'

Fletch looked across the rumpled bed at her, anger simmering in his veins. 'Yes, it is, Tess,' he said quietly, his jaw locked tight, keeping rigid control of his response. 'It's exactly like that.'

And before he could say something he regretted, he did what he'd always done, turned away and walked out of the room.

CHAPTER SEVEN

TESS lay awake long after Fletch had left, staring into the darkness. He didn't come back to bed and she knew in her bones he wouldn't. She fell asleep as dawn was breaking across a velvet sky and didn't wake until the sun was high.

Even then she couldn't move. She just lay on her side and watched a vapour trail leave a white streak across the slice of sky she could see through the bedroom's large windows, her thoughts full of Fletch.

And their kiss.

It was time to admit to herself that living in such close quarters with him had loosened the lid on feelings she'd thought long suppressed.

She was attracted to Fletch.

It was simply undeniable. It had been there from the first moment she'd spotted him at the cemetery. Fletch had improved with age and there was a sexiness to his maturity that pulled at her in places entirely different from those the first time around.

And to someone who hadn't felt attraction or desire in such a long time, *who'd actually shunned it*, it wasn't an easy admission.

It was made worse by the answering flicker she'd seen in him. From the moment he'd looked at her bare thighs that first night to the way she'd caught him looking at her in unguarded moments, it was obvious he felt it too.

It had been wrong of her, stupid actually, to think they could just pick up where they'd left off—two human beings going through the motions, shells of what they'd once been—with this attraction raging between them.

But she hadn't meant to use him.

It had just been so good to forget for a while after Jean's unintended stirring-up of their past.

Her stomach muscles tightened as the kiss played in her head again and for a fleeting moment Tess regretted pushing him away last night. Maybe she should have just got lost in him, like she used to. Let him and the magic she knew their bodies could make obliterate everything.

The time between going to bed and falling asleep was always the hardest—last night particularly—and he could have helped with that.

But she just…couldn't.

She'd known she was getting herself into dangerous emotional waters, a torrent she'd barely survived the last time, and she just hadn't been able to let go.

Her life was too regimented for that.

She'd tried to live her life simply and on a level emotional plane ever since they'd separated. She'd moved far away and started anew. She lived modestly, kept friendships light, actively discouraged men. She worked and she slept and in between times she kept herself busy in her garden or doing online research for the local historical society.

She didn't even have a pet.

Jumping head first into a sexual liaison with Fletch as a way to keep the memories at bay during her stint in his apartment was a huge leap and one that was pure folly. Pretending they were happily married for Jean's sake was enough of a lie without throwing sex into the mix.

Because even she knew with their history and this latent attraction, it could never be that simple.

And she didn't want to need Fletch again like she once had. Ten years of separation had afforded her a true sense of self. She didn't need anybody these days and that was fine and dandy as far as she was concerned.

Because when she was done here she *was* going back to England, back to her perfectly fine life in a small Devonshire village where everyone knew her name and no one knew her pain.

Just the way she liked it.

But first she had to get through the next weeks and to do that she had to get out of bed and go and talk to Fletch.

Fletch squinted against the harsh morning sunshine reflecting off the river as he stood at the railing of his deck. He and his mother had just come back from taking Tabby for a walk along the river path he could see snaking down below.

He took a long swallow of the ice-cold berry smoothie they'd whipped up together on their return. Tess had stocked the freezer with frozen berries, quoting something about their antioxidant properties being good for Jean's memory retention.

He was pretty sure it wouldn't stand up to any rigorous scientific testing but the nutritional value of berries was well documented and blended with ice and a little cream they went down very well on a hot morning.

He yawned as his lack of sleep caught up with him. His neck ached from hunching over the laptop at the coffee table, pretending to work, while his brain had turned the incident with Tess over and over until he'd thought he was going to pass out from the spinning.

He'd been angry with Tess when he'd walked out on her last night. And it hadn't been from some thwarted sexual fulfilment. Or the fact that she had been using him to forget for a while.

Well, not entirely anyway.

It was her rejection of his closeness, her continual refusal to let him in, to talk to him, that had steam blowing out of his ears.

It was déjà vu.

By the time his mother had woken at seven he had been angry with himself. For a start, he'd been foolish to believe he could just share a bed with Tess and not want to get her naked. Despite their history he was still dangerously attracted to her and he'd known that from the first night when she'd put her hand on his thigh.

Secondly, he was angry because he should have never given up on her.

On them.

He should have insisted on counselling instead of the gently-gently approach he'd taken. Demanded she come with him. Picked her up and carried her there if necessary.

Maybe they'd still be together.

He should have said no when she'd asked for the divorce.

But things had been so dark and bleak for so long and he'd just done something utterly and completely unconscionable. Sure, there had been a thousand excuses and justifications but he hadn't believed any of them then and the passage of time hadn't made them any more palatable.

It had been too hard to look at her, and impossible to look at himself.

And she'd given him the perfect out.

Walking away had been the only option. Because telling her hadn't been.

Just as starting something with her while she was here wasn't an option either. Not with so much unsaid between them.

Fletch drained his glass and moved inside, his eyes instantly grateful. His mother was washing up at the sink and she smiled at him as he placed his glass into the soapy water and picked up a tea towel.

'Tess on an early today?' she asked.

Fletch shook his head as he'd done the last six times she'd asked. 'She's on a day off. She's having a lie-in.'

It had been hard for him, watching his mother's memory slowly regress. Worse for Trish who had done more of the hands-on caring over the last couple of years. That she'd remembered Ryan last night had been completely unexpected. And if she'd been in her right mind Fletch knew his mother would have been mortified by what she'd said.

He wished he knew what was going on inside her head. He wished he knew so he could fix it. But there were just some things that couldn't be fixed.

He knew that better than most.

He turned to put the glasses away in the cupboards behind him and he smiled at the little sticker that had a picture of a tumbler and had *glasses* written in neat black print. Thanks to Tess, nearly every single surface in his apartment bore labels—cupboards, light switches, electrical appliances. Her handiwork was everywhere.

She was everywhere.

In a short space of time she'd made such a huge difference—cupboards and drawers had symbols on them, labels above power points reminded Jean to turn the power off when she was finished with it. Tess had added to the book that Trish had instigated containing basic but important information like name, age, address, appointments, etc. A map and directions back to home had been included and Tess wrote in it each day what they going to do so it had become a communication tool as well.

She'd bought Jean a journal and encouraged her to write down her thoughts and ideas, to use the book each day as a way to keep her mind exercised. She'd even made an appointment for Fletch at the family lawyer to review and update the legal and financial documents that he and Trish and Jean had put into place five years ago when his mother had first been diagnosed with Alzheimer's.

And then, of course, there was the dog.

There was no doubt about it—Tess had made herself indispensable. And his mother was more settled, more content than he'd seen her in a long time.

But her presence was a double-edged sword.

It reminded him of what he'd had. What had happened.

And how badly he'd screwed up.

Tess took some deep, cleansing breaths as she walked down the hallway to the lounge area. She could hear the clinking of dishes and Fletch and Jean chatting as she grew nearer, and it felt so domestic she wondered if she hadn't been caught in some kind of bizarre time warp.

The urge to pack up her things and return to her isolation on the other side of the world grew with each footstep closer. But she'd told Fletch she'd stay until after Trish's baby was born and she wouldn't go back on her word.

Fletch looked up as Tess appeared in the kitchen. She was wearing above-the-knee denim cut-offs and a tank top. Her hair was damp and spiky, her feet were bare and she wore no make-up.

She looked utterly gorgeous. A soothing sight for tired eyes. A decade ago he would have teased her about sleeping in. Hell, a decade ago he would have been right in bed beside her.

But their kiss from last night stood large between

them and he gave her a polite smile instead. 'Morning,' he murmured. She gave a wan nod in reply.

'Tess, don't you have an early today?' Jean asked as she squeezed out the dishcloth.

Tess shook her head. 'Not today.'

Fletch watched as she stood there looking awkward. 'Berry smoothie?' he asked.

She nodded. 'I can get it.'

Fletch was already halfway to the fridge. 'It's fine,' he dismissed. 'Why don't you go out to the deck and I'll bring it out to you?'

Tess acquiesced. She figured it was best to get the inevitable out of the way and try and move forward from the awkwardness of last night.

Bright sunshine enveloped her as she stepped outside and headed straight for the railing. She shut her eyes and turned her pale face to the source of the heat, revelling in it as if she were an unfurling flower. The hit of UV was so intoxicating she didn't hear Fletch approach a few moments later.

Fletch was engrossed by the image before him. Tess on his deck, her face raised to the sun in silent supplication. He wanted to stroke the ice-cold glass down her bare arm, drop a kiss against her nape. What had happened last night had changed things between them and despite her rejection of him, he still wanted to touch her.

'Here,' he murmured, holding out the glass to her from a safe distance.

Tess opened her eyes reluctantly. She'd forgotten how good it felt to be deep-down-in-your-bones warm.

'Thank you,' she said, taking the offering but avoiding his gaze.

Fletch took up position beside her but not too close. He leaned heavily against the rail, waiting for her to take a couple of sips before he said what he'd come out to say. 'I owe you an apology over last night.'

Tess shook her head, her gaze fixed on the river below. 'It's okay, Fletch.'

'No, it's not. I was rude.'

She shrugged. 'You were right.'

Fletch glanced at her sharply. He hadn't expected her to say that.

'I *was* using you,' she said, her eyes fixed on the wide expanse of the water below. 'Not intentionally… but deep down…'

Fletch looked at her for a long moment before glancing at the view below. Her candour vindicated him but it didn't make him feel any better. 'I'm sorry things got so out of hand, Tess. I wouldn't blame you if you wanted to turn tail and run.'

Tess looked up for the first time. 'I told you I'd stay until after Trish has the baby and I will.'

He glanced at her again and their gazes meshed. 'Thank you.'

Tess nodded. He looked so serious. So different from the smoky-eyed lover of last night.

'I was thinking…' he said. 'Mum seems settled now with Tabby for company. Maybe I should go back to the couch?'

Tess regarded him for a moment then looked away.

It was a sensible suggestion, given what had happened, but this thing wasn't about them. It was about Jean.

'She's still wandering, Fletch.'

'Not very often.'

'Yes, but you know how upset she became that night when she thought you and I were going to get divorced. I don't know about you, but I don't want her to have to go through that again—it's not good for her or her blood pressure. Actually...' Tess thought back to her own response to the distressing incident. 'It's not good for any of us.'

Fletch nodded. He knew what she was saying was right.

But...

'It would make things easier for us,' he pointed out.

Or him anyway. Sharing a bed with her had been hard enough without last night's little session playing like an erotic movie on slow-mo through his head.

And now he'd tasted her again? And realised he was as hot for her as he ever was? He wasn't sure he was capable of waking tangled up in her and not letting his natural urges take over.

Tess looked at him. 'It's not about us, Fletch.'

Fletch met her calm amber gaze. She was right, of course. But he wasn't so sure he could compartmentalise it as easily as she had.

She'd always been the expert in that department.

A few nights later Tess was woken again in the wee hours. Fortunately this time it was Fletch's pager and not his mother.

It had been a long time since she'd been woken by a pager. When they'd been married it had been a regular occurrence that had barely caused her to stir but all these years later it was disorientating for a moment.

'What's that noise?' Tess murmured as she groped through layers of sleep. The soft pillow beneath her head was warm and pliant and she snuggled into it farther.

Fletch was instantly awake. Tess's head was on his shoulder, her body curled into his, her hand on his belly dangerously close to a piece of his anatomy that had obviously been up for a while. 'Shh, it's okay,' he murmured. 'It's just my pager. Go back to sleep.'

He gently eased away from her as he reached for his pager, dislodging her hand and her head and her thigh crossed over his at the knee. He wished it was as easy to remove the lingering aroma of her hair in his nostrils and the warm imprint of her body against his. He pushed a button on the device and read the back-lit screen.

Displaced, Tess roused further. She frowned. 'You have a pager?'

'I'm on call for the study,' he explained quietly as he swung his legs over the side of the bed and his feet hit the floor. 'They need me to consent an admission. There's no one on that can do it.'

Only certain medical and nursing staff that'd done in-service on the study had been cleared to give consent. A large percentage of the staff across the two units had been trained up to ensure there was always someone on shift who could do it but occasionally it worked out that some shifts just weren't covered.

Tess yawned, her heavy eyes refusing to open. 'What time is it?' she asked as she tried to snuggle into her actual pillow, finding it nowhere near as comfortable.

'Two-thirty,' Fletch whispered as he stood. 'Go to sleep.'

No answer was forthcoming and he turned to look at her. She had taken his advice. The urge to lean over and drop a goodbye kiss on her mouth surprised him with its intensity. It was certainly what he would have done had they still been married.

But they weren't.

Twenty minutes later Fletch was walking into the PICU at St Rita's. He'd pulled on some jeans, thrown on a T-shirt, stuffed his feet into a pair of joggers and finger-combed his hair. He'd quickly brushed his teeth and ignored the fact that he needed a shave.

Time was of the essence where head injuries were concerned.

Every female staff member on the unit practically swooned as he entered. Any distraction from weariness was welcome at three a.m. and Fletch's particular brand of scruffy chic especially so.

'What have we got?' he asked Dr Joella Seaton, the registrar covering the night shift.

'Kyle Drayson. Eighteen-month-old immersion retrieved from Toowoomba area.'

She handed Fletch the chart and continued, unaware that Fletch had stopped listening.

'Incident occurred at a local swimming hole where the family were camping at just after midnight. He'd woken and wandered away from the camp site. Local ambulance arrived within twenty minutes of call. After an extended down time they got a rhythm. He was medivaced out. He's not quite three hours post-injury.'

Joella stopped talking and waited for Fletch to say something. He blinked when he realised they were standing outside room two and he hadn't been aware they'd been walking.

Of course. *Room two.*

'Dr King?'

Fletch looked blankly at Joella. What had she said? 'I'm sorry, Joella, go on.'

'Mum came in the chopper with him. She's obviously very distressed. She's currently with the on-call social worker.'

Fletch nodded as his demons prowled in front of the closed double doors. A glass window allowed him to see some of the activity as nurses scurried about, trying to stabilise the patient.

An eighteen-month-old patient. Who had nearly drowned.

Not a forty-year-old motorcyclist who'd been going too fast around a bend. Or a nineteen-year-old skateboarder who hadn't wanted to look uncool in a helmet. Or a sixty-year-old golfer who'd been smacked in the head with a flying ball.

A boy. A little boy.

And he had to go into the room. He had to go in and stand at the end of bed two and look at little Kyle who had nearly drowned. Just as he'd done with Ryan ten years ago.

As a doctor this time, not a father.

For a moment he doubted he could. Not this room. Not another eighteen-month-old boy.

His pulse roared in his ears. His gut felt as if it had tied itself into the mother of all knots. Right now he would have paid Joella every cent he owned not to.

But he believed in this study. He believed in therapeutic hypothermia for acute brain injury. Had seen over and over how neuro-protective decreasing a patient's body temperature could be. How it could reduce the harmful effects of ischemia by reducing the rate of cellular metabolism and therefore the body's need for oxygen. How it stabilised cell membranes. How it moderated intracranial pressure.

He believed he could give Kyle and kids like him—
kids like Ryan—a better neurological outcome with a simple non-invasive therapy.

And to do that, he had to do his job.

He had to walk into room two and be a doctor.

Tess was getting back into bed from her dash to the loo when Fletch entered the bedroom a couple of hours after he'd left. She glanced at the clock. Four-thirty. There was a moment of awkwardness as their eyes briefly met but his gaze slipped quickly away and he barely acknowledged her before he headed for the bathroom.

'Did you get your consent?' she asked his back as it disappeared. She pulled the sheet up as the light went on in the bathroom. He didn't answer. In fact, she wasn't even sure he'd heard her.

'Yes.'

Tess turned her head towards the bathroom and for a brief moment caught his backlit haggard face before he snapped the light off.

She stifled a gasp. He looked like he'd aged ten years in a couple of hours.

Drawn, pinched, tense.

Old.

He looked like he had that day with Ryan.

She sat up. 'Are you okay?'

Fletch sank down on his side of the bed, his back to her. He shut his eyes for a moment, rubbed a hand through his hair. Kyle Drayson's face, his blond hair and green eyes so like Ryan's, seemed to be tattooed on the insides of his eyelids. He opened them, lifted the sheet and slipped under it.

'I'm fine,' he said, conscious of her face peering down at him.

Tess may have spent nine years apart from Fletch but she still knew him well enough to know that he wasn't fine. Knew that whatever he'd gone to see at work hadn't been pretty. She'd worked in ICU. She remembered too well those times when it was even too much for seasoned veterans.

And she'd been on the other side of the bed too. So had Fletch. Except he was still there, at the coal face.

How did he do it?

'Was it bad?'

Fletch sighed. 'I'm fine,' he repeated.

His voice was telling her to leave it alone but his utter wretchedness provoked her to push. 'Was it the kids or the adults?'

'The PICU.'

His terse reply put an itch up her spine. 'Do you… want to talk about it?'

Fletch shut his eyes. He wanted to do anything but. He wanted to be able to get in a time machine and erase the last few hours. He wanted to go back and stop Kyle from leaving his tent. Or further still. Stop Ryan from leaving the lounge room via a door Tess had been nagging him to fix.

'It might help,' she murmured, looking down into his tense face, his forehead scrunched, his lips flattened.

He snorted, his eyes flying open. 'Oh, and you would know that how?'

How many times had he begged her to talk to him?

Tess blinked at the flash of venom reflecting like a great orb in his silvery-green gaze. He was right. Psychological advice coming from her was hypocritical in the extreme. But something was very obviously wrong.

And she couldn't bear to see him so troubled.

She'd been blind to his torment a decade ago but she could see it with absolute clarity now.

'Forget it,' he said, flicking the covers back and vaulting upright. He swung his legs over the edge of the bed.

Tess frowned at the expanse of his back. 'Fletch?' She reached out a tentative hand and touched his shoulder. He flinched and her hand fell away. The rejection stung.

Fletch buried his face in his hands for a few moments, the spike of rage dissipating as fast as it had arrived. His hands dropped into his lap and his shoulders sagged. 'I'm sorry.'

Tess watched him for a moment, feeling utterly impotent in the face of his turmoil. She wished she had some words for him but she was at a loss.

'It was a little boy. Blond hair. Green eyes. Eighteen months old. An immersion. They'd put him in room two.'

The words fell like stones—like huge boulders, actually—into the silence. If Tess thought she'd been lost for words before, she was practically rendered mute now.

There were no words.

So she did the only thing she could think of. The only thing that felt right. She reached for his shoulder again. This time he didn't flinch. This time he covered her hand with one of his own.

She moved closer then. Parted her legs so his back fitted into her front, his bottom pressed into the place where her thighs joined, her legs bracketing his. She pressed her cheek against his T-shirt just below his shoulder blade. It smelled of detergent and sunshine and man.

She felt and heard the steady thump of his heartbeat. Found comfort in its slow, assured pulse.

She wasn't sure how long they sat there. All she knew was that when she whispered, 'Come on,' to him, he let her pull him back, let her draw him down until his head was resting on her chest, his ear over her own heartbeat, her arm around his shoulders.

'What's his name?' she asked after a while.

'Kyle.'

Tess ran the name around in her head for a moment. 'Did they give consent? His parents? For your study?'

Fletch nodded. 'The mother did.'

And because neither of them wanted to talk about Kyle or Ryan, she stroked his hair and asked him about the medicine. The medicine was safe. It was clinical. Unemotional. Free of baggage.

'Was he part of the treatment group or the control?'

'Treatment,' Fletch confirmed. 'They had the cooling blanket beneath him and were actively cooling him when I left.'

'What's the goal, temperature-wise?'

'We only want to induce moderate hypothermia for forty-eight hours.'

Tess shivered at the thought. She knew that freezing water would currently be running through the latex underblanket and that Kyle's skin would be icy to touch in a matter of hours. He would be oblivious, kept in an induced coma, but still the thought gave her chills and she was grateful for the heat of Fletch and his big arm encircling her waist.

'That's different from your earlier studies,' she murmured.

He turned his head to look up at her. 'You've read my studies?'

Tess allowed a ghost of a smile to touch her lips. 'I've read all your published stuff.'

Fletch was speechless for a moment. A hundred things to say crowded to his lips but he dismissed them all. He'd often wondered if she'd ever thought of him.

It was good to know she had.

Tess let him talk. Listened to the rumble of his voice as he told her about his earlier studies. About his experiences in Canada with cold-water immersions having better neurological outcomes than those he'd seen in Australia. How because of Ryan he'd developed a special interest in the subject, which had fast developed into an obsession.

And somehow hearing her son's name when they were both wrapped up together, keeping their demons at bay, didn't seem so gut-wrenching.

The irony of it all wasn't lost on her. Not even at five in the morning after another disrupted night.

Why had it taken her ten years to comfort him?

This was what he'd needed, what he'd asked for so many times in so many ways, and she'd denied him because she just hadn't been capable.

When he'd needed her most, she'd pushed him away.

She should have been there for him more.

She'd failed Fletch as well as Ryan.

CHAPTER EIGHT

Two weeks later Tess was in the middle of a lesson in making royal icing flowers when the phone rang. She reached across to the nearby wall where it was hanging and plucked it off the cradle, all without taking her eyes off the deft precision of Jean's wrinkled fingers as they created sweet perfection.

Tabby lay at their feet, ready for any morsel that inadvertently landed on the floor, and Tess absently stroked the dog's back with her foot as she said, 'Tess speaking.'

Jean held up a perfectly formed miniature rose for her approval and Tess grinned and silently applauded.

'Oh…hi, it's Trish. How are you?'

Tess heard the disappointment in her ex-sister-in-law's voice. She'd spoken to Trish a few times on the phone since the day they'd turned up with Christopher, just a quick hello and goodbye as she'd handed the phone to Jean or Fletch. But she knew that Trish rang religiously every day to speak to her mother.

'You want to talk to Jean?'

'No. I was hoping to speak to Fletch, actually. Is he there?'

Tess shook her head, even though Trish couldn't see her. 'He's at the hospital at the moment.'

'Oh…do you know when he'll be home?'

There was more than disappointment in Trish's voice. There was something else. Worry?

'Not till about five. They've had quite a few study enrolments the last couple of weeks so he's got a bit to catch up on.'

'Right. Damn it.'

'Is there something wrong, Trish?'

'I was hoping he could watch Christopher for me for a couple of hours. I have an appointment for my thirty-two-week scan. Normally I'd take Christopher but he's unwell at the moment. Doctor says it's a virus, but he's totally miserable so I don't want to drag him from pillar to post. And I can't leave a sick child with any of my friends—they all have kids. It's fine, Doug will just have to stay home and look after him instead of coming to the scan with me.'

Tess remembered how Fletch had been there at all her scans. How he'd revelled in the experience as much as she had. How it had bonded them even closer when they'd been able to share the images of their unborn son together, watch his little heart beat, his perfect little limbs kicking away like crazy.

'What about Doug's mother?' Tess asked.

'She's up north, visiting relatives.'

And they both knew Jean wasn't capable. 'Could you reschedule?'

'They've already squeezed me in on a cancellation. My obstetrician is always booked to the eyeballs.'

Tess felt an encroaching dread as she contemplated the right thing to do. Back in the old days she wouldn't have hesitated to offer her services. But the mere thought of looking after Christopher terrified her.

'Doug won't mind,' Trish assured her. 'He's pretty easygoing.'

Tess hated the awkwardness between them now. That Trish wasn't even asking her. That she was obviously trying to reassure her. Once upon a time Trish would have just asked, secure in the knowledge that Tess would say yes.

She shut her eyes, knowing she couldn't let Doug miss out on this experience when she was perfectly capable of looking after a small child. 'I...I can do it.'

Her voice quavered, her heart pounded, but she'd offered.

Silence greeted her from the other end. Then, 'Oh, Tess... It's fine, you don't have to do that...'

Tess shook her head. 'Doug shouldn't miss out on this, Trish.' More silence. 'Of course I'd understand if you preferred I didn't.'

There was silence on the other end again for a long time and Tess wondered if Trish had hung up. *God, Trish really didn't want her looking after Christopher.* And as much as she didn't want to do it either, it hurt.

'Look, it doesn't matter,' Tess said, gripping the phone hard. 'It was just a thought. Forget it. I know my track record's not...'

She couldn't finish. She couldn't say that the last little boy she'd been left in charge of had drowned.

'What? Oh, Tess, no! I'm sorry, I was just thinking. Christopher doesn't really know you, that's all. It's not about… I didn't mean to…'

Trish fell silent and Tess heard a long, deep sigh.

'I don't blame you, Tess…for what happened to Ryan.' Trish's voice was husky with sincerity. 'No one has ever blamed you. Not Mum. Not me or Doug. And certainly not Fletch.'

'I know.'

And she did know. But what Trish and Jean and Fletch didn't realise was that no matter what they thought, no matter how much time passed, she would *always* blame herself.

'I would very much appreciate it if you could watch Christopher for me, Tess. It would be a big help.'

Tess felt a thunk in her chest and had the insane urge to take the offer back. But it was out there now and Trish's voice was suddenly unburdened of the worry and disappointment that had been present at the beginning of the conversation.

And it meant something that Trish had faith in her.

'What time's the appointment?' she asked.

'In an hour. Do you mind me asking if you and Mum could come here? He's asleep now and I'm pretty sure he's going to be out to it for the afternoon—I'd rather not disturb him. Tell you what, why don't I take Mum with us to the scan? That way it'll be just you and Christopher and Mum will get to see her grandchild.

Not that she'll remember.' The husky note had crept back into Trish's voice.

'I'm so sorry, Trish. It's hard to watch, isn't it?'

'The worst,' Trish agreed. 'She was such a great grandmother, wasn't she? It's awful that my kids are never going to know that. They'll only know the shell she's going to become.'

Tess thought back to how wonderful the older woman had been with Ryan. How the two of them had been practically inseparable. How he'd hung on her every word and Jean had declared him the most loveable child on the planet.

No bias, of course.

'But you'll keep the real her alive for them, Trish. You and Fletch. You'll tell them all about the wonderful, smart, kind, funny person she was and how very, very much she loves them. That person's always going to live inside you.'

'I know,' Trish murmured. 'Sorry. It just gets to me on some days more than others. I blame the hormones.'

Trish laughed and Tess joined in. It wasn't very jolly laughter but it broke the maudlin conversation.

'We'll be half an hour,' Tess said.

'Perfect.'

Tess hung up the phone and looked at Jean and the small pile of white sugar flowers on the bench top. 'Let's go and visit Trish,' she said.

'Oh, yes,' Jean said, her eyes sparkling. 'Yes, please.'

Tess was nervous as she and Jean walked up the stairs of Trish and Doug's massive, beautifully renovated Old

Queenslander. Not even the warm welcome of the big, wide wraparound verandas helped to quell the low-level nausea that had afflicted her ever since she'd bundled Jean into the car.

But they were here now and then Trish was opening the front door and ushering them inside. She followed them down the hallway past rooms that Tess assumed to be bedrooms running off either side and into a large lounge with soaring ceilings. A dining room and kitchen spilled off the edges in a very open-plan arrangement.

'Wow. This is beautiful,' Tess commented as the warm honey of the polished floorboards and the rich tapestry of Middle-Eastern rugs attracted her attention.

Trish smiled. 'Thanks. It's been a labour of love.'

Tess remembered the cottage that she and Fletch had been renovating together and understood the pride and accomplishment on Trish's face.

'So, Christopher is asleep on the lounge. I've just given him something for the fever.' Trish half turned and indicated the little sleeping figure on the lounge chair behind her.

Tess looked over but kept her distance. Christopher was wearing just a nappy and lying on a sheet that had been tucked into the lounge cushions. A ceiling fan directly overhead blew a cool breeze downwards, ruffling white-blond hair with two little cowlicks.

Trish padded towards her son and gently stroked his forehead. She grimaced at the fine red rash sprinkling his torso. 'The doctor assures me the rash is a post-viral thing.'

Tess nodded absently. He looked so still. An image

of Ryan in PICU popped into her head—so still and pale—and for a second Tess wasn't sure she could do it.

Then Trish turned to her and smiled. 'Thanks so much for doing this, Tess.' Her hand stroked her belly. 'It means so much to Doug and me.'

Tess smiled and assured her it was fine.

She handed Tess a piece of paper. 'Mobile numbers. Mine and Doug's. Just, you know…if you need to know where the pickles are or something.' She smiled at Tess then crossed into the kitchen. 'He can have a drink of water and a cup of milk if he wakes up and if he's hungry I've made up a couple of different things to tempt him in the fridge too—he's been off his food.'

Trish opened the fridge and indicated the stacked tower of plastic containers that looked like they could feed a small nation.

'Thanks. I'll try him if he wakes.'

Doug, who had entered the kitchen, rolled his eyes at Tess. 'Is she showing you the food she prepared for the masses?'

The knot of nervous tension eased slightly at Doug's teasing and Tess even laughed.

'We have to go, darling,' he reminded his wife, his arm slipping around Trish's non-existent waist.

Trish looked over at her son and Tess could tell that leaving him when he was sick was a real wrench for her. She remembered how that felt.

'Okay, let's go,' Trish murmured. 'Mum?'

Jean had found a little jug and was watering Trish's indoor plants. 'Yes, dear?'

'Let's go,' she said.

Jean smiled at her daughter. Then she frowned. 'Where are we going?'

'To the hospital. For the scan.' Trish patted her big round belly.

'Oh, yes,' Jean said. 'Splendid. We can drop Tess at work for her shift while we're at it.'

Tess smiled at Jean. 'I've got a day off today so I'm going to stay and look after Christopher.'

Jean looked down at her sleeping grandson. She frowned and looked up at Tess, perplexed. 'What a sweet boy,' she said vaguely.

Trish sighed. 'C'mon, Mum,' she murmured, laying a gentle hand beneath her mother's elbow and ushering her along. She smiled at Tess. 'See you in a couple of hours.'

Tess nodded, then the door closed behind them and then it was just her.

And Christopher.

Tess sat on the edge of the couch opposite Christopher. She felt awkward at first, desperately looking around the room at anything and everything other than him. Art on the walls. A DVD collection. Some bookshelves.

A set of open French doors led out onto a massive deck. Tess could see a tangle of wild, lush greenery from this vantage point and suddenly wished she was out there, digging in Trish's garden, not in here, looking after her most treasured possession.

But she daren't leave him. He looked so still and pale.

She sat back and pulled a book out of her handbag,

determined to distract herself with Fletch's crime novel, which she still hadn't managed to finish.

Or would try to, at least.

But inevitably her gaze was drawn to the sleeping cherub. His little bow mouth, so like Ryan's, clutched at her heart. She dropped her gaze to focus on his chest, watching for the barely perceptible rise and fall, felt the hot spurt of panic as an occasional respiratory pause delayed the onset of the next breath.

Tess shook herself as she realised she was counting Christopher's breaths.

She returned her attention to the book with renewed vigour and for twenty minutes, apart from the odd sneak peek, she managed it. The story finally pulled her in and the only sounds breaking the silence were the fan whirring overhead, magpies warbling in the back yard and the rustle of paper as she turned a page.

Then Christopher stirred. Then he woke and sat up. He took one look at Tess and his bottom lip dropped, his forehead wrinkled.

'Mumma, Mumma,' he called, looking around wildly for Trish.

Tess's heart banged noisily against her ribs as she stood to comfort the child who, for all intents and purposes, was her nephew. 'It's okay, Christopher,' she crooned, approaching him slowly as he started to cry. 'Mummy and Daddy will be home very soon.'

She sat down beside him and he cried louder.

'I know, honey, I know. You're not feeling well, you just want your mummy.' She put her arm tentatively around his skinny little shoulders. They were warm beneath her cool palm. 'She'll be here really soon.'

Then Christopher really lost it. He screwed his face up, which went as red as the rash covering his body, and howled for all he was worth. Within seconds his eyes were streaming and his nose was running and he'd shrugged her hand away.

The poor little guy looked utterly miserable.

She suddenly understood Trish's earlier reticence as the crying child made her feel completely inadequate. Christopher didn't know her. So how could she console him properly? Mild panic set in at the thought that he might cry for the entire time Trish and Doug were away.

No. Think, Tess.

Think!

She'd been a paediatric nurse, for crying out loud. And a mother!

Yes. What would she have done if this had been Ryan? The problem was she'd fought so hard not to think about her son over the years it was as if all that basic maternal intuition had also been suppressed.

Come on, Tess, think!

Distraction.

Yes, distraction.

'Would you like a drink, sweetie?' she asked over the din.

Christopher showed no sign that he'd even heard the question so Tess hurried to the kitchen and retrieved the two plastic sippy cups from the fridge. She sat back down again and offered them to Christopher.

He pushed them both away. 'Are you sure?' Tess asked, offering them again.

Christopher looked at them, then at her, then back at them as his crying died down. He looked at her with red eyes and pointed to the milk. Tess smiled at him and handed it over. He took it on a shuddery indrawn breath and drank half the cup without pause.

'Good boy,' Tess murmured. 'More?'

Christopher went again, slower this time, his huge green eyes never leaving her face. When he'd finished he thrust the cup back at her.

'Are you hungry? Would you like something to eat?'

Christopher shook his head then pointed to the stack of books sitting on the nearby coffee table.

Tess smothered a smile. Christopher obviously knew what he wanted. Ryan had been like that too.

Fletch had called it stubborn. She'd called it decisive.

'You want me to read to you?' He nodded and she picked up the first book. 'This one?' she asked. He shook his head. He shook it four times before one met with his approval. 'You like cars?' she asked as she opened the book.

'Car, car,' Christopher said, nodding his head.

So Tess read it to him. On the first read-through he sat upright beside her, his little legs out in front of him, his ankles just dangling over the edge of the couch cushion. The next time he leaned in closer so his side was jammed against hers. By the third read he'd climbed into her lap.

Tess froze as he snuggled down, making himself at home. She hadn't held a child in a decade and it felt so bitter-sweet. Looking down on his blond head, she had a feeling of déjà vu, like holding Ryan all over again.

She pressed her nose to his hair, feeling the fine down that stuck up at the crown tickle her nose as she inhaled deeply. The sweet little-boy smell lodged in her throat and when he turned his face up to look at her, unshed tears shone in her eyes.

'Car,' he prompted, one little pudgy finger pointing at the words.

Tess bit down on her lip. 'Car,' she murmured, swallowing hard against all the emotion and memories.

Eventually Christopher allowed her to read some other books but after about half an hour he started to feel very warm against her and started to grizzle. Tess felt his forehead.

'Gosh,' she murmured, 'you're burning up.'

She laid him on the lounge and reached for the tympanic thermometer that was also sitting on the coffee table. Christopher lay docilely as she inserted it into his ear canal and waited for it to beep. She read the display and was shocked to see his fever had spiked rapidly—no wonder he was lethargic and looking miserable again.

Trish had said she'd just given him something for the fever before she'd left so that was out as an option to bring the temperature down. Maybe a tepid sponge would help and also be soothing for Christopher.

'It's okay, sweetie. Tess is going to get you something nice and cool. Won't be a moment.'

Tess looked over her shoulder as she scurried towards the kitchen. Christopher lay quietly on the cushion, his gaze tracking her movements. In less than a minute she'd found a glass bowl in a cupboard and filled it with lukewarm water. Under the sink she'd located an unopened packet of dishcloths.

Christopher hadn't moved as she hurried towards him but he was staring now, his gaze not fixed any more. He looked out of it and an itch prickled at the bottom of her spine. She was two paces from him when he let out a little cry and his limbs stiffened.

Tess gasped and dropped the bowl, water spreading over the floorboards, soaking into the rug, as Christopher went into a full-blown seizure.

Tess lunged for the lounge. 'Christopher? Christopher!' she shouted as she threw herself down next to him.

His little body twitched and jerked and her brain came to a complete standstill as terror rendered her utterly useless.

'Christopher,' she whimpered again, not even game to touch him.

Oh, God, oh, God, oh, God!
Don't die, don't die, don't die.

She watched in horror, completely paralysed. She couldn't think what to do. She didn't know how to make him stop.

Some latent part of her brain was screaming at her and it finally made itself heard.

Ambulance.

Tess picked up her phone that she'd put on the coffee table earlier and with useless, trembling fingers somehow managed to dial three zeros. A voice she could barely hear over the roar of her pulse in her head asked her if she wanted police, fire or ambulance, and she knew she was yelling but she just couldn't stop. 'Ambulance, ambulance, ambulance.'

She tried not to think about another time, another call she'd made to triple zero. She'd been an incoherent mess then too.

Another voice came on seconds later. 'I need an ambulance now!' she told the voice frantically. 'My nephew is having a seizure.'

The soothing female voice asked her name and the address. For an awful moment Tess couldn't even remember the number of Trish's house—she just knew which one it was in the street as it had been so long since she'd needed to know. But in a blinding flash she remembered.

'Number sixteen,' she panted. 'Please, please, hurry, you must hurry. He's still fitting.'

The voice told her a car had already been dispatched with lights and sirens but it didn't reassure her. Tess looked down at Christopher, whose stiff, jerky movements continued unabated. How long had it been? Too long. It felt like for ever.

His lips lost their pinkness and Tess wailed into the phone, 'His lips are turning blue.'

'Okay, here's what I want you to do…'

Somehow Tess managed to follow the instructions from the emergency call-taker. Quite how, she wasn't sure. Her fingers were shaking, the roar in her head made it almost impossible to hear and she wanted to throw up. But putting Christopher on the floor and turning him on his side improved his colour even if it didn't stop the seizure.

All stuff that Tess knew but was too panicked to do herself.

'Why isn't it stopping?' she demanded of the woman who had assured Tess repeatedly that she would stay on the phone with her until the ambulance arrived. 'It should be stopped by now.'

As if speaking it had made it so, the jerking reduced to twitching and then stopped altogether. 'It's stopped,' Tess announced victoriously into the phone. 'It's stopped.'

'Okay, that's good,' the calm voice continued in her ear. 'Keep him on his side. He'll be very sleepy for a while. The ambulance is about a minute out.'

Suddenly Tess heard a siren. 'I can hear it!' Her insides practically went to water at the relief that coursed through her system.

'Okay, I'm going to go now. Go and open the door for the paramedics.'

Tess nodded. 'Thank you,' she gasped. 'Thank you so much.' The connection had been momentary but in those awful minutes the stranger's voice had been a lifeline.

Tess pushed the 'end' button then hurried to the front door to greet the paramedics coming in through the front gate.

'This way,' she said. 'The seizure's just stopped.'

The paramedics greeted her as they crossed to a limp-looking Christopher lying on his side on the beautiful Turkish carpet that Tess had admired when she'd first arrived.

It seemed like an age ago now.

They knelt beside him, one in a puddle of water, and Tess apologised profusely. He smiled at her. 'It's okay, it'll dry,' he assured her.

They were hooking Christopher up to a monitor and trying to rouse him when he cried out again, his little limbs stiffening for the second time. 'He's going again,' the female paramedic said.

Tess clamped a hand over her mouth to muffle her wail as she looked on in abject terror. The paramedic kneeling in the water spoke into his radio. 'This is one five three. About to administer midazolam. ETA on the ICP.'

Tess couldn't watch. She just couldn't watch. She needed...she needed Fletch. And, oh, God, she had to tell Trish!

How was she going to tell Trish?

Fletch would tell her. Fletch would know what to do.

She grabbed for her phone as the paramedics worked on Christopher. She turned her back, walked out to the front veranda. She couldn't look. She just couldn't. And he was in better hands with them than he had been with her.

She'd been utterly useless.

She dialled Fletch's number, her hands shaking so hard she had to try three times before she was successful. It went to voice mail. 'Fletch, it's Tess. You need to ring me urgently. Urgently!'

If she'd been in her right mind she wouldn't have left

such an alarming message. Or the five more that followed. But she wasn't.

Another ambulance pulled up and a single paramedic raced into the house. Tess heard them say that Christopher had stopped breathing. That they were going to have to intubate.

A terrible foreboding settled over her. Déjà vu. Ryan all over again.

God! Where was Fletch?

She dialled his number again. 'Fletch! Damn it, ring me!'

She walked back in the house. Christopher had stopped seizing but they had a mask over his face and were puffing air into his lungs. The female paramedic was inserting an IV. The newcomer paramedic looked up at her standing by the door.

'He's stopped breathing. It's probably the drug we used to stop him fitting. It happens sometimes. We're going to put a tube into his lungs to help him breathe.'

Tess nodded. She knew all this, had seen it a hundred times. But this was Ryan.

No. No, wait. She blinked. *Christopher*. It was Christopher.

'Just hurry,' she urged, standing by the door her hands curled into fists. 'Hurry!'

Tess couldn't look away now. She sank to the floor and watched while they put a tube down Christopher's throat, exactly like they'd done with Ryan. Her heart was banging so loudly her whole body seemed to bob to its rhythm. She could hear the blip, blip, blip of Christopher's heart rate on the monitor and almost collapsed on the floor when the intensive care paramedic announced, 'I'm in. Let's get this tube secured so we can scoop and go.'

In five minutes they had Christopher on a trolley and were heading out the door. 'We're taking him to St Rita's. Do you want to come with us in the ambulance?' the female paramedic asked.

Tess wanted to shake her head. Christopher was in safe hands and she wanted to run away. Go straight to the airport and get a ticket back to the UK. Her head felt like it was about to explode. Her heart was being ripped to shreds in her chest.

But she couldn't leave him. He looked small and pale and fragile dwarfed by all the medical equipment and she couldn't leave him alone. She nodded and followed them in a daze. She didn't take her bag or even shut the front door.

Tess sat in the front seat as the ambulance sped away from the kerb, lights and siren on. The intensive care paramedic and the female paramedic—they'd told her their names but she couldn't remember them—were in the back, tending to Christopher.

Her phone rang and the sudden noise was so startling she stared at it for a moment, trying to remember what it was. Fletch's name was flashing on the screen as Tess looked at it and suddenly she realised what she was holding and relief washed through her like a raging tsunami. She pushed the answer button in a rush.

'Fletch?'

'What's wrong?' he asked, his voice frantic after

eight missed calls from Tess with increasingly alarming messages. 'Is it Mum?'

It took a moment for Tess to figure out why Fletch would think something was up with Jean. But, of course, he hadn't known of her plans to look after his nephew. 'No. It's Christopher.'

'Christopher?'

'It's a long story,' she said, suddenly so strung out from an excess of adrenaline she just wanted to curl up in a foetal position somewhere and rock.

'Is that a siren?' Fletch demanded.

Tess ignored him. 'I've been looking after him for a couple of hours while Trish went for her scan. He had a…a convulsion. They gave him midaz… He stopped breathing. They…they t-tubed him, Fletch. We're in an ambulance on our way to St Rita's.'

She swallowed hard as a lump of emotion bigger than the iceberg that sank the Titanic lodged in her throat. 'I'm scared, Fletch.'

Fletch gripped the phone, trying to assimilate what Tess was telling him. She sounded close to hysteria and he shut his eyes, knowing that whatever had happened today Tess wasn't emotionally equipped to deal with it.

'It's going to be okay, Tess,' he assured her, even though he had absolutely no idea what the hell was going on. 'I'm coming downstairs,' he said, already abandoning the computer work he'd been doing and striding out of the unit. 'I'll be waiting for you when you pull in.'

Tess could feel the tight control she'd been keeping

in place slowly unravel as Fletch's calm, soothing voice spoke assurances into her ear.

'Promise?' she demanded. 'Promise you'll be there?'

'I promise.' He paused for a moment. 'Are you okay, Tess?'

Tess shook her head. She was about as far from okay as was physically possible. 'No. But as long as you're there, I will be.' She was surprised to realise just how true that was.

'I'll be there.'

Tess had never heard three more beautiful words in her life.

CHAPTER NINE

FLETCH drummed his fingers impatiently against his thigh as he stood in the ambulance bay, listening to the urgent wail of a siren draw closer and closer.

It couldn't get here soon enough.

His gut churned as worry about Tess's state of mind warred with his fear for Christopher.

What exactly had happened?

He'd left for work a few hours ago and Tess and Jean had been planning on doing some baking, and now he was standing outside the emergency department, waiting for his intubated nephew to arrive in the back of an ambulance with a frantic Tess in tow.

He should have known things had been going too well lately. His mother was content, the study was running smoothly and things with he and Tess were finally…easy.

It was a subtle difference, probably not noticeable to anyone else especially as, from the outside, he doubted anyone would have even noticed that things *hadn't been* easy.

It was just a feeling between them.

Ever since she'd comforted him that night, things had changed between them. The awkwardness that had been there since she'd come back to live with him, which had been exacerbated by the kiss and which they'd ploughed through every day to keep things as normal as possible for Jean, had dissipated.

In all the small ways it felt just like they were married again. Finding mango ice cream in the freezer, putting toothpaste on her toothbrush when he brushed his teeth just like he used to do, a shared memory making them smile.

Even going to bed at night, which had been fraught with anxiety for him, had changed. He didn't wait now for her to be asleep before he came in or get up before she woke. They just got into bed together and went to sleep. Sometimes they talked a bit about their day or discussed Jean, other times they read companionably or she read while he worked on his laptop, but the apprehension was gone.

Or at least it had been.

The siren almost upon him, a portent of doom if ever he'd heard one, was a sign that the dynamic had shifted again. And whatever ground they'd gained was about to be lost.

Maybe for ever.

The siren was killed as the ambulance screamed into the bay. A paramedic jumped from the vehicle and hurried to the back doors, a doctor and a nurse from Emergency joining him there. Fletch headed straight for the front passenger door and opened it. A pale-faced Tess looked down at him with a dazed expression.

'Tess!'

Relief stormed his system. He'd been half-crazy, listening to those increasingly desperate messages. He'd expected her to be a hysterical mess, like she'd been that day with Ryan. Seeing her dry-eyed and relatively calm was a miracle.

It shouldn't be—this was classic Tess after all. Stoic. Controlled. Keeping it all together.

But what she'd just been through would have shaken anyone. Especially someone who'd already been through something this terrible before.

'Are you okay?' he asked as he held out his hand to help her down.

'I don't know what happened,' she said, shaking her head at him as her feet touched the ground. 'He just started fitting.'

Her frightened, confused face grabbed at his gut and an overwhelming urge to protect her coursed through him. He swept her into arms and kissed the top of her head. 'It's fine. He's going to be fine.'

Tess sagged against him, absorbing the heat and the solidity of him. Remembering how good it always felt, how right. 'I didn't know what I was supposed to do, Fletch. I was useless.'

Fletch pulled away slightly, grasping her upper arms, and put his face close to hers so he could make sure she understood what he was about to say. 'You called the ambulance, didn't you?' She nodded, and he acknowledged it with a brisk nod of his own. 'That's what you were supposed to do.'

Tess bit her lip. *She would not cry.* She wouldn't.

'I was so scared it was like…it was like Ryan. All I could see was Ryan lying there. Ryan's blond hair. Ryan's blue lips.'

Fletch pulled her in close again as those images, never far away, rolled through his mind. He'd give anything at this moment to have erased what she'd just been through. No one should have to go through something so shocking twice.

'I'm sorry you had to go through that, Tess. I'm so sorry. But you did good. Trish couldn't have left Ryan in safer hands.'

Tess pulled away from him on a gasp. 'Oh, God, Fletch. Trish! I haven't… I couldn't call her. She doesn't know yet.'

Fletch nodded, already dreading that conversation. 'It's okay, I'll call her. Let's go inside and find out what's happening then I'll call her, okay?'

'Okay.'

She followed him in on autopilot. Into the resus bay where staff swarmed around Christopher, loading him with anti-epileptic drugs and putting in another IV. It looked like chaos but Tess knew that everyone there had a job and that their teamwork would get Christopher through.

Still, she found it hard to breathe. Resus looked the same as it had ten years ago when they'd brought Ryan here, and she couldn't stand it. Flashbacks flared in her head as a doctor fired questions at her just like they had with Ryan.

Yes, a virus. No, she didn't know how long he'd been unwell for. No, she didn't know if he'd ever had a febrile convulsion before. Fletch thought not. Yes, his temp had spiked. No, she didn't know how long he'd had the rash for or how many wet nappies he'd had that day.

They went on and on until there was a roaring so loud in her ears she could barely hear them. She turned to Fletch, who was talking to a colleague, and tugged on his sleeve. 'I can't stay here,' she said. 'I can't…do this. Get me…get me out of here.'

Fletch saw the shadows in her eyes and the tautness around her mouth. 'Come on,' he said, putting his arm around her.

He led her outside. 'Margie, can I use your office?' he asked a middle-aged matronly woman in a nurse's uniform striding by.

Margie narrowed her eyes for a moment but Tess could only assume she must have looked close to a nervous breakdown because the woman didn't hesitate. 'First on the left at the end of the corridor,' she said briskly.

Fletch made a beeline for the office and had Tess ensconced in a chair in twenty seconds flat. He crouched in front of her. 'The consultant thinks it's just fever related and that Christopher decided not to breathe properly after the midaz dose. They're going to wait for him to wake up and then pull the tube.' He placed a hand on her knee and gave it a squeeze. 'He's going to be fine, Tess.'

She nodded. She'd heard the consultant telling Fletch as much. It was just taking a little while to work through the soup that her brain had become.

Fletch frowned. He'd thought she'd be over the moon at the news. 'Tess?'

'Yes.' She nodded. 'I know. That's great.' She smiled at him. 'Really great. It's just a lot to…absorb, you know?'

Yes, he did know. And she was in shock, which probably made it that much harder. 'I'm going to call Trish. Will you be all right in here?'

Tess nodded vigorously. 'Of course. Go, call your sister.' She consulted her watch. 'They must be on their way home by now.'

He was back in ten minutes and Tess looked at him expectantly. 'How is she?'

He shoved his fingers through his hair. 'Pretty frantic. They've just got out of the scan. They're coming straight here. They're only five minutes away.'

Five minutes but Tess knew it would feel like an age to Trish. She knew intimately how her sister-in-law would be feeling. The lead in her belly, the tightness in her chest, the rampant fear knotting every muscle.

The if-onlys.

If only I'd been there. If only I'd cancelled the scan today. If only I'd taken him to the hospital for a second opinion.

Fletch sat beside her and Tess looked at him. 'What are you doing?' she asked.

'I'll wait with you until they get here,' he said.

Tess shook her head. 'No.' She pushed his arm, urging him to get up. 'You can't leave him in there by himself, Fletch.'

'He's surrounded by people, Tess.'

Fletch knew his nephew was in good hands but he didn't have a clue what was going on in Tess's head. He could do nothing for Christopher now—he was being taken care of by experts.

But he could be here for Tess.

She shook her head vigorously. 'Not by people who love him. He's so small, Fletch. He looks so tiny and fragile surrounded by all that…stuff.' She pushed at his arm again. 'You have to be there with him. Don't let him be alone.'

Fletch didn't dare argue. She was breathing hard and there were two bright red spots high on her spare cheekbones. She hadn't wanted to leave Ryan alone either. Not even after he'd been declared dead. She'd sat for ages and just held his hand.

'Okay, Tess,' he said quietly as he stood. 'It's okay, I will. I'll be with him until Trish arrives. Apparently they have Mum…' In all the drama Fletch had temporarily forgotten about his mother. 'So I'll bring her back here to be with you if you don't mind?'

Tess nodded. 'Of course. Just go,' she urged again.

Tess checked her watch every minute for the next fifteen as the four walls pushed in on her. She read the posters for hand washing and a couple of anti-violence ones designed to warn emergency department patients that violence against staff would not be tolerated.

A wall-mounted bookshelf was crammed with thick, heavy textbooks. Some had fallen over and others were leaning drunkenly against each other. The desk was controlled chaos with a lot of paper and a computer displaying a screensaver.

A cork board behind the door had postcards and work photos tacked to it. Smiling nurses and doctors snapped in the middle of their jobs or temporarily acting the fool for the lens.

It looked like a happy work place. Where people liked each other and got along.

But how anybody could deal with the kind of things that came through those doors, things like Christopher—and Ryan—and stay as normal as the snaps suggested was beyond Tess.

They all deserved medals.

Or to have their heads read.

Fletch appeared in the doorway with a worried-looking Jean and a red-eyed Trish. 'Here's Tess,' he said to his mother, injecting a light note into his tone.

'Oh, Tess, there you are.' Jean's voice was light with relief. 'I don't know why we're at the hospital, do you?'

Tess smiled reassuringly at her then looked over Fletch's shoulder to a devastated Trish. She looked like she was close to collapse and it was only Fletch's arm around her waist that was holding her up.

'It's okay, Jean,' Tess said, focusing back on her mother-in-law. 'I'm going to take you home. I think Tabby needs to be walked.'

'Oh, goodness, yes!'

'Just have a seat here for a sec,' Tess said, helping Jean into the chair, 'And we'll be on our way in a jiffy.'

Jean sat down with minimum fuss, which left Tess facing Trish. It was like looking in a mirror. 'How's he doing?' she asked.

'Oh, Tess,' Trish wailed, her face crumpling as she pulled Tess into her arms and gave her a fierce squeeze. 'He looks so small.'

Tess stared over Trish's shoulder at Fletch as his sister purged her emotions. 'I'm sorry,' Tess murmured, hugging her tight. 'I'm so sorry.'

'No,' Trish said, pulling back and wiping at her tears with the backs of her hands. 'This is not your fault, Tess. It was a febrile convulsion. I need to thank you. Thank you for being there. I would have been completely useless.'

Tess shook her head. 'I just called the ambulance.'

Trish nodded. 'Exactly.' She pulled a tissue out of her pocket and blew her nose. 'I know this can't have been easy for you today, Tess. Looking after Christopher was a huge step for you and then to have this happen... it must have bought up a lot of stuff with Ryan that I know you don't like to think about.'

Tess froze at the mention of her son. She'd been trying so hard not to think of him during this whole ordeal but the very essence of him was building inside her, demanding to be let out, and she just couldn't let it.

'It's fine,' she dismissed quickly.

She didn't want to get into this. Not now. Not ever.

Trish shook her head. 'I don't think I could survive if something happened to Christopher. I don't know how you've managed, Tess.'

Tess looked over Trish's shoulder at a grim-looking Fletch. 'Some would say I haven't managed very well at all.'

'Then they don't know what it's like, do they?'

Tess glanced back at her sister-in-law. 'No, they don't.'

Trish sniffled and wiped her nose with the tissue again. 'I have to go…I have to get back to Christopher. Doug's not very good in hospitals. They're transferring Christopher to the PICU where they're hoping they'll be able to take the tube out in a couple of hours.'

Tess nodded. 'Best place for him. Give him a kiss for me.'

'Do you want to… Do you want to come and see him?'

Tess recoiled from the suggestion. Circumstances had dictated that she be part of this nightmare scenario but now it was over, she just wanted to put it away in the same place she put her Ryan stuff.

Deep down and out of reach.

Besides, Jean was getting restless, pacing around the small office and anxiously asking every ten seconds when they could leave.

'Ah, no. I'm going to get Jean home. I think the stress of this environment is increasing her anxiety level and you guys just need to be able to think about Christopher today.'

Trish nodded. 'Take our car,' she said as she reached into her handbag for her set of keys. 'It's parked in the two-minute emergency parking and needs shifting any-way, and it's not like we're going anywhere soon.'

'Thanks,' Tess said, taking the keys.

'I'll follow shortly,' Fletch said.

Tess shook her head. 'No, Fletch, you need to stay with Trish—she needs you now. So does Doug.'

It was such a cowardly thing to set him up for. She couldn't bear to do it herself so she was putting it on him when she knew it had to be just as difficult for Fletch to go into the PICU—as a relative, not a doctor—and sit with his sister while she watched a machine breathe for her little boy.

A little boy that looked remarkably like his own little boy.

It was cowardly to ask him to have to relive the whole nightmare of Ryan again while she fled to the safety of home.

But Trish and Doug shouldn't go through it by themselves either, not when they had someone with a wealth of ICU experience in the family. Not when they'd been such a tower of strength to her and Fletch a decade before.

Trish needed her brother now.

And, yes, she probably needed Tess now too, but Tess had given all she could.

'I'd like you to stay, Fletch,' Trish whispered. 'I'm sorry, I know that's asking a lot.'

Fletch smiled at his sister. 'Of course.' He squeezed her shoulder. 'Whatever you need.'

'Are we going yet?' Jean asked again.

Tess nodded briskly. 'Yes, we're going right now. Come on, let's be off.'

She gave Trish a quick hug, mouthed 'Thank you' to Fletch and then ushered Jean out the door and didn't look back.

'I'm sorry, Fletch,' Trish said as they watched the two women disappear around the corner. 'Will she be okay?'

Fletch grimaced. 'I don't know, Trish. I don't know how much longer she can go on like this, just keeping it all bottled up, keeping it all inside.'

Trish squeezed his hand. 'You still love her, don't you?'

He looked down at his little sister as her words seemed to make sense of the jumble of emotions that had been tangoing inside him since Tess had been back in his life. 'I don't think I ever stopped.'

And the guilt he felt at what he had done all those years ago magnified tenfold.

Tess kept busy when she got back to the apartment.

Busy, busy, busy.

They walked Tabby, baked a double batch of muffins—one for Trish and Doug—and then cooked a huge lasagne for tea, half of which could also go to Trish. They cleaned up the kitchen and watched Jean's television game shows. They took Tabby down again for one last toilet stop before bedtime.

Normally Tess loved the river at this hour of the late afternoon as the shadows turned it an inky velvet and she and Jean and Fletch too, if he was home, would watch it for a long time, chatting about the different boats, and Jean would usually tell a story from her childhood.

But Tess didn't want to indulge in anything that didn't involve brisk activity. The events of the day had stirred up too many memories and if she stood still for too long they might just take over.

When they returned to the apartment Fletch still

wasn't home. Tess felt a spike of worry and pushed it away.

It would be fine. Christopher would be fine.

They ate the lasagne without him, Jean doing him up a plate and covering it with cling film just as she always used to when she'd come to stay with them and he was on shift. Then she washed up.

'Oh look, *Vertigo* is on,' Jean said, pointing to the television as she dried her hands on a tea towel. 'Jimmy Stewart is magnificent in it, don't you think?'

Tess marvelled over the complexities of the human memory and the bizarre progression of a disease like Alzheimer's. Earlier Jean hadn't known what a whisk was but she could remember a film that was over fifty years old.

'Shall we watch it?' Tess asked.

Fletch still hadn't returned by the time the movie faded to black and Jean declared she was off to bed. Tess watched as she and Tabby headed for the bedroom.

Then there was just her, a quiet apartment and the relentless pulse inside her of things she didn't want to think about.

She texted Fletch. *Everything okay?*

He texted back. *Extubated twenty minutes ago. Will be home soon.*

Tess didn't know if she was relieved that he would be coming home soon or not. It was good to know that Christopher had been successfully extubated but it had been a momentous day and she was pretty sure Fletch was going to be physically and mentally exhausted.

She remembered how shattered he'd been that night

after being woken to do the study consent on the immersion. How much worse would he be after hours in the very PICU where his son had died, watching as a machine pumped air into a carbon copy of him?

She took a shower and tried not to think about it. She hummed out loud to keep the images of Christopher and Ryan at bay as they rose and blurred in her head unbidden. She scrubbed at her body vigorously with the towel afterwards, rubbed at her hair so hard the sound of it temporarily obliterated everything else from her head.

Then she heard 'Tess?' and her heart contracted with the force of a sonic boom then tripped along at a crazy clip.

Fletch.

'In here,' she called out. 'Just a sec.'

She looked around the bathroom for something to wear. With Fletch not home yet, she hadn't thought to bring her pyjamas in with her. There were two options—the towel she was using or the T-shirt he'd been wearing to bed, which he'd hung on the towel rack that morning and had left there.

She shied away from the whole idea of the towel. A towel said *I'm naked under here.* A T-shirt said *I'm dressed.*

So she quickly threw it over her head and was immediately surrounded by the very essence of Fletch. That strange mix of aftershave and deodorant and pheromones that all combined to make a wild, heady aroma. She inhaled deeply and her nipples tightened against the fabric, rubbing erotically on the inside where his own naked skin had imprinted.

Dear God! Get a grip.

She'd worn his shirts a hundred times in the past and with what they'd been through today her nipples and his pheromones shouldn't even be registering.

She was just stalling.

And she doubted he'd even notice.

'Hi,' she said as she stepped out of the bathroom, flicking the light out and leaving just her bedside lamp to illuminate the room. He was sitting on his side of the bed, taking his shoes off, his back to her.

'Hi,' he said, turning to look at her. She was in his shirt and a rush of emotion filled his chest. He wanted to lose himself in her so badly at the moment he had to turn away from her lest she see it and run screaming out of the apartment.

'You're wearing my shirt,' he said, for something to say other than *I love you.*

Tess grimaced. *So much for him not noticing.* 'Yes. Sorry. It was…at hand.'

'Don't apologise,' he said. 'My shirts always looked better on you.'

Tess walked around the bed, approaching his side tentatively. She stopped when she was standing in front of him an arm's length away. 'Are you okay?' she asked his downcast head.

He lifted his head and pierced her with his wattle-green eyes. 'What do you think?' he demanded, his voice low.

Tess looked at him. His salt-and-pepper three-day growth looked more salt suddenly, his eyes bloodshot and the lines on his forehead and around his mouth

deeper. His tie was pulled askew, his top button undone and it looked like he'd worn a track in his hair
from constant finger ploughing.

'I'm sorry,' she whispered. 'I just couldn't…I
couldn't stay.'

Fletch reached out a hand and squeezed her forearm, dropping it again straight away. 'I know. You did
enough today…it's fine.'

'Is he okay?'

Fletch nodded. 'Grizzly but curled up in Trish's lap
in a recliner by the bed when I left.'

Tess visibly sagged at the news—she hadn't realised
she'd been holding herself so upright. She knew from
her past PICU experience that it would happen that way
but the whole drama had been too close to home and
deep down she'd been preparing herself for disaster.

'Oh…thank God,' she murmured, clutching a hand
to her breast.

Fletch rubbed a hand through his hair and then
scratched at his chin. It rasped like sandpaper in the
still of the night. 'He's just so much like…Ryan, you
know?' he said, marvelling at how Tess had managed
to keep it together at Trish's today when it must have
been the most horrendous experience for her.

'I just kept seeing him…Ryan. Looking at
Christopher's chest rise and fall and thinking it was
Ryan.'

Tess saw the moisture in his eyes and felt a corresponding moisture in hers. The tears she'd been trying to keep at bay all day—no, all decade—burned for
release. But still she wouldn't let them. She'd already

shed more than her allotted amount since coming to stay with Fletch.

And the tears threatening were world-is-nigh tears and she knew once she'd shed them there was no way back. That part of Ryan would go with them and as much as she tried not to think about him, she wanted to know he'd be there if and when she was ready.

'It was awful,' he murmured.

'I know,' she said, remembering how hard it had been to separate Ryan and Christopher in her own head. 'I know.'

And it seemed like the most natural thing in the world to take a step closer. To step right into the circle of his arms and enfold him in hers.

Fletch shut his eyes as she fitted against him. She cradled his head against the soft part where neck met shoulder, and he inhaled the scent of her. Her shampoo and her perfume and the strange heady mix of his shirt on her skin. He drew her close and just absorbed her.

He felt the kiss at his temple first. It was so light he didn't even realise for a moment. But his mouth must have because his lips were nuzzling her neck and then her fingers were in his hair and his hand was sliding down her back and she moaned in his ear as his hand skimmed her bare skin where buttock met thigh.

He pulled back, one hand clamped on the back of her leg, the other firmly on her opposite hip. His heart banged against his ribs as desire ran thick and undiluted to every nerve in his body.

'Tess?'

Tess read his question loud and clear and knew the

answer even before he'd asked it. She could already feel the taint of the day sliding away with her inhibitions. The memories of Christopher and Ryan and ambulances and hospitals fading with every fan of his breath on her neck.

She couldn't remember a time when she'd needed him more.

CHAPTER TEN

'MAKE love to me,' she whispered.

Fletch drew in a shuddery breath at her request. That he could do—loving her had always been easy.

Loving her had never gone away.

He tilted his head, his gaze zeroing in on her mouth. The flesh of her thigh was hot and pliant beneath his palm and he squeezed. A tiny, almost imperceptible gurgle at the back of her throat went straight to his groin and his breath stuttered out between them.

He opened his palm and traced the inside of her thigh with his fingertips. He watched as she shivered and her eyes widened before fluttering closed. His fingers traced higher, over the sweet curve of a naked buttock, into the dip that formed the small of her back, across to the bony prominence of her hip.

Tess sucked in a breath. 'Fletch,' she murmured, opening her eyes.

Their gazes meshed as his fingers trailed upwards. The curve of her waist, the bumps of her spine, the fan of her ribs. Each slow, lazy stroke ruching his shirt ever northward.

Tess bit her lip as cool air caressed bare, heated flesh from her waist down. It pricked at her skin, leaving thousands of goose-bumps and two erect nipples in its wake.

'Lift your arms,' he whispered against her mouth.

She clutched his shoulder at his husky command. Long-forgotten muscles clenched deep inside. Then she did his bidding, slowly raising her arms above her head, her gaze never leaving his.

Fletch swallowed at the directness in her gaze and her complete compliance with his command. His palms skimmed up her sides, hooking his T-shirt as they went, past the swell of her breasts, up over her shoulders and finally over her head.

His breath hissed out as she stood between his legs totally naked.

He dropped his gaze to look at her. She was different now. Thinner, less round, her breasts smaller, her bones more prominent. But there was still a slight curve to her hips and her waist still dipped and her breasts were still dominated by large areolas that had deepened to mocha during her pregnancy and were as fascinating tonight as they'd always been. He swallowed, just anticipating taking them into his mouth.

He dropped a kiss at the hollow at the base of her throat and whispered, 'Tess,' against her neck, his erection straining painfully against the confines of his trousers. 'My Tess.'

Tess shut her eyes as his lips moved along a collar bone and his palms stroked up and down her back, urging her closer.

She *was* his Tess. Had *always* been his Tess.

He turned his head and made for the other collar bone and she whimpered as his hot tongue lapped at her skin like she was dusted with honey. Fletch pulled back, already breathing too hard as the aroma of her swirled around him in an intoxicating haze.

A trail of glistening skin shone in the lamplight where he'd laved her collar bones but her mouth, so tantalisingly close, looked parched in comparison. He claimed it then, biting back on a groan as she instantly granted him the entry he craved. His tongue plunged inside then flicked over her lips, desperate to also make them moist with his possession.

His hands slid down to her smooth bare bottom, pulling her pelvis into the cradle of his. One hand moved lower, stroking down the backs of her thighs, the other moved higher, seeking the fulfilment only a round female breast could offer.

Years ago one of her breasts would have spilled out of his palm but now it fit perfectly, the hard nub in the middle scraping erotically against the dead centre. He squeezed it and she whimpered. He flicked his thumb over the tightly ruched nipple and she cried out, breaking their lip lock.

'Fletch,' she moaned.

Fletch felt her fingers plough into his hair as he kissed down her neck, homing in on his target. His mouth salivated at the feast that awaited. His hand at the back of her thigh moved up swiftly to her other breast and by the time his mouth had closed over her nipple his fingers had claimed the other.

Tess gasped, her knees buckling slightly. She felt his arm tighten around her waist as she clasped his head to her chest. Partly to stay upright, partly because she *did not want him to stop*. The heat and the pull of his mouth as he paid homage to her breasts was turning everything liquid.

Her head spun as he continued to use his mouth and tongue on nipples so aroused she wanted to throw her head back and howl her pleasure. She dropped a hand to his shoulder to steady herself, her palm instantly lamenting the feel of thick starched fabric instead of hot male skin.

She opened her eyes, suddenly aware that whilst she was buck naked, he was still fully clothed.

That wouldn't do. It wouldn't do at all.

She groped for his buttons, her eyes rolling back as he switched attention from one nipple to the other, taking it from cool and puckered to hot and hard in a second as he sucked it deep into his throat.

Her fingers fumbled and somehow found his loosened tie despite the havoc he was creating. She only just managed to strip it out from his collar as his teeth grazed the sensitive tip in his mouth and she lost all coherent thought for a beat or two.

Determined to plough on whatever the provocation, Tess straddled his lap and started in on his buttons, pleased to hear a guttural groan escape his mouth as she rocked herself into him. He released the nipple he was torturing, placing his forehead against her chest and breathing hard as he grabbed her hips and held here there.

She smiled then slowly pushed at his shoulders until he was lying back on the mattress and she had him at her total mercy. His eyes, smoky with desire, glittered up at her as she rotated her pelvis again and he swore under his breath, his fingers gripping her hips hard.

She marvelled that ten years of abstinence hadn't dulled her sexual instincts. But, then, it had always been instinctive with Fletch. There'd been guys before him but they'd always been such hard work. With Fletch it had been easy.

So very, very easy.

Still, she'd have thought she'd be nervous about having sex again after such a long dry stretch. Or that she might even have forgotten how. But towering over Fletch's reclined form, she knew that her body knew what to do.

And she knew it was going to be better than ever.

Tess leaned forward slightly, her gaze locking with his as she reached for his first button. It popped easily and she lowered her mouth to where it had been and pressed a kiss there. She repeated the process with each button until they were all undone and his shirt had fallen open.

Fletch let out his breath on a hiss as she sat up to admire her handiwork and her breasts bobbed enticingly. Once upon a time her long hair would have flowed down her front and covered them and he liked it that they were free to his gaze. He reached up and traced a finger from her collar bone to the tip of a rapidly hardening nipple and repeated it on the other side.

She arched her back and thrust her hips forward a

little, and he curled up to claim her mouth because he doubted she had a clue how provocative she looked, straddling him stark naked, her breasts thrust out, while he was practically still fully clothed. She whimpered against his mouth, opening to the insistent thrust of his tongue and the bruising crush of his lips as he ground his pelvis into hers.

Tess could barely breathe as the onslaught of Fletch's out-of-control kiss sucked away all her oxygen. She desperately dragged in air through her nostrils as she rode the wild bucking of his hips.

'Tess,' he groaned against her mouth.

Tess could feel the hard length of him rubbing against the centre of her splayed thighs and she wanted more. She wanted him naked and inside her. She didn't want the barrier of two layers of fabric and a metal zipper. She wanted him thick and hard and proud the way she remembered him in dreams she couldn't always quell. She wanted to feel him in her hand. She wanted to relish every inch of him as he entered her and took her to a place far, far away from this world where they just didn't do things like this.

She broke away from his mouth, pushing him back again, more urgently this time. She looked down at his erection clearly outlined beneath the taut pull of fabric. She reached for it, walked her fingers up it, walked them back down.

'Tess.'

The growl was deep and low, stroking deep and low inside her as he looked at her from beneath half-shuttered eyelids.

She heeded his warning, quickly unbuckling his belt, popping the button and peeling back his zip. The opening of metal teeth was loud in a room where the only other noise was the rasp of breath.

One glimpse of the long hard length of him and she was pushing aside the flaps of his fly and grasping him still encased in his underwear. Her insides clenched and she rocked against him, a completely involuntary movement.

Fletch shut his eyes on a groan as she rubbed herself against his thigh while she stroked his thickness and then impatiently broke through the last barrier to put her hand around him, skin on skin. He cried out as the muscles in his groin and belly and deep inside his buttocks shuddered.

He vaulted up again, his hands sliding to her breasts, his mouth slamming into hers, their tongues thrusting as their hips rocked to a rhythm pounding simultaneously through both of their bloodstreams and she milked the length of him.

Fletch couldn't bear it a moment longer. It had been so long and he'd dreamed of them coming together again too many lonely nights to count. He grasped her thighs and tumbled her to the side, rolling on top of her in one easy movement.

'I need you,' he muttered against her neck.

'I'm yours,' she whispered straight into his ear.

Fletch felt everything stutter to a halt. He shut his eyes as the familiarity of the words slugged him right between the eyes. He felt her mouth at his neck and her hand pushing beneath the loosened waistband of his trousers, sliding beneath his jocks to grasp his buttocks, but everything inside him had turned cold.

The words played in his head over and over. A different place. A different time.

A different woman.

He saying, *I need you*. She saying, *I'm yours*.

It was like a blast of arctic air in his face. *He couldn't do it*. He couldn't go ahead with it. Because he knew with a certainty that came from deep in his bones that he loved Tess and he wanted more than this, more than one night.

He wanted every night.

He wanted his wife back.

But there were things that had to be said first.

It took a moment or two for Tess to realise that Fletch wasn't responding when she pressed her mouth to his. She pulled back. 'Fletch?'

Fletch looked down at her, a frown knitting her brows together. 'I'm sorry...' He dropped his head on her chest, giving himself a moment to take stock. 'I can't do this...' he said.

His voice was muffled but Tess could sense his withdrawal in every muscle of his body.

No, no, no. She mewed her disappointment as Fletch pushed himself away from her. *She needed this, damn it!*

Fletch's hands trembled as he gripped the side of the mattress, keeping his back to her. He tucked himself away with difficulty, pulling up the zip over his bulge, feeling instantly uncomfortable. His fingers shook as he did up a couple of buttons to cover his chest. He bent down and retrieved her shirt, *his shirt*, from the floor, dropping it behind him without looking.

The shirt landed on her belly, cold against her heated flesh, and Tess just stared at it for a moment. Her blood was still thrumming thick and sludgy through every cell in her body, rendering her completely useless.

'There's something you need to know,' he said, staring out at the darkness beyond his floor-to-ceiling windows.

Tess blinked at his back as a sense of foreboding pushed the sticky remnants of desire violently aside. She scrambled upright, throwing the shirt over her head, then wriggled off the bed to stand in front of him. 'Whatever it is, I don't want to know,' she said.

Because it didn't take a genius to figure out this was something to do with Ryan. She didn't want to talk about Ryan. Surely he knew that by now? She didn't want to think about him or reminisce about him. She didn't even want to say his name.

Didn't he realise how much it hurt to even say his name?

Fletch almost gave up. But that was what he'd always done with her because her grief and her guilt had been so great he'd tried to make everything else easy for her. He'd let her avoid and deny and shut things out because she'd asked him to and he'd been at a loss as to how to help her.

Well, not any more.

He wanted something real with her. Warts and all. It meant making some hard decisions but he was finally going to fight for her instead of letting her slip away again. 'I need to talk about this.'

Tess crossed her arms. 'Damn it, Fletch, why do you think we're on your bed, making out like teenagers? Especially after today? So we don't have to talk.'

He shook his head. 'I don't believe you, Tess. You want more than that.'

'No,' she denied.

Fletch felt a wellspring of frustration and anger bubble up inside him at her stonewalling. 'Well, if all you wanted was for me to *screw* you then why did you ask me to make love to you?'

Tess blinked at his profanity. 'I guess because asking you to *screw* me was just a little too crass,' she hissed.

'Well, at least I would have known where I stood,' he snapped.

'Oh, come on, Fletch. You can't tell me you weren't trying to forget about today just a little bit too.'

Fletch snorted. He stood and stalked passed her, stopping in front of the windows, his reflection staring grimly back at him. *God, he looked like hell.*

He turned his back on it. 'I was doing what you asked me to do, Tess. I was *making love* to you.'

They stared at each other for long moments, their chests rising and falling rapidly, this time in anger.

Fletch ran a hand through his hair. 'It's not about Ryan,' he said. 'Not directly anyway.'

Because they both knew that everything in their lives since Ryan had always stemmed from Ryan.

'Don't, Fletch. Please, don't.'

He heard the plea in her voice and knew it would be

so easy not to tell her. To take the coward's way out. He'd decided nine years ago to keep it to himself—why not just stick to it?

Because their relationship nine years ago had been a train wreck and he couldn't go there again.

He wanted to be with her, he wanted to make love to her.

But he couldn't make love to her with this on his conscience.

It's why he'd walked away all those years ago without a fight.

They had a lot of work to do with their relationship. A lot of honesty and dealing with their unresolved grief and unspoken feelings around Ryan. There was going to be a lot of soul-searching and it demanded total honesty.

And that had to start now.

Fletch knew it was the only way they could build a relationship that could survive and thrive the second time around. And if he had to drag her kicking and screaming along with him, he would.

Because he knew deep down that she still loved him too.

And this time he was fighting for that love.

'I'll give you fair warning. I'm not just going to let you disappear out of my life again, Tess.'

Tess blinked at his audacity. 'You don't get a say, Fletch. I'm leaving here and going back to England as soon as Trish is home from hospital.'

Fletch ignored her. He'd move heaven and earth to keep her with him and with several weeks left before Trish was due, he had time on his side.

There would be no more playing it her way.

'Before we can go forward, there's something you need to know first.'

Tess glared at him. 'There is no forward, Fletch.'

He ignored her. 'There was a woman…'

The four words free-fell into the space between them and seem to stay suspended, hovering there for an age.

When they finally landed Tess felt each one slam like a bullet straight through her heart.

Fletch had…cheated on her? 'Do you mean you—?'

'Yes,' he said, cutting her off because he couldn't bear to hear her utter his transgression aloud.

Tess stared at him. She'd known on some level just how messed up she was and that she'd been closed off and shut down and it was not fair to Fletch, but she'd never have thought in a million years he would find someone else.

Her faith in his fidelity had always been rock solid.

Fletch's stomach clenched at the look of shock on her face. She was looking at him like she had that day after the ambulance had whisked Ryan away. He wanted to reach out to her but knew her well enough to know that it wasn't the right time.

'It was at the intensive care conference I went to the weekend before we split up,' he continued, his hands shaking, his voice husky. 'She was in the bar late on the Saturday night. I couldn't sleep. She smiled at me, we talked for a while…' He shook his head. 'It was just the once… Hell, I don't even know her name. I left her room straight away afterwards, but…' he shook his head '…I couldn't believe I'd done it. Knew I'd never forgive myself. Knew that we were over…that I'd signed our marital death warrant. So when I came home on Sunday night and you asked me for a divorce, I agreed.'

Tess remembered that weekend. Remembered the overwhelming sense of relief as he'd left, knowing she didn't have to look at him for forty-eight hours. The sudden realisation that their marriage was over. That they'd drifted too far apart.

She remembered him coming home from the conference that Sunday evening. *How could she not?* Asking for a divorce had been her first act of courage in a year.

She also remembered his lack of fight. Remembered being surprised by it even as she'd rejoiced in his capitulation.

But she hadn't demanded to know why, had just accepted it at face value, knowing she could move on in her own way, in her own time. No more listening to him talk about Ryan and what had happened, ad nauseam. No more analysis of every single detail. No more requests for her to go to counselling.

It had been a green light to deal with things her way and she'd embraced the end of her marriage as a way to begin again—far away from everything that hurt so much.

And things had been just fine—until now.

Now she had to face the fact that her husband had picked up some woman in a hotel bar while she'd been at home grieving for their son.

'Why are you telling me this?' she asked him, shaking her head as the knowledge hurt much, much more than she expected. 'Why didn't you just keep it to yourself?'

'I can't, Tess. I love you and I want you back. And this is something that's been eating at me, would continue to eat at me. It would erode any chance we had for the future.'

'So you get to feel better and unburdened and I get to feel like shit?' She lunged forward and pushed him hard in the chest. 'Gee, Fletch, thanks a lot!' She glared at him wild-eyed. 'I don't even get an orgasm to take the sting out of it!'

Fletch took a step back as his body absorbed her shove. 'I'm sorry. I'm so sorry, Tess. But would you rather we'd had sex and then I told you?'

Tess looked at him, flabbergasted. 'I'd rather you hadn't done it in the first place, you lousy, cheating bastard!' she hissed, conscious of Jean sleeping down the hall. 'Then, yes, I'd have preferred you'd kept it to yourself.'

Fletch snorted. 'Do you know most wives would have demanded to know why I did it, not why I told?'

'Well, I guess you already knew I'm not like most wives!'

He shook his head. 'You're not even curious?'

'I'm assuming that one year without sex was your personal limit and seeing as you weren't getting it from me, you got it where you could.'

Fletch's hands curled into fists as he almost roared out loud at the unfairness of her assessment. *She didn't have a clue*. Not a single clue. He turned away from her, planting his fists up high on the windows, hanging his head, fighting for control.

'Hell, Tess,' he said after a long moment or two. 'It wasn't about the sex.'

Tess turned so she was looking at his back. 'So it was love?' she scoffed, her voice ripe with sarcasm.

He waited until his temper was truly in check before he turned around again. He placed his hands behind his back and lounged against the glass, trapping them there.

'It wasn't about sex or love, Tess, it was about affection. She looked at me like I was a man,' he said in a low voice. 'An interesting man. An attractive, interesting man with interesting things to say. Not as a grieving father. Or an inadequate husband. She didn't look at me like I'd let her down. Like I'd failed her. Like I'd killed her child.'

Tess gasped, wrapping her arms around her body to fend off his shocking words. 'I didn't do that, Fletch.'

'She didn't flinch when I touched her, Tess,' he continued ignoring her protestation. 'She looked at me, *at me*, Tess. Not at what I *hadn't* done but what I could do.'

He shifted, bringing his arms up to cross his chest. 'It's not an excuse for my behaviour. I was weak and it was wrong and I've regretted it every day since. And I'm sorry that you'd rather not know about it, but I want to start anew with you, Tess. We've spent all this time avoiding the hard stuff—second time round it has to be warts and all.'

Tess couldn't even begin to assess the revelations that had just occurred. Knowing that Fletch had indulged in a one-night stand was mind-blowing. Hearing his reasons had been shocking.

Confessing that he wanted her back was just way too much altogether.

It was too much. It was all too much.

She was trembling but she wasn't sure if it was from anger or shock.

She dropped her arms. 'I'm sorry too, Fletch,' she murmured, then turned away from him and headed for the walk-in wardrobe.

'What are you doing?' he asked as he watched her disappear inside.

Tess grabbed the overnight bag that she'd arrived with just over a month ago. 'I'm packing,' she said.

Fletch frowned. He pushed off the glass and strode briskly to the large open cupboard space. She was emptying the drawers he'd cleaned out for her. Grabbing her few paltry belongings off hangers.

He folded his arms. 'I thought you were staying until Trish had the baby.'

Tess steeled herself against the guilt of her broken promise. Fletch's family was not her family.

Not now. Not for a long time.

'Nope. Not any more.'

Fletch heard the finality in her voice and realised she was serious. 'Tess, don't,' he said, shoving his hands in his pockets. 'This is crazy. What about Mum? You promised you'd stay.'

Tess hardened her heart. 'That was before your little revelation tonight.'

She zipped up the bag with a vicious flick of her

wrist, dragging it past him and throwing it on the bed. She went into the bathroom, clothes in hand, and threw them on. As usual she didn't bother with any make-up and she refused to look in the mirror as she gathered her paltry toiletry supplies.

She felt like she was about to shatter into a thousand pieces and she didn't want to see what that looked like. She'd made a habit of avoiding mirrors this last ten years—tonight would not be a good time to start. Her heart was pounding and her ears were ringing when she strode out two minutes later.

'Where are you going?' he demanded. 'It's the middle of the night.'

'To the airport,' she said, more calmly than she felt.

She knew she had to go now. If she waited until the morning, when both Jean and Tabby were looking at her with their big eyes, she'd knew she'd cave in.

Much easier to look into the eyes of an adulterer and walk away.

Fletch wondered if he hadn't maybe tipped her over the edge. She looked so calm and yet was acting so crazy. 'You haven't even got a flight booked,' he reasoned.

'I have a credit card.' She shrugged, picking up her watch from the bedside table and slipping it on. 'I'll get on the first airline with a flight out to London.' She shoved her feet into her shoes by the bed and grabbed her bag.

'Tess.' He put a stilling hand on her arm. 'Please, don't go. Don't run like you always do. Stay and help me work it out.'

Tess looked down at his hand. 'Don't touch me,' she warned. 'Don't you ever touch me again.'

And then she turned on her heel and marched away and she didn't look back and she didn't stop until she got to the safety of her car, where she locked all the doors and burst into tears.

CHAPTER ELEVEN

Six weeks later Tess was just about cried out—talk about the straw that broke the camel's back!

She'd cried big, fat, silent tears for twenty-four hours solid on her plane trip home. The air hostesses had been so concerned about her that three of them had surrounded her outside the loos about four hours into the flight and asked her what was wrong.

'My husband cheated on me,' she'd told them, because it had been easier than the whole truth and it had hurt too much to keep it inside any longer.

Before she'd known it and in a startling display of female solidarity, she'd been whisked into business class for a little more privacy. Silent tears had rolled down her face as she'd thanked them.

She'd cried louder tears in her car, hurtling down the motorway towards Devon. She'd cried herself to sleep, she cried when she woke up and she cried at work. Hell, she'd even cried at the supermarket yesterday when a baby sitting in a trolley had smiled a dribbly smile at her.

She doubted she'd ever cried this much in her life. Not even in those first two months after Ryan had died.

Even sitting here right now snuggled in her pink polar fleece dressing gown in front of her fire on a chilly November night cradling a photo of Ryan in her lap, she could feel the tears pricking at her eyes again.

She shut them. 'Please, no,' she whispered. 'No more.'

The phone rang and her eyes flew open. The muscles in her neck tensed as they'd formed the habit of doing every time it rang since she'd returned home. Her answering machine was full of messages from Fletch, who had taken to ringing several times a day for the first couple of weeks.

Wanting to talk. Wanting her to understand. Wanting her to come back.

The last time had been two weeks ago when he'd rung to tell her that Trish had given birth to a bouncing baby girl and he was an uncle again. Her heart had swelled with joy and happiness for Trish. She'd been standing right beside the phone, listening to the message as he'd left it, and she'd almost picked it up that time to share the occasion with him.

But she'd gone to bed and cried instead.

The answering machine clicked in and the tension oozed from her muscles as old Dulcie Frobisher, the secretary of the historical society, informed her she was sending Peter around with some jam she'd made because she knew how much Tess enjoyed it.

Tess rolled her eyes at the message, knowing that Dulcie also thought that her great-nephew, who after years of frustrating bachelorhood had finally come out of the closet three months ago, just needed the love of a good woman and that Tess, being practically the only single woman in town in his age bracket, filled that criterion.

Tess was used to well-intentioned villagers trying to fix her up with their sons, grandsons, nephews and widowed neighbours.

She looked down at her wedding ring, which seemed to mock her in the firelight. It may have been a force field to keep men at bay but she'd always believed in what it had represented.

Love, commitment, fidelity.

A knock interrupted her thoughts and she gave an inward groan. Dulcie must have nagged the poor man into action immediately because she just didn't get visitors at eight o'clock at night. She grimaced as she stood, mentally preparing herself for the encounter. She flipped on the outside light as she pulled open the door.

'Hi, Tess,' Pete said apologetically, holding out three jars of jam.

'Hi, Pete, thanks. Dulcie just called.' She took the jars from him. 'Do you want to come in?' she asked, hoping sincerely that he didn't.

He shook his head. 'No, I'd better get back. I have some pots firing.'

But he seemed reluctant to leave so she asked, 'How are things?'

'About the same.' He sighed.

'You know, you really need to go and live in London for a while, Pete,' she said gently. 'Gay men are pretty thin on the ground in this neck of the woods.'

He nodded glumly. 'I know. But I can't leave Dulcie.

Or the art gallery. And I'm sure I'm way too country bumpkin for the big smoke.'

Tess put her hand on his arm. 'You're a nice man, Pete, and very nice-looking to boot. You're smart and articulate and arty. Any man would be lucky to have you.'

Pete gave a half-laugh. 'You're good for my ego, Tess,' he said as he leaned in to kiss her on the cheek and sweep her into a hug.

It felt good to relax in a man's arms with no expectations and she hung on for a little longer than she normally would until a sudden harsh cough behind them had them both leaping apart guiltily.

It was Fletch.

Standing on her garden path, his strong, beautiful jaw clenched tight, his hands jammed in the pockets of a warm, heavy coat.

He looked from Pete to Tess then back to Pete again.

'Hello, Tess.'

Tess blinked. 'Fletcher?'

Fletch threw a steely glare towards Peter. 'Yes.'

'What are you doing here?' she asked dazedly.

'We need to talk,' he said tersely, his gaze not leaving the other man.

Peter took one look at the magnificent, tight-lipped guy staring him down and concluded that if this was a London man, then he truly did need to get there pronto. 'Is everything okay?' he asked Tess, dragging his eyes away from the stranger. 'Do you want me to stay?'

Tess could see Fletch bristling and came out of her daze, stepping in before things got any more tense. She introduced the two men—Fletch as her ex-husband and

Peter as a jam-bearing friend—and assured a rather disappointed Peter she'd be fine.

She saw Fletch through Peter's eyes and sympathised. He cut a dashing figure in his heavy wool coat, which only seemed to emphasise the power of his chest, the breadth of his shoulders. The alcove light caught the streaks of grey at his temples that had been tousled to salon perfection by the brisk November breeze. The three-day growth looked shaggy and touchable. He looked tired. But solid and warm and sexy.

Very, very sexy.

'Tell Dulcie I'll ring her tomorrow,' Tess said as Peter turned to go.

Fletch watched the man retreat down the path and out the gate, giving Tess a wave as he turned left down the street. Even though he was obviously gay, Fletch felt a spike of jealousy. He didn't want *any* man's hands around her unless they were his!

He turned back and looked at her, capturing her gaze. She looked so good in her pink polar fleece he wanted to sweep her up in his arms and bury his face in it. But it was freezing out here and there were things to say.

'Can I come in?'

This was not the way that Tess had expected her day would finish up. She didn't usually hug gay men on her doorstep or have her ex-husband turn up out of the blue.

But, then, not a lot had been normal lately.

'Sure,' she said, standing aside.

He brushed past her, ducking his head to fit under her low cottage doorway, and every cell in her body went onto high alert. He shrugged out of his coat to reveal charcoal slacks and a round-necked, fine-knit sweater in navy blue, which clung to every muscle in his chest, and those same recalcitrant cells went into overdrive.

But the full lights inside accentuated rather than softened the lines around his eyes and mouth and he looked every day of his forty years.

'You look awful,' she said.

'Thank you.' He grimaced as the cosy atmosphere wrapped him in a big warm hug even if her observation hadn't. 'Don't suppose you have proper coffee? I've just got off possibly the longest transpacific flight in living human memory with a grizzly baby behind me and a man who sounded like he had whooping cough in front of me.'

Tess smiled despite her state of confusion. 'Sure,' she said again, and headed for the kitchen. She made them both a cup while Fletch watched her with brooding silvery-green eyes.

She passed him a steaming mug and led him over to the lounge area where a three-seater couch and a coffee table stood a safe distance away from the glowing fireplace.

She sat at one end and he at the other. 'How's Trish and the baby?' she asked, because it was easier to start with the inane stuff.

Fletch took a reviving sip of coffee, shutting his eyes as the caffeine buzzed into his system. 'Great. She went into labour at thirty-six weeks but the obstetrician was happy with that.'

He fished around in his trouser pocket and pulled out

his phone. He touched the screen a few times and pulled up the pictures of baby Katrina and handed it to Tess.

Tess swiped her finger across the screen, smiling at the pics of Trish and Doug and their daughter. One of Christopher holding his sister very carefully scrolled up and Tess felt her heart contract.

'You can tell they're brother and sister,' she murmured as Katrina's two cowlicks became more evident next to her brother's. 'Christopher looks no worse for wear,' she mused, examining his sweet little face for signs of long-term damage.

Tess had learned from one of Fletch's many phone messages that Christopher had been discharged from hospital two days after his seizure and that nothing had turned up on any of the investigations the hospital had run.

'Oh, yeah.' Fletch smiled. 'Back to normal.'

The next one that scrolled up was of Fletch holding his little niece. He was smiling but she knew him well enough to see that it didn't reach his eyes.

He'd always wanted a daughter.

Then it was Jean's turn. She looked fit and happy but Tess could tell from her eyes that she didn't feel any kind of connection with the little bundle in her arms. Not like the hundreds of pictures they'd had of Jean holding Ryan as a newborn, where her love and pride and awe had shone from her eyes like a beacon.

'How's your mum?' Tess asked, touching Jean's cheek with her finger.

'She's okay, I guess. Not as settled as when you were there, although Tabby has helped enormously.'

Tess could tell that Fletch was trying to keep the accusation out of his voice. 'I'm sorry,' she said, looking up at him, 'for leaving you in the lurch.'

Fletch shrugged. He couldn't really blame her. 'I managed.' It had been a huge juggling act but somehow he'd got through the last six weeks. 'She went back with Trish yesterday. Or…' he looked at his watch '…the day before…whatever the time is now.'

Tess gave a half-smile. Jet-lag and time zones always left her at sixes and sevens. She handed him back his phone and they sat and watched the fire without saying anything for a minute.

'I'm sorry too,' Fletch said. 'For a lot of things, but especially for not coming sooner. I wanted to follow you… I would have followed you but…'

Tess nodded. She'd flown to the other side of the world because running away was what she did best but part of it was also about knowing he was stuck at home with Jean and couldn't follow.

But he was here now.

He'd come after her this time.

Last time she'd asked him to leave her alone and he had. This time he'd come anyway.

Fletch put his mug down on the coffee table, feeling the boost of the caffeine bolster his nerve. He'd made a vow that he wouldn't come back to Australia until Tess was with him, and the time to make his pitch was now.

He noticed a face-down photo frame near where he placed his mug and he picked it up and turned it over. A close-up of Ryan stared back at him, his green eyes sparkling. Not even a party hat at a jaunty angle was able to disguise how his blond hair stuck up on top from that impossible double cowlick.

He'd taken the picture at Ryan's first birthday party.

He looked at Tess, surprised—she'd taken all the photos of Ryan down two months after he'd died, declaring she just couldn't look at them any more.

It had been as if he'd never existed.

'Reminiscing?'

She nodded. 'I've been looking at that picture for six weeks. It doesn't hurt to look at it any more.'

'That's good,' he said tentatively, encouraged that Tess finally seemed to be facing things instead of locking them all away.

Had their argument the night she'd left been the catalyst?

Tess looked into the depths of her milky coffee. 'You never blamed me,' she murmured. Then she looked at him. 'Not once.'

Fletch frowned then scooted to the middle cushion, folding one leg under him till he was turned side on in the lounge. He placed a hand on her arm. 'It wasn't your fault, Tess.'

She shook her head as tears welled in her eyes and rolled down her cheeks. 'I fell asleep, Fletch. I was supposed to be watching him and I fell asleep.'

Fletch had finished a run of five night duties and had been sleeping in the bedroom. Normally Tess would have had Ryan outside to keep him quiet for Fletch or even taken him out, but it had rained quite heavily overnight and had still been drizzling that morning. And she'd felt too ill herself to go anywhere. So she'd set him up with a DVD on low and his building blocks on the lounge-room floor. At some stage she'd drifted off sitting upright in the lounge chair as she'd watched over him.

'Tess, you'd been up all night with him, teething. You'd had only marginally more sleep than me for the three previous nights and you had a really bad migraine that you'd taken something for. You were exhausted.'

Fletch had offered to stay up with Ryan for a few hours while Tess had got some sleep but she had assured him she'd be fine and he *had* been very grateful. He'd been so tired he hadn't been able to see straight.

Normally in that kind of situation they would have had Jean come and look after Ryan but she'd been going off to the coast for the day so they'd decided they'd tag-team and manage between the two of them.

'He was shut in the lounge room with you,' Fletch continued. 'You had no reason not to think he was safe. If *I'd* fixed the dicky latch on the door you'd been nagging me to do for a week, he wouldn't have been able to get out.'

Tess shook her head, wiping at the tears. 'I should have turned the bucket over the day before. Put it away like I always did.'

Tess had been playing with Ryan the afternoon before in the sand pit. She'd pulled the deep bucket out of the shed because Ryan had loved to fill it with sand. But because his clumsy toddling kept knocking it over and he was becoming frustrated, she'd dug it into the sand a bit and wedged it into the angle of wooden framework to stabilise it.

And then the phone had rung and they'd raced to answer it so it wouldn't wake Fletch but it had and they'd all had some family time together before Fletch had gone off to work again and she'd forgotten all about the bucket in the sand pit.

'Tess, you weren't to know it was going to pour down with rain that night. It was an accident, Tess, a freak accident. A freak set of circumstances. Don't you see we can go back and forth for ever like this? You shouldn't have fallen asleep. I should have fixed the door. We should have put the bucket away. I should have done a better resus job.'

He cupped her cheek and swiped at a tear with his thumb. 'At some stage we've got to forgive ourselves.'

Tess raised her hand to cover his. 'He died, Fletcher. Our little boy died.' She looked into his eyes. 'I keep wishing I could go back to that day and change just one thing, you know?' she implored him. 'I'd stay awake. Because then none of that other stuff matters—if I had been watching him, everything else would be moot.'

Fletch couldn't bear the pain in her amber eyes. He would have given anything to take it from her. But he knew that by finally talking about it she was taking the first steps towards expunging it herself. Steps towards living a full life again instead of the half-life she'd allowed herself tucked away in the middle of nowhere.

He pulled her towards him and wrapped her up tight. 'The door,' he said against her temple. 'I should have fixed that door when you first complained about it.'

Tess heard her own anguish echoed in his words and when the sob rose in her chest she didn't try to stop it.

She let it out. And the low wail that followed it. The gut-wrenching wail that cut like razors on its way out but instead of leaving her bloodied it left her feeling infinitely lighter.

Fletch held her while she sobbed. It was the first time apart from at the hospital and the funeral that she'd let him hold her while she'd cried. His own tears mingled with hers as they finally grieved for their son together.

Tess didn't know how long she cried for or even where the tears had come from, considering how much she'd already cried these past six weeks. But she did know that she felt better for it and that it had felt right to share her tears with Fletch.

She eventually lifted her head from his shoulder. She was surprised to see his eyes also rimmed with red.

She smiled at him as she gently fluttered her fingers over his eyelids. 'I'm sorry,' she murmured.

He shook his head, his eyes closed. 'Don't be.'

She traced the slopes of his cheekbones down to the corners of his mouth. 'Why didn't you tell me about… the other woman? Back then? Was I that fragile?'

Fletch opened his eyes. 'Yes, you were. But mostly…' he shrugged '…I was just ashamed and sick to my stomach over my actions. I could barely face you. I certainly didn't feel like I deserved you after what I'd done. When you gave me the chance to end it I grabbed it with both hands. It seemed like a better alternative than having to confess.'

Tess traced his bottom lip with her thumb. 'I guess that couldn't have been an easy thing to tell.'

Fletch felt the stroke of her thumb right down to his

groin. 'You don't seem so mad about it any more,' he said tentatively.

Tess nodded realising he was right. 'I've done a lot of soul-searching since coming home. I wasn't easy to live with, Fletch. You tried so hard…every day…you were so patient with me. But I was so caught up in my denial stage, avoiding even the slightest mention of Ryan, that I forgot you were grieving too. That you needed someone to lean on as well. I don't blame you for finding a little solace somewhere else for a few hours.'

She dropped her hand into her lap. 'Don't get me wrong, it hurts…but I need to own my part in that.'

Fletch picked up her hand from her lap and pressed a kiss to the back of it. 'I'm sorry. I'm so sorry. I didn't just stop loving you because you were done with me, Tess, but we went to bed each night and there was this great divide between us that I just couldn't breach, no matter how I tried.'

Tess nodded, swallowing a lump that had risen to her throat. She'd been so inside herself she hadn't realised just how much he'd been suffering too.

'But I want us back together, Tess.' He raised her chin so they were looking into each other's eyes. 'I think you still love me and I don't want to live any more of my life without you in it.'

Tess nodded. He was right. She did still love him. She didn't need a clanging of gongs or a light bulb over her head to know it. It hummed quietly in every cell, as it always had. She just hadn't been listening.

And the truth was their marriage hadn't ended because they'd fallen out of love—it had ended because they'd given up on that love when everything else had got too hard.

'I do, Fletch. I do love you.' She sniffed and wiped at yet another tear. 'But do you really think we deserve a second shot when we screwed it up so badly the first time? Do you think we can truly be happy?'

Fletch cradled her face, pushing his long fingers into her hair. 'Yes, Tess, yes. Everyone deserves a second chance. I'm not pretending that the road ahead is going to be all roses and sunshine. We need counselling, Tess, both together and separately. We have a decade's worth of guilt and grief that needs to be talked about and I imagine that's going to be pretty harrowing at times. I know you've never wanted to talk about this before but we can't go on like that again. We have to do it differently this time round.'

Tess could see the love and determination mingling in his silvery-green gaze. 'I don't want to walk around with this stuff inside me any more, Fletch. I'm so tired of carrying it around.'

Fletch leaned in and brushed his mouth against hers. Finally he felt that everything was going to be all right.

Tess pulled back from his kiss, a swell of emotion blooming in her chest. He looked warm and solid and calm and she needed him more than ever. 'I love you,' she murmured.

Fletch smiled. 'Then the rest will come,' he whispered, claiming her mouth once again.

And for the first time in a decade Tess looked forward to the future.

* * * * *

A sneaky peek at next month...

Medical Romance™

CAPTIVATING MEDICAL DRAMA—WITH HEART

My wish list for next month's titles...

In stores from 7th Septmber 2012:

☐ Her Motherhood Wish — Anne Fraser

& A Bond Between Strangers — Scarlet Wilson

☐ Once a Playboy... — Kate Hardy

& Challenging the Nurse's Rules — Janice Lynn

☐ The Sheikh and the Surrogate Mum
   — Meredith Webber

& Tamed by her Brooding Boss — Joanna Neil

Available at WHSmith, Tesco, Asda, Eason, Amazon and Apple

Just can't wait?

MILLS & BOON® Book Club — 2 Free Books!

Get your free books now at
www.millsandboon.co.uk/freebookoffer

Or fill in the form below and post it back to us

THE MILLS & BOON® BOOK CLUB™—HERE'S HOW IT WORKS: Accepting your free books places you under no obligation to buy anything. You may keep the books and return the despatch note marked 'Cancel'. If we do not hear from you, about a month later we'll send you 5 brand-new stories from the Medical™ series, including two 2-in-1 books priced at £5.49 each and a single book priced at £3.49*. There is no extra charge for post and packaging. You may cancel at any time, otherwise we will send you 5 stories a month which you may purchase or return to us—the choice is yours. *Terms and prices subject to change without notice. Offer valid in UK only. Applicants must be 18 or over. Offer expires 31st January 2013. **For full terms and conditions, please go to www.millsandboon.co.uk/freebookoffer**

Mrs/Miss/Ms/Mr (please circle) _____

First Name _____

Surname _____

Address _____

_____

_____ Postcode _____

E-mail _____

Send this completed page to: Mills & Boon Book Club, Free Book Offer, FREEPOST NAT 10298, Richmond, Surrey, TW9 1BR

Find out more at
www.millsandboon.co.uk/freebookoffer

Visit us Online

0712/M2YEA